A Lunatic Love Life

A Novel By

Stephen Leon White

Contents

Dedication

To four generations of Ladies and Lassies in my lunatic life:

Ann, my mother

Mus, my wife

Shannon and Lauren, my daughters

Lulu and Trixie, my granddaughters

WITH LOVE

Epigraph

According to The Compact Edition of the Oxford English Dictionary, L (el), *the twelfth letter of the modern alphabet and the eleventh letter of the ancient Roman alphabet represents historically the Greek lambda and, before that, the Semitic lamed. The earliest known Semitic forms of the character are Z and L, both of which occur in early Greek inscriptions. The latter was adopted from the Greek into the Latin alphabet and is the ancestor of the modern Roman forms, but in Greece itself the letter was superseded by the inverted form I, which eventually became A….*

A Brief Prelude

Luckily for Oliver Sandwich, on the day he turned nine, his adoring mother, Grace, arranged through a woman friend to take him to lunch at the Magic Castle, a hangout for magicians in Hollywood. There, Oliver encountered Irma the Magic Piano, as well as other wondrous and amazing feats performed by prestidigitators. The experience fired his imagination. Though he knew the performers used tricks, he preferred to believe they veiled some greater meaning, an entryway to an unknown world. He began to dream that possession of a magical word, zigzag, for example, could make him disappear whenever he wished.

Eager to share the afternoon's excitement, a supercharged Oliver greeted his father, Fred, at the door that evening. Fred proceeded to yell at Grace for further filling Oliver's already impractical head with additional nonsense. During the argument, which lasted through dinner, Oliver zigzagged into his room, pulled his maps from the drawer, and concentrated with all his might on his current favorite project, that of tracing the flow of the Ganges. As he sat and copied each curve of the holy river, he tested out magical words capable of taking him to that exotic waterway.

But no matter the word he called aloud, his body remained trapped in his chair. He sat stuck like a fly to a piece of flypaper. In a last desperate act, he closed his ears to sounds and his eyes to the world. With intense attention, he transported himself onto a boat manned by oarsmen, who paddled in unison as they glided a sleek, highly decorative craft down the river.

Distractions

Late on a Saturday afternoon, a few minutes past four, Oliver Sandwich stood facing the pot-bellied corner mailbox, a Brentwood colossus that accepted letters as well as packages. In his role of dutiful son, Oliver had first pondered his mother's unusual request as he struggled to remove the twelve-foot-long aluminum ladder from behind the garage. Since his mother had left no postage for him, he rummaged through her top desk drawer to locate the self-adhesive roll from which he peeled off four first-class stamps, placing them on one of the ladder's side runners.

His mother's verbal request, wafting through the closed bedroom door, had come in its muffled state at a most unfortunate moment. Bored by his review for an English test, Oliver had abandoned his book to resume his latest set of geographical tracings of detailed maps of the exotically named and reasonably recent Soviet Republics. Uzbekistan, Turkistan, and even Soviet Armenia now had independent borders that he wanted to commit to memory. But after a moment or two of racing, his mind began to drift. As often happened under such circumstances, his brain tuned in to his favorite internal station. The call letters were #span_smallcaps LYSANDER!span, a chestnut-haired beauty in his college English class who had managed to divert his attention since the semester began.

Lysander crossed the border of Oliver's mind somewhere between Russia and Georgia as he sat tracing the Black Sea. He retrieved from his wallet the student card containing her picture, which she had dropped in the hall following class one day. He decided not to return it—the boldness of his act made him blush— and then placed the ID card carefully in his billfold. Now he stared down at her face. Her beautiful mouth showed just a hint of a smile. Her hair tumbled down below her neck in slight disarray. Her round cheeks invited kisses from imaginary suitors, and her blue *eyes* seemed to penetrate the lamination that protected the surface of the card.

As Oliver wrapped himself up in an imaginary embrace with this beauty, his mother's distorted request came through the door: "Olislur, would you fun to the mailabox to send a ladder for me? I'm dreaded down to Gloe's for a spinet."

"Sure, Mom," came his rote response. His mother had broken the spell. Lysander jumped from his arms back to the surface of the card. Once he had collected himself, he left the room to choose a proper ladder among several that hung in a neat arrangement on the wall on one side of the garage.

After stamping the ladder but forgetting he needed to add an address label, he carried the long object one block to the mailbox and leaned it upright against the side of the repository. A bird chirped from the telephone pole above. Oliver looked up, first at the bird, then at the height of the ladder, which towered over him and the mailbox.

Unlike other mailboxes, which did not accept packages and would instantly reject such a lengthy object, this neighborhood box, the last of its kind, proved itself a worthy representative of the postal system. Nicknamed "MaiLA" by the postal employee who picked up its contents, this old-fashioned receptacle represented the outdated American idea that the customer's needs should be met. This mailbox went the extra mile in spirit and duty. Despite its good intentions, MaiLA would soon find itself obsolete, the victim of a meltdown in the service of the United States Postal Service.

Throughout two decades of service on that corner, MaiLA

never received a challenge equal to the task of consuming a twelve-foot, single-rung aluminum ladder. At most, those twenty years of service had brought a smattering of slightly oversized packages, which the mailbox had accepted with ease once minor adjustments were made to widen the entry door. Any package had proved a piece of cake for this mailbox, even the oversized ones. MaiLA had always managed to expand itself in an unobtrusive manner that did not alert the customer to its unique talents.

Cast in heavy metal like every standard-issue blue variety, bearing the self-same words #span_smallcaps U.S. MAIL!span on the side, MaiLA displayed a wide body and a large package drawer at its rounded top. Riveted bolts finished the vertical belts running down each corner. Little squat legs raised the box to a convenient height for depositors. Below MaiLAs package and letter drop, the schedule offered a single 5:00 P.M. pickup Monday through Friday.

Oliver realized the ladder might not fit inside the mailbox and that he would need a course of action. He took a firm grip on each side bar directly in the middle of the ladder.

As he released a loud grunt, he stiffened both arms to hoist the bulky object horizontally above his head. For an instant the ends swayed up and down like a teeter-totter. Then the entire ladder stabilized.

At that point, he lowered the awkward object onto his broad shoulders with his head sticking up between two middle rungs. One hand, meant to pry open the package door, could now be freed. But the front of the ladder extended past the rounded top of the mailbox. As he kept the ladder balanced from its center, he found no room to maneuver. Somehow he needed to place one end into the package door, a seemingly impossible task.

Just as Oliver considered abandoning the project and returning home, a somewhat pudgy red-haired boy passed by.

"Would you mind giving me a hand?" Oliver asked.

The boy didn't seem in the least surprised to see the twelve-foot ladder perched across Oliver's shoulders. "Which hand?" he asked with an adolescent giggle.

"The right one will be best," Oliver answered, instructing the boy to hold the middle of the ladder as high as possible while he advanced to the front rung in order to guide the top into the package door.

"Raise your end a little more," Oliver told him. "Now let's back up a few steps."

The boy lifted the ladder as high as he could, then backed up. He increased the angle just enough for Oliver to slide both side supports through the package door and into the mailbox.

"I can take it from here," Oliver said as he stepped back toward the middle to secure the ladder. "Thanks a lot. Let me know if you ever need a favor. Name's Oliver Sandwich. Live down the block in that white house there."

"Sure," the boy responded, continuing his walk.

Oliver raised the ladder's angle upward in order to slide the front end further into the box. As rung after rung slipped inside the mailbox, the ladder's weight and angle kept the door flat, which allowed Oliver to use both hands to maneuver its entry. Each step he took back allowed him to raise the angle a bit higher: the steeper the incline, the smoother the ladder's descent.

Then came a snag. Halfway digested, the ladder stopped dead, refusing to travel another inch. No matter how hard Oliver wiggled the sides back and forth, the ladder would not budge.

"Dddddamn," Oliver cursed, irritation ruffling his normally placid disposition.

An obstacle in MaiLA blocked any further progress. Even after Oliver released his grip on the ladder, it remained firmly in place. He reached through the package door to try to yank the ladder loose. No matter how hard he pulled, the aluminum held as if cemented in place.

Head tilted back, Oliver explored the ladder's position. Angled at about 110 degrees, the undigested half resembled a fork stuck into a plump side of beef.

"Dddddamn you," he cursed again, giving a firm kick to MaiLA's metal front. "I need to mail this stupid ladder."

How could Oliver know his angry, rhetorical outburst would further upset MaiLA, who was already incensed and humiliated by the kick? "Take the rest of the ladder, dammit, before I climb in there myself."

MaiLA's sense of inadequacy deepened. Presented with its first serious challenge ever, the mailbox had failed miserably. But rather than give up, MaiLA became as determined as Oliver. To complete the task at hand, it would try anything, even widen to admit the angry young man himself, if necessary.

Unable to pry the ladder loose on its own, MaiLA anticipated Oliver's entry. Through a calculated and painful process, the receptacle expanded its package drop and box capacity in a single simultaneous stretch. Finally, the mailbox activated a trapdoor feature that added incredible depth. Just as Oliver decided to act, MaiLA completed its heroic task.

Oliver's eyes fixed on the portion of the ladder still outside the box as he stood a few steps back to survey the scene. At this point his thinking process, never dazzling to begin with, deteriorated even further. His mind wandered into space with Lysander while his body continued like an inattentive driver on cruise control.

Oliver's innate gymnastic agility helped him swing onto the ladder. Through a concerted effort, he stretched his body flat along the rungs that remained outside the box. He needed every ounce of his strength to lie steady at this steep angle. A controlled descent edged him forward rung by rung, like a worm crawling down steps, until he passed through the package door to enter the unknown.

Dark as a cave, dank-smelling as well, MaiLAs interior loomed before Oliver. As he descended the part of the ladder inside the mailbox, each rung brought him closer to the heart of a forbidding darkness.

Oliver never thought to question his easy access through the package door. An interior space wide and deep enough to accommodate him and the ladder appeared perfectly normal in his befuddled state. As he twisted his head upward, he spotted a sliver of light from outside that barely penetrated the chilled blackness. But confident to a fault, Oliver showed little concern for risks or logistics. His thoughts shared a warm bed with his beloved, chestnut-haired Lysander.

One hand scouted his descent, until some six feet below the package opening, his fingers located the tip of the wedged ladder. At that point, Oliver extended both hands across the thin metal ledge that kept the ladder embedded firmly in place.

A series of bounces by his prone body did little to pry the ladder loose as the angle prevented any give. He had to acknowledge failure. "Oh, Lysander, what I do for my dear mother," he muttered aloud. Each word, hollow and deep-throated, bounced back from the mailbox's depths.

Before he accepted abject failure, Oliver decided to try one more maneuver. To accomplish this feat, he needed to lower himself so that his entire body hung between the first and second rung facing the direction of the snag. That part of his plan went off without a hitch. Dangling high above a black hole, he swayed back and forth as if he'd returned to the monkey bars of his childhood. Extraordinary effort helped him raise one leg to the point where he could propel his foot forward, until the sole of his Nike pressed solidly against the wall directly in front of him.

Encouraged, Oliver raised the other leg, drawing his knees tight against his chest. A loud groan escaped his lips, a sound generated by the intense effort of pressing both feet flat against the side directly below the small ledge that kept the ladder wedged. Unable to maintain this awkward position, he used his powerful leg muscles to push off. At the same instant, he jerked back the first rung with his strong arms. Freed, the ladder swung loose.

In an instant, all the flaws in Oliver's plan became evident. A loud thunderlike sound came from the top half of the ladder as it crashed through the mailbox opening. Suspended in space, the ladder went into free fall and roared past him almost immediately. A jarring clamor, like a pinball overdosed on steroids, echoed as the ladder bounced against the insides of MaiLA.

The falling ladder separated Oliver from the ledge he intended to grab. Just as he realized this, the mailbox door slammed shut. The last sliver of light vanished. Disoriented, Oliver made a wild swipe at the ledge, but he grasped only empty air. For an instant he hovered. Then, like the legendary Humpty Dumpty, he had a great fall.

Flipped twice, like a flapjack on a griddle, Oliver landed on his rear end, buried to his waist in a pile of soft letters. In total darkness, he flayed about like a drowning man about to go under for the third time. He felt around for solid ground, but buried waist deep in letters, he found nothing to hold onto.

MaiLA had opened its direct link to a central repository. Inside, an antiquated machine controlled a giant drum filled with dead letters. The ladder had disappeared beneath the pile of letters just before Oliver slammed into the mass of unbound mail. The young man's added weight provided the catalyst needed to unleash the action of the powerful leviathan. In an age of technology, this industrial hangover still functioned.

The huge engine stirred, making loud, cranking noises, much like an early Model T Ford. The machine began to rotate in order to empty the giant drum of thousands of letters. A creaking sound followed a crash in the darkness. Oliver shuddered with fear. The start of the machine instantly sprang a trapdoor at the bottom of the drum. As it opened, the large wood door banged against the side of a metal chute below.

With jerk after jerk, Oliver bounced around as the drum began to move in fits and starts. A slow rotation increased to a steady circular motion about the speed of a merry-go-round. In pitch darkness and now flat on his back, Oliver could not gain his bearings or his footing. Great piles of dead letters shifted about, keeping him off balance. The sharp corners of the churning envelopes tattooed random patterns across the exposed parts of Oliver's body and face. Each spin dropped another crush of letters through the open trapdoor at the bottom of the drum.

Oliver's heart pounded as he felt himself swept toward his fate like a piece of flotsam carried out to sea. The motor accelerated. The loud clatter echoed in thunderous waves. A sudden jolt, and he crashed feet first through the trapdoor. A pitiful yelp escaped from his vocal cords and exploded into a hollow roar as the remainder of his body, mummified in letters, vanished into the passageway.

"I'm sorry, I'm sorry," the young man babbled amid the racket as a quiet chill settled over him.

Mile after mile of corrugated mail chute flew by at a slow, steady pace. Oliver's nose faced outdated, unpainted, government-issued, subcontracted metal. Battered, constricted, and unable to raise a hand, Oliver dropped like an Idaho potato solidly encased in its skin. After a lifetime of imaginary trips, he'd embarked on a route not found on any of his maps.

Reactions

Letting go and holding on, Grace fought the battle of all mother's. One day, woeful and miserable—another day, happy and successful, Grace had watched her beloved boy mature into his young manhood. Grace had relished his triumphs and shared his pain. She always hoped for more. Now, what she regarded as her own failure had become her secret torment.

These fragmented thoughts tortured Grace Sandwich as she sat before the stained oak breakfast table in the country-style kitchen of her modest Brentwood home. Surrounded by shelves of aging knick-knacks, worn appliances, cheerful slogans, and outdated brown vinyl linoleum, she could slip into her solitude like a uniform. After all, she felt more of closeness to these objects or to her obese black cat Terrance than she did to Fred, her own husband. Her eyes fixed on Terrance, who sat on the sill of the half-open kitchen window and stared out vacantly while an evening breeze cooled the room.

Teardrops flowed blackened trails of mascara down Grace's cheeks. Two fingers tightly gripped the handle of a happy-face coffee mug she'd filled an hour earlier. For the first time, Grace shared the pain every mother experiences—the bitter taste of disappointment.

Not that her son had failed her. On the contrary, he'd always remained a constant source of joy. Only a few hours earlier, they'd shared their traditional Saturday morning ritual, beginning with a yoga class that allowed Grace to gloat over the attention Oliver received from her friends. After the workout, they pursued the same silly game they played each week —aging movie star/young hunk, a pas de deux performed over lunch at a Montana Avenue eatery. They'd returned home in the early afternoon. The last she'd seen of her son, he'd excused himself to enter his downstairs bedroom to prepare for an upcoming English test.

An hour later, she shouted her request to him through his closed bedroom door: "Oliver, would you run to the mailbox to send a letter for me? I'm headed down to Chloe's for a minute." A muffled affirmative came back at once. Without asking him to repeat her request, she departed for a brief visit with her friend. Upon her return in the late afternoon, she found, much to her chagrin, that Oliver had vanished, while the letter to be mailed remained on the table beside the front door.

Hours later, when the night grew dark and foreboding, she could only torment herself as she recalled their last lunch together. "Am I too fatalistic?" she asked aloud rhetorically in the style of her former idol, Angela Lansbury. Still, if for an instant she'd suspected she might never see her son again, what would she have told him? How many times would she have repeated her love for him? More than he'd want to hear, no doubt. What else? Would she have mentioned his terrible shyness? How could she have anticipated his disappearance, perhaps forever? The thought brought her hand to rest against her forehead.

On the plump side of middle age, nearing fifty, Grace Sandwich looked pained. Her face sat distorted in her hand. To think, even for an instant, that her son might take off without warning to pursue some fancy. Totally unimaginable. No coincidence that her maiden name was Manners. Hadn't she passed on every courtesy she'd learned in life? Hadn't he always displayed proper manners, saying goodbye when he left and greeting her when he returned? How dare he vanish as suddenly and casually as a yawn.

Grace sat constructing in her mind an appropriate missing person's notice. If Oliver didn't return by morning, she intended to tack a description of him onto every telephone pole along each block of her affluent Los Angeles neighborhood. The words flowed through her mind:

#div_bq #bq-ind *Missing: Twenty-one-year-old boy, six feet tall, baby blue eyes, dark-blond curly shoulder-length hair, beautifully arched eyebrows, high cheekbones, pointed chin, nice build, quiet disposition, often subject to distraction. Last seen wearing blue Levis and a blue T-shirt with the slogan* #span_smallcaps *WAVE THE SHALES*!span *written across the chest. Answers to the name Oliver. Liberal reward.*!div

After some thought, Grace deleted the part about the reward. Though her son might wander about like a lost puppy, a reward made him appear too much like one. Why give someone money for returning her son to his God-given home?

She allowed her mind to rest long enough to sip the cup of cold coffee. The taste brought a frown. She put the mug down, ran her fingers through her graying hair, and cursed under her breath. Who could she blame for her plight but herself? She'd interrupted Oliver's studies for a frivolous request, a command, in fact, to mail her letter of resignation to an unimportant club whose meetings she never attended. She conceded this one fault of hers: she needed Oliver to prove his love daily through small tasks.

Never mind she'd spent a year deciding to resign. What harm to have waited another day? Or why, she probed, had she not mailed the letter herself when she went out? Why this constant need to prove her son would do whatever she asked?

"Stop staring, Terrance," she warned the cat, as he lumbered down from the windowsill to march out of the room.

About five in the evening, Oliver's father had returned from his club only to brush aside Grace's missing-person theory. He had offered a simple explanation for his son's absence: Oliver had gone to visit a friend. According to Fred, he'd departed to avoid his promise to clean out the garage over the weekend.

At half past five, Grace walked the street, knocking at doors up and down the block to ask if anyone had noticed an unusual occurrence between three and four-thirty in the afternoon. Neighbors, none of whom she knew, tried to be helpful, though Grace refused to divulge the reasons behind her query. Why appear foolish? What would they think of a mother in search of her twenty-one-year-old son in broad daylight at five-thirty on a Saturday afternoon?

Over dinner, Grace had continued to voice her hysterical litany of concerns while her husband ignored her. Afterward, Fred departed with his bottle of Southern Comfort to watch a Dodger game on the television in the den. Grace knew that in her husband's heart of hearts, he would be delighted to have the boy leave home for good. Once Fred determined that Oliver would not be suited for his own small export-import business, he often pushed him toward a Horatio Alger future with the words, "It's time to move on, son, because you're free, white, and twenty-one."

Grace stared at the coffee mug as she once more tried to analyze the sudden departure. He'd taken no clothes or other personal effects. His old Toyota remained parked in front of the house. If he'd gone off voluntarily, he certainly would have taken his car. Either he walked off, or someone picked him up. Kidnapping seemed the least likely explanation and would certainly be considered an oddity in their Brentwood neighborhood.

With each passing minute, Grace's fear increased. When the hall clock struck 9:00 p.m., Grace whispered to herself, "Ask not for whom the bells toll." She broke into tears before finishing the thought.

As her mind circled, her gaze settled on a colorful picture of a kitten playing with a ball of yarn. Below the picture hung the month of May beside the refrigerator. So many days to make a month. What if Oliver didn't return? Would all those days and weeks to come, all those pages waiting to have a turn, become as wide and empty as a black hole in the universe? Would the hole now growing inside her one day be as large as the hole that snatched her treasured son away?

She screwed her lips to one side as if afflicted by palsy and pressed her clenched fists hard against the wood table surface until her manicured fingernails broke through the skin on the palms of her hands. She gravitated toward the worst-case scenario. Oliver would never return. Little clues told the story. Her son would never leave on his own without first closing the door to his room. Three generations of Manners tradition—house code, meal code, visiting other people code, and a plain old everyday code—dictated his every move.

Why did she feel so certain he'd vanished with no corroborating evidence? A mother's instinct, she decided. On that lonely night, immersed in her pain, alone in her kitchen, she sipped her cold coffee and grimaced. No one could answer her questions.

Letterland—One "L" of a Place

Little luminous lights flashed on and off to form a sentence before Oliver's eyes as he crashed through the bottom of the chute.

#div_bq #bq-ctr #span_smallcaps CONGRATULATIONS!span

#bq-ctr #span_smallcaps YOU HAVE CHOSEN THE GOLDEN PARACHUTE!span!div

Brushing against the sign, Oliver's nose activated a parachute that dropped from out of nowhere. As the parachute Velcroed itself onto the boy's shoulders, it unfolded billowy golden wings to carry him, light as a feather, into the blue sky.

Aware by now that he had no control whatsoever, Oliver chose not to struggle against his fate. He would leave his destiny in the capable hands of the postal service. Alive, he might still have a chance of returning home.

But what if he never came back? The thought filled him with terror. What if he returned home a corpse left at his parents doorstep by express mail with #span_smallcaps RETURN TO SENDER!span stamped on his forehead?

Fearful, he floated through a blue sky with thousands of letters dropping around him like pieces of confetti. Looking down, he spotted a sign made from brightly colored circulars laid out in the shape of huge letters across the flat top of a mountain.

Forming the words #span_smallcaps LETTERING HEIGHTS!span, the circulars spread over a mountain of mail almost as tall as the U.S. Bank Tower in downtown Los Angeles, an impressive 1,018 feet, the tallest building Oliver had ever seen in person. The flat surface at the top of the mountain provided an ideal landing strip. With a practiced sense of direction, the parachute glided in. Letters settled in all around him. Oliver touched down softly, as if plopped onto a pile of freshly raked leaves.

As he picked himself up and tried to balance himself on the uneven surface, he unloosened the Velcro straps of the parachute. In a sudden move, like a young, frenzied girl late for a party, the parachute made a dash for the sky in the direction of the metal chute before Oliver could grab hold of the strings.

His eyes followed the disappearing parachutes path through still clouds painted into a clear blue sky. With a pitiful look on his face, he surveyed the almost-perfect circle that formed the mountaintop. All across the top, white envelopes and chunky ends of packages blanketed the surface like snow. He inhaled pleasant and clean country air, then made his way with careful steps to the edge of the clutter.

Far below, at the base of Lettering Heights, Oliver's eyes followed a road that disappeared into the lonesome distance. The flat and repetitious landscape reminded him of childhood visits to the Manners family home in Texas. But Texas wouldn't have a mountain of mail as tall as this. Despite his confused state of mind, Oliver realized he had not parachuted anywhere near Texas.

As he peered over the edge of the mountain, Oliver noticed at its base myriad odd-shaped creatures scurrying about. He blinked a couple of times, thinking they were just small dots in front of his eyes. On closer inspection, however, he observed that the dots moved about like little broomsticks as they swept along a path in left-right, left-right motion.

Oliver set off along the perimeter of the landing field to

search for a pathway down. Suddenly homesick in this alienating landscape, he paced around the entire edge of the flat top looking for signs of a path. Round and round he walked, like a loop running through a movie projector. He saw not a familiar sign anywhere as he continuously peered over the side at the scenery below. Every view repeated itself with monotonous regularity in all directions. At the base, busy little broomsticks scurried around, no matter which way he looked. He concluded no path led to the bottom. But he did count six roads leading in different directions from the base of Lettering Heights. Two roads seemed to come the closest to what appeared to be far-off clusters of buildings. Were these towns, cities, or merely mirages?

How to descend posed the greatest problem. Oliver found that the incline sloped at too unpredictable a grade to risk a step-by-step descent. Layer after layer of white envelopes formed the semi-steep slope, with the occasional odd-shaped package jutting out along the side of the mountain.

An occasional climber, Oliver knew the risk of dropping into a deep, unseen crevice. He imagined his body drilling through dense layers of old mail and finally grinding to a stop in last-century letters moldy with age. There his body, tattered and rotting, would lie forever, encased in the heart of a mountain of envelopes.

His arms folded, Oliver looked down the slope at the curious creatures below. He decided they moved like hockey sticks over ice rather than broomsticks. As he shifted his attention back to the slope, he bent down, extending an arm to trace in his mind the exact angle of descent. As he bent over and noticed his blue T-shirt, he encountered the words #span_smallcaps WAVE THE SHALES!span written across his chest.

He had bought the T-shirt on an impulse one afternoon at

the Santa Monica Mall. He knew full well that the nonsense words were some sort of play on Save the Whales. He had no more interest in whales than the average person. But Wave the Shales captured his imagination; the words sounded poetic and mysterious. And ever hopeful, he thought the unusual slogan might attract the attention of a certain cute girl. So he bought the shirt.

#span_smallcaps WAVE THE SHALES!span! #span_smallcaps WAVE THE SHALES!span! Eureka! The idea crashed over him like a wave hitting the shore. He began to flap his arms like an awkward pelican. The words on his T-shirt offered the first clue as to how he might reach the base.

He moved around the mountain until he reached the area above the two roads that looked the most promising. Then he sat down with both legs dangling over the edge. To steer himself properly, he locked his knees and kept his legs pressed to the surface of soft letters, as if preparing to descend a gigantic playground slide.

He spread his arms wide apart at shoulder level. Propelled by the angle, he pushed off to gather speed as he flapped his arms past layer after layer of Lettering Heights. His excited voice called out, over and over, "Wave the Shales, Wave the Shales." Without a serious hitch, he swooped at a steady pace along the soft surface of letters to the base of the mountain. A sudden stop, and he splashed to the ground like a huge bird-dropping.

Despite the hullabaloo, the hockey sticks acted sublimely unaware of Oliver's unsightly landing. Not even for a moment did they take their eyes off their assigned tasks. Perhaps, he thought, they hadn't even heard his tumultuous descent since up close he could see they didn't have any ears.

Once again upright on terra firma, Oliver focused his

attention on one of the creatures, an odd-looking L-shaped mechanism that busily hovered over several stacks of letters. The stacks, one piled neatly beside the other, stood in a long row. Each stack reached as high as the worker.

Shaped like a pie tin, the hockey sticks head consisted of extended edges surrounding a flat circular center. Two puncture holes in the middle of the tin had to be nostrils while, directly beneath them, a horizontal slit could pass for a mouth. Above the nostrils, protruding and circular orbs resembled colorless egg yolks served sunny-side up. Without pupils, eyelashes, eyelids, and eyebrows, the hockey-stick figure projected the austere and critical expression of an angry father.

Remove the facial features, and Oliver's mother could have filled the tin-shaped head with piecrust and apples ready for baking in the oven. With features, such as they were, the creature's head resembled a metallic version of the man in the moon.

Oliver didn't know whether to fear this odd creature or approach it for help. A piece of metal fitted in a straight line supported the circular head. If indeed a neck existed at all, Oliver could not determine the point where it joined the long, narrow frame. That straight frame, no more than six inches wide, ran directly from the base of the head to the swiveling joint at ground level. This metal man measured about four feet from the top of his pie-shaped head to his "feet," which consisted of a single horizontal metal section that resembled a ski and trailed behind the rigid body. The ski measured about two feet long, with the same width as the body. To describe the shape in alphabetical terms would be to compare the creature to a rather rigid upper-case letter L with the head facing the wrong direction.

A thin, circular piece of support tubing secured the metal

man as he worked. A vise-like clamp supported the L from the rear, directly below the pie-shaped head. From there the pole angled toward the end of the horizontal ski-like foot. A second clamp of similar metal at the end of the joint secured the tubing. The round pole angled through the clamp to the ground. This support section formed a triangle with the body and extended foot. The pole functioned like a rudder, allowing the horizontal ski to swing swiftly from side to side.

To make this odd-looking creature even odder, a monitor about the size of a mini portable television hung suspended in space about a foot from its forehead. A narrow beam of blue light attached the monitor to the forehead section of the flat face. One by one, envelopes glided through the air, pausing for an instant at the center of the beam. A loud zap greeted each letter that floated through space to place itself on top of the closest pile in the line of stacks on the opposite side of the creature. With so many creatures around, the zapping noises made a deafening roar. Oliver glanced at his watch, counted the number of letters the metal man in front of him zapped, and concluded the creature could do over a hundred zaps a minute.

A great number of identical looking Ls zapped letters all around the base of the mountain, while others, busily rotating on their hockey sticks, moved among the workers to pick up the large stacks of sorted mail and place them in neat piles on the ski behind them. Oliver noticed that despite the erratic movements of the Ls, the mail never tumbled off.

Other Ls, scurrying here and there, used their joint to pivot the horizontal section back and forth as they emphasized the rotating hockey-stick appearance. Slower-moving Ls produced a sound like a sweeping broom while the faster moving Ls produced a louder, whirling sound. Each L appeared controlled in its movements by the tiny monitor joined to the forehead by the blue beam. Overall, the area had the constant hum of a busy factory.

Incredulous, Oliver watched the organized chaos created by all the Ls, monitors in front, poles angled behind, turning every which way. Somehow, unlike the traffic at home, these creatures maneuvered around without the slightest risk or incidence of a traffic jam or accident.

As the L nearest to Oliver finished up a pile, it used the monitor to retract the support pole to its parallel position. Freed, it rotated on its joint to face Oliver head on. This meant that the monitor partially obscured the Ls face. The joint rotated back and forth at a steady rate, allowing the L to retain a stationary position. Unbeknown to Oliver, from the moment he flap-landed at the base of Lettering Heights, the Ls had been immediately informed of his arrival by their monitors, but chose to ignore him while they completed their assignments.

The shock produced by the Ls and their activities caused Oliver to momentarily lose his power of speech. He followed the Ls rotation with his eyes, waiting for the right time to make contact with the creature. He suspected it did not speak English. After some thought, he decided to use a hand signal, a raised arm with an open palm such as he'd seen used in films as a sign of friendship between Native Americans and settlers. He would then follow the hand signal with the words "Me, Oliver." He hoped this would prove a good beginning.

Startled, Oliver heard the L speak first in clear and precise English. Even though the monitor obscured its mouth, the words remained crystal clear. "An impossible task, an impossible task," it muttered. "That LLiterally LLucid is to blame. Look how that mountain of letters only grows larger. All these letters must be re 'l'orecated in order to be used again. Is there no end to this?"

Without moving its monitor so much as an inch, the creature shifted its attention to Oliver. "Just who in 'l' do you think you are?" the figure demanded to know. It spoke English without even the trace of an accent.

"Never seen one of you fancy 'l'omputed types here," it continued. "I didn't think you important town folk would mix with us lowly letter 'l'orticians. All we do is reclaim these infernal dead letters, one after the next, and send them off for distribution by Word Central. We're nothing at all, nothing at all. Why waste your time here with us? I thought your kind preferred to act important while you pretended to be somebody you're not."

Oliver realized he must have been mistaken for someone else. But whom? Every creature looked identical to the one in front of him. Before he had a chance to defend himself, a low-pitched, guttural cry emerged from deep within the L: "LLuLLxicleipclcalsesosaslllllweaaaalll, lalalalalala!" By the time the painful lamentation ended, Oliver could have sworn that the visible part of the grayish moon face had changed to a pale metallic pink.

Hearing the dismal cry of a fellow creature, eight other Ls stopped dead in their tracks as if frozen by a noon lunch whistle. In an instant, each of the eight rotated its joint to converge, monitor first, in a semicircle around Oliver. Alarmed, he took a defensive posture.

All the advancing Ls harmonized the last letters of the original cry that sounded like a Greek chorus chanting in a Euripides tragedy. Dissonant sounds in a polyphonic chorus filled the air as they chanted over and over in rondo form, "lll-lweaaaalll, lalalalalala." Humming, they continued to sing as they shifted into a capital L formation between Oliver and the L that had sounded the initial alarm.

Five Ls rotated their joints in place, side by side, to form the vertical part of the capital L, while another three completed the shorter horizontal extension. As suddenly as they had assembled, they stopped their chant. Then they dispersed in a simultaneous motion. Oliver's challenger swiveled before it rotated in reverse back to its original position between the piles of mail. The Ls pole swung forward to clamp into the support position. Again, the L went back to work as if Oliver no longer existed.

"Excuse me, sir," Oliver persisted, using the formal approach his mother had taught him to use when in doubt. The young man assumed a forthright stance in an attempt to look solicitous.

"Excuse me, sir." Anxious from a lack of response, Oliver forced himself to push his appeal. "I'm lost, sir. I wonder if you would be kind enough to tell me what town I'll reach if I walk along the road in this direction." Oliver pointed his index finger toward the road that began directly in front of him.

"'L'ompute it, yourself, Cookie," grumbled the L.

Though this L spoke quite clear English, it seemed more closely related to a letter in an alphabet soup than to a person. Oliver pondered why it refused to be polite when addressed in a proper manner. However, the response bolstered Oliver somewhat, and he continued meekly, "Is this a place where letters live?"

Oliver did not yet realize he had encountered his first non-computed, short-tempered 'l'ellow. Like its colleagues, this L did not suffer fools of any kind easily. Without meaning to, the young man's questions had managed to mock the L. How could Oliver know that the L mistook him for a fellow L, one of a privileged group computed to look like a real person, rather than a visitor from another land? The L naturally expected him to know about his own letter origins and his own direction in life.

A glance down at his battery-operated self-winding faux Chronosport wristwatch informed Oliver that the current Los Angeles time was 5:45 p.m. At least his watch still worked. Noting the hour and beginning to feel hungry, Oliver decided the time had come to move ahead.

But first he posed one final question to the L: "Do cell phones work here? I should like to call my mom. She might be worried."

Getting no response from the old pie face, Oliver turned his back on the unfriendly figure to begin his long trek along the dirt road.

Roadside Distractions

Lost and overwhelmed, Oliver tried to concentrate on his surroundings as the huge mountain of mail receded in the distance. The barren plains, distant hills, far-off clapboard buildings, and barbed wire reminded him of the landscapes he had seen in the Western movies and videos provided by his uncle Bob Manners during summer visits to Texas throughout his childhood.

Uncle Bob had been a great enthusiast of early video taped off cable—as well as a faithful advocate of the Beta system. Bob viewed the triumph of VHS over his beloved Beta as the last great Communist plot to win the hearts and minds of the American people. Though both had half-inch tape, Beta had always provided a sharper picture, and he constantly pointed that out to young Oliver during hours of viewing Bob's favorite programs taped from reruns. Dressed in his cowboy hat and pearl-buttoned Western shirt, Uncle Bob would make selections from the rows of neatly arranged tapes on the shelf and play them on one of his three Beta players that he kept in immaculate condition.

Every summer, during those endless years of his childhood, Oliver rode out the hot Texas afternoons on a couch in Uncle Bobs cool den, where together they relived the glory days of *Bonanza, Little House on the Prairie, Gunsmoke, Palladin, Death Valley Days, Mister Ed, May berry R.F.D, The Honeymooners* and numerous other shows.

Suddenly, Uncle Bob's videos, each episode titled and dated, flashed through Oliver's mind as he noticed for the first time that all color around him had vanished. All the surrounding scenery now appeared in black-and-white. The landscape resembled the hills and valleys of those early episodes of *Bonanza* and *Gunsmoke* from precolor television days. When had the change occurred? This place made no sense. In a television wilderness, he almost expected Marshal Dillon or his sidekick, Chester, to ride up to greet him.

But nobody came to greet him. Trapped by his dreary circumstances, Oliver felt a gloom as dismal as his surroundings settle over him. He longed for home, his mother, and yes, even his father. He missed his bed and his maps. But mostly he wished to be in class staring at his beautiful Lysander.

He pulled his cell phone from his pocket. His worst fears were immediately realized when the words #span_smallcaps NO SIGNAL!span appeared on the screen. No signal meant #span_smallcaps NO HOPE!span: no friends to call, no family to reassure, no contact with the world he knew. He checked his other pocket. All he turned up were a stick of gum, a pen, and fourteen cents. He'd left his room to mail a ladder, and he'd arrived here unprepared, with a useless cell phone, almost empty pockets, and only his wallet for company.

Noticing that his clothes had lost all color, he thought of living out his life as a black-and-white cartoon. He felt pushed to the brink. Terror urged him forward at breakneck speed. With the pounding pace of a scared rabbit, he ran as fast as he could along the center of the endless dirt road. Finally, a sneezing, wheezing fit forced him to slow down. A cloud of dust trailed behind him like a black tail. A sharp pain in his side made him double over. How far had he run? He couldn't tell. Each foot of drab scenery looked identical to the last.

Out of breath, he pushed himself forward step by slippery step. Every bone and joint in his body ached from the jolting his feet took against the uneven road. The road felt real, though his predicament seemed anything but. Muscles aching and blinded by sweat, he suddenly stumbled upon an unexpected intersection in the middle of nowhere.

With the back of his hand, he wiped the sweat from his eyes as he stood panting in bewildered silence. Four roads, each lifeless, appeared to lead nowhere. A black-rimmed rectangular monitor suspended in space at the edge of the crossroads caught his eye. The screen seemed to pulsate in movements from light to dark and back again. Similar in design and size to the smaller monitors worn by the Ls, this one offered a choice of four buttons on the rim directly below the screen.

Gun-shy, he hung back. He tried to catch his breath. He pushed away the thick matted strands of long, wet hair that had plastered the back of his neck during his mad run away from the mountain of letters. Mesmerized for several minutes by the shifting light of the monitor's pulsating beam, he finally recovered enough strength to make a tenuous advance.

Once inside the contact zone, his presence activated a beam, and the monitor, as if on an invisible stand, adjusted immediately to the height of his forehead. The beam's arc, connecting the monitor and Oliver's forehead, startled the youth, who jumped back. Deactivated, the beam returned the monitor to its original position. Another step forward, and the monitor raised again. As the beam made the connection a second time, Oliver extended a hesitant finger to push a button set off at the far left. Light filled the screen the same way as his computer monitor at home. Seconds later two menu choices appeared:

#div_bq #bq-ctr #span_smallcaps COLOR!span

#bq-ctr #span_smallcaps BLACK AND WHITE!span!div

A familiar voice from the past spoke, but he couldn't put a face to it.

"Select the first button for a color preference or the second to retain current black-and-white programming."

After a moment's hesitation, Oliver chose the first button.

Four new menu items appeared on the screen:

1. #span_smallcaps WINTER!span

2. #span_smallcaps SPRING!span

3. #span_smallcaps SUMMER!span

4. #span_smallcaps FALL!span

"Push the button of your preference to activate the season of your choice in living color."

Until now, Oliver had encountered nothing in L Land that made any sense. Though he understood the words, the meaning or the consequences of his choices eluded him. Hardly in the mood to play a game, but with no control over his situation, he made a selection. Sweaty and hot, he chose #span_smallcaps WINTER!span.

In Los Angeles, with its year-round mild climate, winter meant putting on a jacket at night. LA might have eighty-degree weather the same day a storm dumped a foot of snow on a nearby mountain.

The word #span_smallcaps WINTER!span flashed on and off on the monitor. Instantly, a howling wind, sleet, and snow charged across the barren landscape. The arctic sweep knocked Oliver flat to the ground. The monitor followed, gliding gently to the ground a foot away, beam intact.

In a second, the boy's sweat-soaked T-shirt freeze-dried to sit stiff as a signboard over his trembling body. Blinded by the onslaught, Oliver kept his eyes shut to protect them against the sting of the relentless wind. Reduced to a shivering, horizontal mass of protoplasm, Oliver clamped his arms tight against the frozen shirt stretched across his chest. His numb ears felt as if they had dropped or popped off. He prayed for a second chance. "Please, please," his weak voice piped from his rigid lips. "Let me choose anything else."

By the time the monitor responded, his red nose held its first icicle. Once more the list of choices appeared on the screen. "If you wish to change your selection, please do so at the sound of the beep. This is a recording."

Oliver unglued his closed eyes just long enough to read through snow-decked eyelashes the same four selections. With a shriveled stick of a finger he pushed with all the strength he could muster against the third button, #span_smallcaps SUMMER!span.

"All right, already," the recorded voice snapped. "Not so hard."

As sudden as the full force of winter had attacked, the cold departed, leaving behind an air of sweet gentleness. A day filled with hues of summer enveloped the surrounding landscape like a mother embracing her cherished child. Fields only moments earlier covered by snow now teemed with flowers and butterflies. Shade trees in lusty green lined what had been a naked road. Larks and loons filled the silence with their mating calls.

Oliver turned onto his back to stare upward at a cloudless blue sky. He let the warm air breathe new life into his trembling limbs. As the last signs of ice melted, his normal skin color began to return.

Glowing like a newborn baby, his attention slowly shifted back to the monitor on the ground beside him. The crossroads appeared in a diagram on the screen. A name identified each termination point with a corresponding number on the menu.

1. Lawyertown

2. Liberaltown

3. Lecturetown

4. Lettering Heights

"If you wish to purchase information about any of the-above locations, please identify your choice by pushing the appropriate button," the voice said, as if nothing at all out of the ordinary had occurred.

Little flickers of hope danced across Oliver's brain. Somewhat relaxed for the first time since his unfortunate descent into this gray world, he tried to decide in a deliberate and calm manner which name had the most appeal. He'd already learned the hard way that choosing without considering the consequences could have immediate and dire results. The arrows in the simple diagram indicated the road he had taken from Lettering Heights led to Lawyertown.

The name Lawyertown made Oliver uncomfortable. Early on, Fred Sandwich taught his son to avoid all practitioners of what he termed "the expensive art of jurisimpudence." Fred claimed he changed lawyers often because each one he met saw him only as an expensive business suit ripe for a trip to the cleaners.

Fred had repeated his favorite lawyer joke with tireless abandon throughout Oliver's childhood. "Do you know the perfect Christian names for a married pair of lawyers?" Fred would quip at every opportunity. Nobody ever knew. "Bill and Sue, because Bill can sue and Sue can bill." Fred never tired of the telling.

liberaltown, the next menu choice, conjured up a word as familiar as the Beverly Hills ZIP code 90210. The word "liberal" resembled a ping-pong ball tossed back and forth around the Sandwich household. Amid shouts and repeated accusations, the word surfaced on Fred's lips as predictably as the consistency of Los Angeles weather. Fred blamed liberals for the family's constant state of poverty, rather than his own talent for being embroiled in lawsuits, often as claimant, but more frequently as defendant. His small export-import business seemed to produce a constant tangle of problems requiring legal help. Fred claimed that Grace's small acts of generosity, stemming solely from her liberal roots, caused them to make continual sacrifices. According to Fred, she'd managed, in the name of charity, to give away to her many liberal causes what little money remained from their income after taxes and the legal feeding frenzy of useless lawyers. Of course, Fred counted Oliver as one of the primary recipients of her endless donations. On more than one occasion, in a fit of anger, Fred threatened to export Oliver to regions unknown.

Time and again while growing up, Oliver had retreated to his room to shut out his parents' angry fights, curling up into a fetal position on top of his bed. His name would fall into the middle of each loud confrontation like a shoe stepping into a puddle of mud. After the house quieted down, he would seek solace from his mother, but she would be silent and withdrawn, sometimes in tears. Despite these confrontations, the word "liberal" conjured up a comforting feeling.

Lecturetown appeared next on the monitor. The sound of the name brought up images of hell. Oliver envisioned thousands of cranky pie-faced Ls identical to the ones he encountered at Lettering Heights eager to lecture him on his shortcomings and remind him of his ignorance. Lecturetown sounded about as appealing to Oliver as letting himself be dipped in honey and then led into a swarm of killer bees. The fourth choice, Lettering Heights, home of the worker Ls, offered no incentive to return.

So after brief but serious thought, in the end, Oliver selected liberaltown.

The screen first beamed a panoramic view of a small and tidy Western town awash in brilliant colors. Then the camera focused in on a close-up of Main Street, a dusty road with wooden sidewalks, whitewashed buildings, painted signs, and hitching posts that mirrored every cliché from *Shane* to *Little House on the Prairie* to Wild West attractions at Disneyland. The view looked as tranquil and inviting as a favorite pair of old shoes.

Where, however, were the people, horses, automobiles, bicycles, or even the Ls with their pie-tin heads? Only signs on storefronts offered any hope of finding a normal town. As the camera panned down Main Street, Oliver read signs reading Lego 'L'avings and Loan, LLitebrites Letterless Library, Larks 'L'ascending, liberaltowns Luscious 'L'ectasies, Lucky Lady Saloon, Lapidarian, and Ludicrous Linguistic Liabilities.

"liberaltown was 'l'omputed by Big Mac some time ago for a migrant population," the voice of the monitor informed Oliver. "Currently the town holds a population of 1,036 'l'omputed Ls as well as unspecified numbers of noncomputed Ls. Bad feelings between liberal town and Lawyertown initially erupted from a border dispute between them. Recently, Lawyertown legislators, of which there are twenty-two, decided to challenge the upper case L in the name of liberal-town. Their bill, introduced by Lester Lisp before the legislature, demanded that the capital L in the name liberaltown face left rather than right to reflect the true leanings of the town. Lister Leeds, the sole representative of liberaltown, defended the town during a legislative debate. He explained that the name bore no relationship to the meaning of the word 'liberal.' The name, in fact, originated from its founder, Liberal Liability. Long ago Liberal Liability, no longer able to stand all the hyperbole, departed Lecturetown in disgust to settle in a new place. Eventually, other disgruntled Lecturetown citizens followed suit. Together they formed liberaltown.

"But," the announcer continued, "under Lisps urging, the legislators voted in the law. They ordered liberaltown to reverse the capital L in its name. However, the town refused. In what can only be termed a lexicon standoff, the town has begun to spell its name using a lowercase l."

Along with the lengthy narrative, the monitor displayed pictures of residential streets in liberaltown. Block after block showed a consistent turn-of-the-century design: two-story wood-frame homes typical of a small Western town. Curiously, single-story 1950s tract houses out of *Leave It to Beaver* or *The Adventures of Ozzie and Harriet* were interspersed with the older ones. Now and then a house of post-and-beam construction appeared.

As the tour concluded, the voice offered the following summation: "liberaltown is a safe and pleasant place to visit, but some citizens are leaving out of concern that the legislature has marked the place for future extermination."

Oliver and the monitor rose in unison. Before Oliver could walk away from the monitor, the voice spoke again: "Seventy-three Legos service charge, please. Legos must be deposited in the box extended from the bottom of this monitor. One hundred Lego bills will be given correct change. L.T. & T. thanks you for your patronage."

"I know that voice," Oliver blurted out. Right then the screen produced a large, intimidating eyeball. Having no Legos in his pocket, Oliver decided the time to depart had arrived.

In a flash, the monitor tossed a laser-beam lasso to snag Oliver before he could get away. Restrained, the lasso forced him to stand still while the energetic device constructed a geodesic dome around the two of them. Crisscrossing light beams created an instant mini-prison.

The friendly familiar voice now took on the tone of a scolding parent: "When undisciplined behavior persists, L.T. & T. is inclined to become user unfriendly. L.T. & T. does not enjoy threatening its customers, but we will not hesitate to use proper restraint. Do not try to escape by altering or touching the laser beams in any manner. Attempts to deface them may make you subject to abbreviation or elimination. Deposit seventy-three Legos at this time or, for convenience sake, use your library card to charge services. L.T. & T. thanks you for your patronage. We wish you a nice day."

Oliver dug his wallet out from his left rear pocket. Two of his fingers extracted and placed his library card into the drawer in one rapid motion. As the drawer retracted, Oliver dipped into the wallet again, bringing out Lysander's student ID.

"Scanning indicates this library card is not known in L Land." Here a different voice interjected the words: "Los Angeles does not appear on any list. Conclusion: The library card is rejected. No solution is available for this problem." The drawer ejected the card.

Before Oliver could slip his library card and Lysander's ID back into his wallet, every beam uncriss-crossed. His immediate sense of relief proved short-lived, however. Instantly, the monitor vanished as did any trace of summer. Sunshine, trees, birds, flowers—all were replaced by a flat, gray sky and a desolate black-and-white landscape.

Confused and frustrated by the sudden shift, Oliver began his long trek down the road that led toward liberaltown. At first, he walked timidly. Then he sped up into a trot. Keeping the pace of a slow jog, he ran mile after mile on the hard dirt. *Where is liberaltown?* He asked himself over and over. The black-and-white terrain never altered, and Oliver didn't see a sign of a town anywhere.

Fatigue threatened to devour his last reservoir of energy. Tripping over his own tired feet, Oliver finally wilted like a flower. Spread-eagle and exhausted, he feebly scanned the horizon from ground level. Far away in the distance, he noticed a cloud of dust barreling in his direction at the pace of a twister. A chorus of atonal sounds, like a hundred electric lawn mowers, thundered toward him.

A thick, transparent wall suddenly caught his attention. *Where did that come from?* he wondered. As high as his chest, the wall stood some five feet off the road along both sides as far as the eye could see. Why hadn't he noticed this wall before? He crawled toward the transparent structure on his knees, then forced himself up to press his palm against the flat top. Like a bowl of soft Jello, the wall yielded to his touch.

As Oliver turned his head, he realized he'd left the road just in time. A noisy, orchestrated buzzsaw rushed by him. He shut his eyes in an attempt to avoid the onslaught of flying dust. A left-right, left-right cadence marked the noisy progression of hockey stick Ls swiveling in rows, six across, and moving in unison like a marching band. These Ls appeared to be faster and far more organized than the chaotic group operating below Lettering Heights. As the Ls whirled past, they raised a terrible clatter. Oliver covered his ears in a futile gesture to keep out the deafening thunder. As suddenly as the marchers appeared, they vanished in the direction of the crossroads, leaving only a cloud of settling dust behind.

Through the thick grayness hurried three ragtag little Ls. Tiny 'Tellows, they'd remained far behind, unable to catch up. Valiantly, they pushed on to stay as close as possible to the pack. Back and forth they pivoted, as fast as their miniature hockey sticks would swivel. But spotting Oliver in the midst of a sneezing attack, they made a trilateral decision. The words #span_smallcaps WAVE THE SHALES!span, resting on the chest of what they assumed to be a computed young L, gave them an acceptable excuse to forsake their endeavor to keep up with the others. They had found a home. Without notice or further ado, the small Ls hopped aboard and settled easily among the letters on the shirt. The new slogan read #span_smallcaps WAVELL THE SHALLES!span.

Still coughing dust, Oliver backed up to lean against the wall, pressing his elbows into the edge for support when he heard, "Greetings and salavations young man seeking revelations, which you will not find, friend of mine, by leaning against my personal wall, clear and transparent as a crystal ball."

Oliver jumped at the unexpected voice, seemingly coming from the gray sky. Afraid, he backed away from his resting place. He had heard no hint of threat in the rhyme. The voice, in fact, sounded like a youthful Johnny Carson. Oliver knew Carson's voice well. He had heard his light-hearted refrain on many a hot summer night as a child when, lying in bed, the sound drifted down from his parents' open second-story bedroom window. Carson jokes had comingled with the steady rhythm of his father's loud snores.

Oliver turned around to stand face-to-face with the speaker. Instead of a pie-tin-faced L, he encountered an odd-looking lion. Making fun of Oliver's former resting position, the lion aped every nuance of the young man's stance just as nimbly as it had imitated

Carson's voice.

Oliver didn't know whether to laugh or cry. A lion covered in lamb's wool! A curly black mane crowned the broad and powerful features of the lions head right down to his whiskers, while a fleece as white as snow stretched across its powerful lion body.

"Don't laugh at me, my fine young 'fellow. You, who sneezed on my wall of Jello and acted like you knew where you were headed in high hopes of being fed and bedded. I'll now guide you in the right direction to a small town that will worship your erection."

Despite the personal reference to his private parts, Oliver attempted to respond with a degree of dignity. "I don't need your help to find liberaltown, thank you," the young man answered with an edgy tone. "I'm sure it's just up the road."

A sarcastic look, mingled with a touch of pity, was the lion's only response. Rear legs crossed, he posed against the wall like a laureate poet basking in the glory of his own vulgar rhymes. Who could pay serious attention to such a ludicrous spectacle?

Oliver realized he had no choice but to be polite. In a soft, solicitous tone he began to ingratiate himself. "Maybe you can be of some help after all. I'm sorry about being so rude a minute ago. But you caught me off guard. You see, I'm lost, and I'm trying to find my way home. That's why I'm headed for liberal-town. I would appreciate whatever help you could give me."

Crossing, then recrossing, then crossing once more his hind legs, the lion looked as if he were seriously reflecting on Oliver's change of attitude.

"If you hope to return home as you claim to be tryin', whom better to kiss up to than a lamentable lion? First, can you explain where your home might be? Your manners and customs are unfamiliar to me."

Fast as a sneeze, Oliver caught the contagious rhyming disease.

"I'm from LA, quite far away," he responded.

The black, curly corkscrews on the lions head bounced back and forth in a nod. Seeing this as a sign of encouragement, Oliver continued.

"I've landed in a place called L Land, but all here is black, white, and bland. I'm headed toward liberaltown, though it's hard to see if it's around. I'm so hungry I feel like cryin', and I'm getting tired of tryin', and that's the whole truth, friendly lion."

Continuing in a rap style, Oliver felt his agitation increase. "My mother's worried, that much I know. She just can't figure where I would go. My father must find it a scream, but as for me, man, it's one bad dream."

A hearty laughter interrupted Oliver's effort. Flushed once again, his black-and-white face darkened like a rain cloud.

The lion covered his face with both paws in a vain attempt to hide his silly grin. Not able to conceal his smirk, he went on.

"I see plainly from my point of view that you don't know an IUD from an IOU. You can't divorce the stinger from the bee or the dog's bark from the bark of a tree. Wake up, my boy, is what I say, if you seek the way to old LA."

Oliver continued in a desperate state, "Are there people in liberaltown? Where exactly can the town be found? And what exactly is a Lego? Real money or more like play dough?

The lion groaned. "Your questions all have answers, just as your answers have questions. But all of your nonsense gives me indigestion.”

The lion dropped onto all four feet in a proper lion stance. Unfortunately, this move did not improve the deleterious effect he had upon Oliver. Unflappable, intent only upon finding some signs of intelligent life in Oliver, the lion added after a long pause, “Its riddleiculous indeed, clarification you still need. I’m from the city of Lyin’, a place that’s dyin’, because we have given up tryin’.”

Startled by this confession, Oliver asked, “Do you mean to say you’ve been lying? There’s no reason for me to keep trying?” Hysteria had by now crept into his voice. “If I don’t know, where can I go? If I don’t know, how can I go?”

The lion countered with a riddle, “Big Mac had a little lamb who thought he was a lion. When Oliver came to him, he sent the lad off cryin’.”

Again the lion broke into uproarious laughter, which he followed by an incredible backward flip. His acrobatic bounce landed him squarely in the middle of the clear Jello wall. Bending both forelegs as low to the ground as a lion is able, he bowed elegantly as if to acknowledge some silent applause.

Mired in this lion’s insane version of a good time seemed to Oliver strangely enough a better place to be for now than walking along an empty road looking for a town that might not exist. So, in desperation, Oliver continued the conversation. “I’d like your perception about my direction.”

The lion’s taunting voice filled his ears. “Time, which does not exist here, reveals all to those who hear. Continue the same way, I say, and soon you’ll settle down to a leisurely life in liberaltown. Turn every dimension upside down until an LL you’ve found. That boy will guide you back home, you see. It’s all as easy as A to Z. Now

I've spoken far too much. Find yourself another crutch."

As the last word sounded, the lion, along with the clear wall, vanished, just as everything else had in this place. Three little Ls on Oliver's T-shirt were all that remained.

Alone on the desolate road once more, Oliver reevaluated his predicament before he moved forward. Five hours earlier his life had been ordinary and blissfully predictable. He sifted through the events that had led him here. The only answers he found that gave any kind of clue came from a gnawing at his heart and a hunger in his stomach.

He noted the time: past eight o'clock on Saturday evening. If only he could use his cell phone. Oliver pictured his mother sitting alone in the kitchen. Concerned, perhaps in tears, she would be upset by his sudden disappearance. Absorbed in the Dodger game, his father would be settled into his favorite easy chair in the den, a bottle of Southern Comfort by his side.

Saturday night, Oliver would be at the Leanmeaneating Machine, where he held a part-time job. Often at this time, he would be there hanging out with his friends. Customers would be at the counter placing their orders, then sitting down with friends or family to eat. Unconcerned and unaware of his absence, tomorrow they'd do the same. Almost all the residents of Los Angeles would continue their lives as if Oliver never existed.

Cutting short these disturbing thoughts, Oliver moved forward with slow, heavy strides. Not ten feet had passed when a vision in the middle of the road stopped him dead in his tracks. Lysander, transparent—the perfect outline of her tall, thin body— shimmered in a mirage.

"What is your name?" the beautiful vision asked. She sounded exactly like Lysander. Overcome, Oliver found it difficult to concentrate on what she was saying. "Aren't you the boy who sat beside me in English class? The one who disappeared? Whatever happened to you?"

The words stung like venom. But then again, they also flattered. To think Lysander might remember him! He recalled well the day just a month earlier when they had departed from class, walking side by side toward the parking lot. They talked about classes, the registration process, parking problems, various professors they'd heard lecture. Not a word had penetrated. Instead, he had practiced over and over in his mind the words he didn't have the courage to utter: "Maybe we could go to the movies one night."

Again tongue-tied, Oliver saw a streak of light appear from the gray sky. The light struck instantly, eliminating Lysander's luminous apparition. In her place, he saw the rhyming lion, balanced on his two hind legs. In a continuation of Lysander's own dear voice, the lion offered a final, brief observation before he too vanished: "As you make this perilous journey inside, measure each step and take it in stride."

Oliver pounded the palm of his hand against his forehead, thoroughly confused. What made sense anymore? He didn't want to partake of some incomprehensible adventure. He longed to return to his day-to-day life. Even giving up the thought of winning the heart of his Lysander was no big deal, really … since he had never had a chance to begin with. If it made any difference or mattered to anyone out there, he would confess and shout loudly enough for the whole L world to hear that he never wanted to be different, never was a somebody, never would be a hero … not here, not anywhere.

Crossbar Confusion

Listless, thirsty, Oliver trudged on with a heavy heart and sore feet, searching for some familiar sign, anything to lift his low spirits. But all he came up with was his dependable watch. Then and there, he made up his mind that for him to get through this journey and back home again, he would have to go on just as his watch did, and as the lion suggested, one step at a time.

Strangely comforted by the watch's round and cozy features, Oliver kept an eye on its face. Why, he thought, was a watch called a watch and not a watchim? Didn't his watch watch over him? Couldn't he have the time and day at his bidding? This connection with home would help him to stay the course. His watch remained on his wrist just for him. The thought soothed him. From now on, he resolved, his true and only trustworthy friend would be Watchim the watch. Just Watchim!

Looking fondly at Watchim, he passed minute after minute of distance while challenging himself to spell out the name of each Soviet Republic. At the very moment he wrestled with the correct spelling of Novgorod-Karabash, he caught a drift of smoke rising from out of nowhere. He strained to locate the source.

A few steps further brought him up a small hill. From there, he saw smoke rising from a shack beside the road, perhaps two hundred yards ahead. The small structure seemed, from a distance, to be made of pieces of rough wood with a roof of corrugated metal. Afraid the shack might prove to be another mirage, Oliver broke into a fast run.

Getting closer, he slowed as he noticed a crossbar beside the shack. Six inches thick, the long strip of wood blocked the entire width of the dirt road. The white painted bar extended horizontally from a constructed base. Cradled in a metal U-frame, the crossbar appeared to be intended to control the nonexistent flow of traffic along the road. On the side of the shack that faced the road Oliver saw a window with four panes and a sign that read:

#div_bq #bq-ind #span_smallcaps LIBERALTOWN CITY LIMITS!span

#bq-ind #span_smallcaps LAWYERS BARRED!span!div

The dirty windowpanes and the darkness inside the shack made it difficult to see clearly through the glass. Nevertheless, Oliver was pretty certain he detected a form stirring behind the window just as he heard something hit the floor with a loud crash.

"Hello, anybody home?" Oliver called out in his friendliest tone.

"Just a doggone minute there," came the call from within. Why did that voice sound as familiar as the one in the monitor? As he gripped the top of the crossbar, Oliver attempted to twist his head and shoulders into a position that would allow him to peer inside the open doorway.

Afraid to appear nosy, Oliver straightened up the instant a human figure emerged from the shack. The man froze in place when he spotted Oliver. An instant later a warm smile spread across the man's face. He held a chart in one hand, which he glanced at, while he waved with the other. "Howdy doody, pardner. Welcome to liberaltown." Oliver twisted his neck to look behind him, convinced the man aimed his friendly gesture at a larger audience. But the surrounding landscape remained as empty and bleak as before.

Oliver judged the man's height to be about the same as his own. He wore a gray Western-cut suit with a matching vest over a colorless plaid shirt. A pair of shiny cowboy boots, string tie, and oversized Western-style dress hat completed the outfit. Altogether, the gatekeeper gave the appearance of a prosperous rancher. The only discrepancy in the picture was that, instead of a branding iron, in his left hand he held a clipboard, which he kept glancing at every few seconds, as if it held cue cards. Despite his warm greeting, the man seemed intent on giving Oliver the once-over before he was allowed another step.

Under normal circumstances, the appearance of a real person would have eased Oliver's fears. But fresh memories of the lion and the vision of Lysander kept him on edge. He cautioned himself that familiar features and a recognizable voice might once again be the work of the lion, who seemed always ready to play a trick. Then again, perhaps the rancher was another L creature in disguise. Oliver had fast adapted to his new environment: he had come to expect the unexpected. If necessary, he planned to duck under the crossbar in a mad dash for freedom.

After a long and mutually pregnant pause, the man made the first move. Amazed, Oliver recognized the gait, just as he had the face and voice. The rancher paused no more than five feet from Oliver on the other side of the crossbar, and his identity became clear at once.

The eight years of his presidency had coincided with the first eight years of Oliver's life. As a child, Oliver had observed him a thousand times on television in front of a gaggle of shouting, demanding microphones. Even now, in this desolate place, Ronald Reagan had not abandoned his style. Reagan looked as young and fresh as he had in Uncle Bob's videos. The host from *Death Valley Days*, one of Bob's favorite programs, carried his role off magnificently, greeting the lone visitor to liberaltown as if he were the equivalent of the finest crowd of reporters.

His walk had a youthful bounce and his rubbery face had nary a wrinkle. The neck looked tighter and the hair, if possible, was fuller and shinier than Oliver recalled. This Reagan incarnation looked as if he had been dipped into the fountain of youth.

No words could describe Oliver's awe at meeting Reagan in the flesh. At a complete loss as to how to address him, Oliver hesitated, hoping the man would offer him a hint from the other side of the crossbar.

After giving Oliver another once-over, Reagan consulted his clipboard again. "Welcome to liberaltown. My name is Lexi Lenticular, keeper of the crossbar." Lexi delivered the line with skillful ease, extending a hand to Oliver over the crossbar. Grasping his hand, Oliver was surprised to feel Lexi's skin so cool to the touch, especially as the outside temperature remained pleasantly neutral. "Please state your name and destination," Lexi went on.

"My name is Oliver Sandwich, Your Excellency," Oliver said in a timid and respectful voice. "I'm trying to find liberal-town. I guess I've found it. Could I ask what you're doing here? I thought you lived in Bel-Air."

Lexi's face registered confusion. He didn't seem to have the slightest idea what this young man meant by "Your Excellency." Instead of answering, Lexi asked, "What kind of name is Sandwich anyway? Not a lawyer name, I hope." He added with a little laugh, "Here we eat lamb sandwiches."

Lenticular scratched his head as he went on. "Sandwich is an S name. How did you come here from S Land? Must be some kind of trick." Lexi had deviated from the script on the clipboard. Now he paused for a moment to regain control, seemingly aware he'd made a mistake by striking out on his own. Then he continued by rote. "What is the stated purpose of your visit to liberaltown?"

"I need your help returning home. But I hope you realize that I am not from S Land or a lamb for eating," Oliver pleaded in a half-joking manner.

Lexi just smiled.

"I really do need help," Oliver said.

Lexi consulted the clipboard. "Howdy doody, pardner. Welcome to liberaltown." He had begun the loop all over again.

"Can I pass?" Oliver finally asked, avoiding further discussion about his last name.

"I have to ask you the questions first," Lexi said, staring directly at the clipboard in his hand. Lifting one page, he read to himself quietly as he mouthed each word on the list.

Though eager to reach town, Oliver stood quietly waiting patiently for Lexi to continue. Why do anything more? With his new perspective on life, Oliver cleverly realized that an actor always runs the stage.

"Please state your name and destination," Lexi finally demanded again. Then he added as an afterthought, "And don't tell me you're Oliver Sandwich. You're going to be known as Liver Landwich here."

"Do you want my destination?" Oliver asked meekly, adding, in an equally soft tone, "Why do you call yourself Lexi Lenticular?"

"Sure ask a lot of damn questions, whippersnapper. I'm supposed to be the one asking. Call myself Lexi Lenticular 'cause that's my name. You think I don't get teased for looking like Ronald Ray Gun? First, the town council makes me 'l'ompute myself to look like him because they think he looks like the kind of 'l'elia that guards a gate. You think I don't know who he is? How many times have I been called Ronald Ray Gun, fastest pun in the West? Want to guess? Unscramble your brain, boy. Now, let's get down to brass tacks. Raise your right hand the same as I do."

Lexi promptly raised his left arm, and Oliver raised his left one as well. "Do you swear to tell the whole truth and nothing but the truth, and that you aren't one of those lawyer varmints?"

"Sure I do," Oliver consented. "And I'm not."

"Now I've got these here questions I have to ask you. Try to wait until I finish before you answer." Lexi consulted the clipboard again. "These are lawyer questions because we don't want no lawyers in liberaltown. Lawyers have wrecked things for us here. See this long bar across the road? This is one bar no lawyer can pass. That's why it's here."

"I'm not a lawyer," Oliver stated again.

Ignoring his comment, Lexi started reading the list. His expression turned serious in the act of performing his official duties.

1. Are you now or have you ever been a member of the bar?

2. Have you ever been served at a bar?

3. Have you ever used a bar of soap?

4. Have you ever swung from a monkey bar?

5. Do you sing bar-i-tone?

6. Do you now or have you ever lived in a bar-rio?

7. Have you ever been bar-red from any activity, organization, or Boy Scout camp?

8. Have you crossed any great bar-rier reef?

9. Would you consider yourself a bargain hunter?

10. Do you now or have you ever gone swimming bar-assed?

11. And this is the final question. Have you ever been bar-ried?

"Bar-ried?" Oliver repeated. "Maybe you mean 'married' or 'buried'?"

Lexi scratched his head with his one free hand directly beneath the rim of his ten-gallon hat. "Darned if I know. Says here 'bar-ried.' It don't matter much. Just answer one way or the other. Only one questions worth a hoot and a holler as it stands."

Oliver thought the questions totally ridiculous. How should one respond to such nonsense? They reminded him of some of the questions his college professors asked on exams.

"Would you please repeat number four again?" Oliver asked, even though he already knew all the questions by heart. In an attempt to look serious, he put on the mannerisms that he thought were expected of him. He pretended to think hard about the answers. First, he rubbed his forehead, then he stroked his chin, and then he nervously pursed his lips. Finally, he glanced toward the far-off black-and-white hills. "Wow," he concluded. "These are hard questions."

Lexi stood, pencil poised, ready to jot down each answer on his pad. Oliver began to recite his answers.

1. No.

2. Yes, when I became legal age.

3. Yes.

4. When I was a kid.

5. I sing off-key.

6. No.

7. Once in the sixth grade I was barred from playing baseball because I threw the ball at a nasty kid.

8. No.

9. I've gone bargain hunting with my mother. But I don't consider myself to be either a bargain or a hunter.

10. I have been swimming bar-assed, but not since I was a kid visiting my family in Texas.

11. If I'd been buried, I probably wouldn't be here. So it's no.

While Oliver recited his answers, Lexi wrote each response down in furious strokes on a piece of paper he'd placed on top of the clipboard.

With a burst of air that escaped his lungs after his last answer, Oliver looked straight at Lexi. But the expression on the man's face gave Oliver no clue as to whether he had passed or failed the quiz.

While Oliver looked for some sign, Lexi ripped the paper loose and crumpled it into a ball. "Think I can hit the basket there?" he asked, motioning toward an office-size wastebasket on the ground beneath the window. Oliver had not noticed the basket before.

"Sure," he answered in a disheartened voice, certain he had somehow failed the test.

Lexi moved a couple of strides to his right before he jumped to arc the wadded ball into the basket, where it popped against the metal bottom.

"Lamb's-eye," he cried, beaming with pleasure from his accomplishment. One hand gripped the crossbar below in order to raise it high enough for Oliver to pass.

Amazed at his good luck, Oliver realized he'd passed the test. But he didn't know how or why. Lexi now allowed him to pass the barrier even though he had jump-shot his answers into the wastebasket.

"Did I pass, then?" Oliver knew that he would be foolish to question anything right now, but he couldn't contain his curiosity. "I asked you if I could score a lambs-eye, didn't I?"

"Sure. But what does that have to do with the test?"

"You must be the thickest 'l'elia in all L Land, worse than a dumb non 'l'omputed L. Those questions I asked were only for me. Answers were for you. If answers are for you, they're not for me. Now, is that so hard to understand? Don't worry. Didn't I ask you if I could hit a lamb's-eye? Didn't you say yes? Didn't I do it? Didn't I tell you only one question counted? Now, you just mosey along the road here, and you'll hit town faster than I can lap up a glass of 'l'aspirilla. I'll go ahead to warn them a stranger's coming. Nobody much likes surprises anymore. Tend to shoot first and ask questions later."

With his words still hanging in the air, Lexi disappeared without a trace. Staring at the empty shack, Oliver shook his head in disbelief. What next?

New Man in Town

Leaving the crossbar area, Oliver watched as a monitor rose up from the ground, liberaltown appeared, not in person, but as a mere name beneath what was yet another miserable monitor. By now, the tired young man had accepted the existence of liberaltown. He had left the toll-booth area expecting to see a town like the one he'd previously seen on the screen. He had passed a test to be admitted. So how could he be tricked like this again?

Nothing looked different! Beside the road, in the midst of the typical black-and-white nondescript terrain, stood a monitor identical in size and appearance to the one that had imprisoned him at the crossroads. A single word appeared below the screen beside a black button, liberaltown had been spelled out in lowercase letters. Suspended in space, the monitor seemed poised, like a hangman sworn to duty.

Oliver burst into tears. In that instant, he knew his dreams were lost. He knew he would never again experience the early sun glide above the low-cut hills warming the morning chill. He would not see white clouds the texture of cotton candy drift across the horizon as he sat at a Wilshire Boulevard cafe eating pancakes. He would never again inhale the smells of frying bacon and freshly brewed coffee.

Caught in the hopelessness of his situation, he dried his tears on his shirt before he stepped forward to confront his future. As soon as the monitor adjusted to his forehead and a beam made the connection, he pushed the button. Two choices appeared:

#div_bq   #bq-ind   #span_smallcaps   BLACK-AND-WHITE!span

#bq-ind #span_smallcaps COLOR!span!div

User-friendly once again, the familiar coded voice offered instructions: "Push the button once for black-and-white, twice for color."

Before he could push twice, Oliver stopped his finger in midair.

"How many Legos will this cost?"

The announcer responded as if he had been sitting inside the monitor waiting for that very question. "You are entering liberal town. There is no charge to the calling party."

Oliver pushed the button twice. More choices appeared.

#div_bq #bq-ind #span_smallcaps LIBERALTOWN!span

#bq-ind #span_smallcaps OPEN!span

#bq-ind #span_smallcaps CANCEL!span!div

"Press once to enter liberaltown," the smooth voice directed. "Press twice to cancel the selection. L.T. & T. wishes you a nice visit."

One push did the trick. Instantly, Oliver found himself standing at the edge of town exactly at the point where Main Street began. Relief and exhilaration flooded his being, liberaltown! The place existed complete with a three-dimensional Main Street identical to the street on the crossroad monitor. But unlike the uninhabited town he had viewed on the screen, this Main Street bustled with life and color.

Oliver saw normal-looking people dressed in old-fashioned clothes walking down the street. Some entered and left wooden buildings with signs identical to those on the monitor. Others stood around in small groups, talking, liberaltown seemed a carnival of bright colors against a backdrop of clear, deep-blue sky. Behind him, the road led through open spaces, stretching toward green hills touched by muted shades of purple and gold.

Basking in his good and glorious fortune, Oliver stood quietly for a moment. As he counted his blessings, he followed the stride of a tall and powerful man whose big boots slapped the wooden sidewalk with a resounding crunch. The sure-footed walk, along with the man's broad shoulders and unusual height, exuded confidence and authority.

No duded-up ranch sissy like Ronald Reagan, this man dressed in basic Western clothes. As he drew closer, Oliver made out worn boots, brown leather pants, and a red-and-black plaid shirt. A dusty white Western-style hat, tilted to shade his head, and a red cotton bandanna around the man's neck finished off the outfit. Once the sidewalk ended, he hopped off to continue directly toward Oliver, his expression fixed as if he were headed for a shootout with a group of unsightly varmints.

Awestruck, Oliver backed away. "Wow" was the only word that came out of his mouth. No question about this man's identity. Oliver recognized the face that starred in *Stagecoach, Red River, Flying Leathernecks, The Conqueror, The Shootist, True Grit, The Quiet Man, The Searchers.* The list went on and on: a young cowboy, a dying cowboy, a military commander, an aging cowboy, an Irish rebel, a barbarian, a flying ace, always a hero. He recognized every ridge and fold in that manly face. Until someone explained otherwise, Oliver knew he stood face-to-face with undeniable proof of resurrection.

The voice of John Wayne boomed out at him: "Howdy, Mr. Liver Landwich. Lexi popped by to inform me you were headed our way. I'm the mayor here in liberaltown. Name's Lefty Littleleather. Don't get many visitors anymore after them lawyer varmints turned the damn legislature against us on the issue of our capital L. See what happens when you mind your own business? Some idiot thing comes back to bite you in the ass like an angry sidewinder."

Lefty folded his arms in front of his chest as he spoke. Shouting as if Oliver were deaf, Lefty sounded like a television set with the volume turned up several notches too high.

Hawkeyed, the mayor tried to size up the newcomer. At once he noted that Oliver did not respond like a typical L. *Where could this odd-looking creature have come from?* he wondered. *Could he be a spy from Lawyertown? Or could he be from G Land, the seat of government for all letters?*

"Know why they did it, don't you?" Lefty continued, as if Oliver knew what he meant. "Hate us here. They used to come over for visits looking like that Perry Mason character or some other LTV lawyer trying to stir up trouble. We wouldn't have none of it. Tell me, young 'l'ella, what brings you to liberaltown? Someone from the government hire you to make a case against the town council or something like that?"

Intimidated and confused, Oliver remained silent. But since his lack of response drew an angry glare, he decided that he better spill the beans fast. As the mayor shifted his weight from foot to foot, the boy outlined in graphic detail the many adventures that led him to liberaltown, not excepting his embarrassing and tearful breakdown when confronted by the last monitor. He elaborated upon and enhanced each incident to gain the maximum amount of sympathy.

"That there has to be the saddest story I've ever heard, sadder than any program on LTV," Lefty replied. "Fell down a mailbox, did you? Claim to be some stranger from a strange land, huh? Well, we'll see about that."

He chomped on the last words the way an angry man clamps

down on a cigar. "Let me give it to you straight, Liver, if that's your real name. Since those lawyers got on our tail, we don't take kindly to strangers here. We've got our ways of checking things out. If I find you're lying to me, you'll wish you were a period at the end of a sentence." While the two vertical lines on his forehead emphasized his angry expression, crags expanded like churning rubber across his cheeks.

To be threatened by a man long dead rattled Oliver to the bones. Puddles gathered in his *eyes* and tumbled down each cheek.

"Son of a gun," Lefty uttered, as his jaw widened. He whistled through his teeth like the professional he imitated.

Ashamed, Oliver raised the back of his hand to wipe away the tears. But Lefty took a sudden step forward, grabbing the young man's wrist with one of his powerful, cool hands. Only inches apart, the mayor towered over Oliver. Much as a child collects a field specimen on an outing, Lefty used the index finger of his free hand to scoop up a bit of the fluid that had pooled beneath Oliver's eyes.

"Son of a gun," he repeated as he stared at the magical dew-drop on the back of his finger. Lefty appeared every bit as startled as Oliver had been earlier when he realized his eyes followed the big boots of John Wayne as they stomped toward him.

When Lefty spoke again, his voice lacked any trace of suspicion: "Why, you aren't some renegade legal beagle or a spy from G Land. There ain't no letter from A to Z, far as I know, that can rain from his eyeballs that way. Son of a gun, I'll bet every dadburn word in that sad story you laid on me is the absolute bona fide truth. Come on, son. We'll do all we can to help you get home. Can't put you up in a hotel because we don't have none. But the little lady and me will give you some good old-fashioned Littleleather hospitality.

Fix you up with a little grub. Bed you down, and you'll be good as new. Then my little girl, Laurie, can show you around town after you've got yourself together."

With a powerful arm wrapped around Oliver, Lefty urged him forward, tugging at his shoulders until he began to move. Side by side down the middle of Main Street they walked. Everyone knew the mayor, and each person greeted him as they passed. Most of the townspeople looked human. Only an occasional L-shaped pie-tin head whisked by, ignoring both the mayor and his young companion.

But why did everything about the street look so staged? Oliver felt like a tourist visiting the newest attraction at Universal Studios. A mother took her child inside the Lapidary Store. Noise came from the inside the saloon as they passed by. Life went on, but for Oliver the whole town had the appearance of a cardboard cutout. He imagined one of those photographer's studios on a boardwalk where a person could become a sailor or a Hawaiian beauty just by sticking his or her head through a hole.

Three tough-looking macho types dressed in Western clothes with empty holsters sat on a bench in front of the saloon. Lefty returned their good-natured banter as he passed by, "When you gonna marry, Larry? How's it goin', Lowen? What's new, Lew?"

Why did those men, Lowen, Lew, and Larry, crowded together on a bench, remind him of something he had seen before? Just as he wracked his brain to remember what and where, Marilyn Monroe crossed the street in front of them. His brain froze. Oliver gawked at her like a rube at a county fair sideshow.

Dressed in old blue jeans and high heels, Marilyn looked quite alive. Her little-girl voice greeted the mayor as she flashed Oliver an adorable, dimpled smile. She cradled her bag of groceries under one arm as she continued across the street.

Wasn't she dead like John Wayne? Hadn't she killed herself? Oliver vaguely remembered a television program he'd seen about her mysterious death. Her face triggered a flashback to when she had dominated his every thought as he sat alone in his room, pencil poised, tracing his maps from Mozambique to Montenegro. Her innocent smile had beamed down at him from a poster above his bed. For years, she remained the focus of many an imaginary journey.

While people kept pausing to greet the mayor, Oliver soon realized that he himself was a curiosity and that the townfolk wanted to view him too. As he stopped to gaze after Marilyn, he noticed people staring at him as if he were a manikin in a department store window. Most of all, they seemed fascinated by his wrinkled T-shirt with its unusual words on the front. Every person they encountered duplicated, in some way or other, an actor in the movies or on a television series he'd watched with Uncle Bob. Or he recognized them as people from some other walk of life, even if he did not know their names.

Sure, he thought, to meet John Wayne was awesome. But what about Lucy and Ricky standing in front of the general store talking to the Flying Nun, who had shed her habit in favor of lay clothing? Those kids playing in the street were Beaver Cleaver and two Dennis the Menace look-alikes. Hadn't he also spotted former president John Kennedy trying to saddle a llama? And Goober of *Mayberry R.F.D.* walked by with a beautiful woman, looking just as he had on the show.

Why did every person look and act real when many of them were long dead? Why did these kids look as young as they did when years had passed and they would now be aging adults? These questions weighed on Oliver as he walked alongside Lefty.

As they continued making their way to the Littleleather home, long-faded memories came back to Oliver. Bobby Kennedy lived again. Oliver saw him walking hand in hand with Carol Burnett. The second Dennis the Menace ran down the street chased by Lassie, or a dead ringer for the dog, at any rate.

How many years had passed since Oliver last visited Uncle Bob in Texas? He could not help but think of his uncle more fondly now. If not for him, Oliver would not have recognized any of these characters from the past. But were they characters? Or actors playing characters? Or Ls playing actors playing characters? The questions could give any red-blooded American male a major headache.

Where were the celebrities of his own generation? Where was Sting, Madonna, or a Macaulay Culkin clone playing with other kids? Not a sign of Bill Clinton anywhere. He wanted to ask Lefty about this but realized he better get the lay of the land first.

Two blocks down Main Street, Lefty turned left onto an intersecting sidewalk that led them into the residential section. As he trailed behind, Oliver heard his stomach screech with hunger like a demented cat. Oliver caught up with Lefty at the end of the block.

Wood-frame homes almost identical in style to one another lined the dirt streets and retained the pure, wholesome, and clean sameness of Mayberry R.ED. Oliver's knees began to buckle at the end of the second block. By the time they reached the corner, Oliver's face had drained to an ashen gray. He tried to focus on an incongruous 1950s' tract house directly across the street.

"Mr. Leatherlittle?" Oliver called out.

"Littleleather."

"Mr. Littleleather …"

"Just call me Lefty," the mayor interrupted.

"Lefty. I wonder if you would explain why there are so many famous people living in liberaltown."

Littleleather had stopped when Oliver first called his name. He'd waited for the young man to draw up alongside him. As Oliver asked the question, the mayor removed his hat to run a hand through his wavy brown hair. "Don't know what you mean, exactly."

"I mean," Oliver began, "that is, a woman crossed the street in town, a very pretty blond-haired woman in blue jeans and a blue shirt, one with a mark on her left cheek. She carried a bag of groceries. She told you hello. Her name is Marilyn Monroe."

Lefty shook his head. "Lana Locaine. She only 'l'omputed herself after that Monroe beauty she seen on LTV. She's been Lana Locaine all along. Lilly Looper did the same thing, and Laricent Langgang. Lucky Luck did too, just to see how it felt. But he switched back to looking like a man. Popular, that Monroe woman."

"Most of the people in your town look identical to characters on programs I watched when I was a kid. Or famous people from back then. That man at the gate, for instance, was the president of the United States a while ago. Did you know that?"

"Lexi Lenticular. President?" Lefty asked, his tone as incredulous as his face.

"His name was Ronald Reagan."

Lefty let loose the kind of deep-throated laugh John Wayne used just before he popped a bad guy. "Sure, we still call him Ronnie Ray Gun, fastest pun in the West," Lefty informed him. "But Lexi wasn't president of nothin'. We don't have presidents here in Letterland. There's only Big Mac to tell us what we can or can't do, and I'm sure someone is tellin' him the same. Only we don't know who that is. Maybe you're mixing him up with the 'l'elia who lives in LTV? Now you got me thinking… ."

Though his head throbbed and his stomach ached, Oliver tried to listen with respectful attention. How many times since his arrival had he received answers that made him more confused than before he asked the question? He couldn't count them.

"Must be that you come here from LTV. If you're not a letter, you're not from any state in Letterland. There's no other place left, ain't that right?" Lefty continued, as much to himself as to Oliver.

Left, right! Left, right! Everything began to revolve in slow circles. Oliver felt as if he were spinning around in the drum below MaiLA again. Even though the bright, outside light made it more like high noon in liberaltown, a glance at Watchim revealed the time to be around midnight.

"What's that?" he managed to cough out.

The mayor chuckled. "What's LTV? Why Tevisions all we got. Guess there's no reason you should know anything about us seeing as you don't come from these here parts. LTV's what Big Mac gave us after he took away our travel and books some time back. See, those of us who could 'l'ompute ourselves had to look like something, didn't we? No sense in being able to 'l'ompute yourself if you don't look like someone. It's no different than when we head off for Word Central to become the lead L in a word. Don't that word have to go somewhere as well? Why would you have a word if you didn't have a place to put it?

"So we reckoned Big Mac gave us LTV to learn about the places we're headed as an L word down the road. We could 'l'ompute ourselves after those folks on LTV to get to know the folks that those words were written for. But us 'l'omputed letters are just copies of you or other LTV folks. We just look the same. You're the only genuine article around here, far as I know. If I wanted to 'l'ompute myself to look just like you, I could, and then there'd be two of you instead of one. You're the first visitor to come here from LTV. So you must live there when you're not here. Isn't that right?"

Exhausted and hungry, all Oliver could do was nod his head.

"So which of them LTV towns do you live in?"

"Los Angeles, I guess," Oliver mumbled.

"I know that town, sure as shootin'. Now, you tell me if I got this figgered right. As mayor, I hear the town council argue a lot about the facts from LTV. But now I've got a genuine authority to tell me true. Isn't Hollywood a big country same as Letterland? Some of us reckon each of those big LTV towns, New York, London, Chicago, Metropolis, Los Angeles, Sunset Strip, they're all in Hollywood like all the different letter lands are in Letterland. Others think those towns are in different dimensions, like letters live in L Land, or D Land, or G Land if they work for the government. That's one thing."

Oliver nodded his head again.

"Next is about how we 'l'ompute. You said Lexi looks like that Ray Gun 'l'elia cause at home in LTV, you see Ray Gun playing the president of all Hollywood Land, just like Big Mac runs Letterland. Is that it? You figgered, because he's president there, maybe he's president here, too. Believe me, Liver Landwich, Lexi ain't president of nothin' around here. Only special trick he has is to disappear when you need him most. Guess you watched him vanish like a double LL. Don't ask me how he does it. He won't say.

"See, here in liberaltown we don't really have much to do. We talk lots about what you LTV people do, all kinds of business and such. We try to follow them LTV people with our actions. Them young Ls, like my daughter and her friends, try to act like young folks in LTV land, and older ones like me settle on being one character, at least most of the time. It's mighty confusing trying to understand how you folks live. Maybe you'll straighten us all out."

Under ordinary circumstances, Oliver would have been flattered to help unravel the mystery. But now he could barely raise one hand to wipe the cold sweat off his forehead. He tried, but as he did his head made a full tailspin. "Maybe I should sit down," he suggested, just before he collapsed onto the wood-planked sidewalk.

The mayor couldn't believe what he saw. Many times people fainted on LTV. But most of them were women. Their eyes would go into orbit just before they dropped to the floor like rag dolls. Laurie and her friends practiced fainting sometimes for fun. They would laugh and giggle as they hit the ground. Closing their eyes, they pretended to be asleep. No L had the physical resources necessary to do anything other than playact.

More convinced than ever of Oliver's authenticity, the mayor squatted beside the unconscious fellow. Again, he used a finger to gather a sample of his sweat. How better to understand an LTV creature than to taste him? Lefty wondered if the fluid on Oliver's forehead contained 'l'alt, the only flavor any letter could taste. Holding his finger to his lips, he stuck out his tongue. Sweat, Lefty concluded, resembled a mild form of 'l'alt.

To revive a fainted person required certain procedures, the mayor recalled from LTV. He sat down cross-legged beside Oliver and cried out loudly, "Give him air! Give him air!"

Sure enough, Oliver soon revived to the sensation of a big,

clumsy hand dabbing his forehead with a genuine Western bandanna. He blinked his eyes in slow motion until he could once more see clearly.

"Could you stand up and fall down again like you did?" Lefty requested.

Oliver focused on the famous face beside him. Was that a compliment? Did he really want him to faint again?

"Maybe I should try to eat something," Oliver suggested. "I'm really hungry. Usually I eat every couple of hours."

"Well, come on, boy, let's get on with it. I'll give you a hand. Reckon the little lady can whip up some victuals, if that's what will fill the bill. Course there ain't no bill at the Littleleather house." Lefty laughed amiably.

Oliver used Lefty's powerful shoulder for support as they crossed the final street before reaching the Littleleather home, which stood directly in the middle of the block.

Lefty's gears were spinning. A real live LTV person in liberaltown had to be the biggest coup in the history of L Land, maybe even in Letterland. Like all letters, he thought only about perfecting the art of imitation. What new gestures and motions could the boy demonstrate? What did Liver look like under his clothes? What could the boy show them that would make Ls become more authentic? Lefty was burning with longing, the L equivalent of curiosity.

Liver's arrival, Lefty decided, would soon be the talk of the town. Finally there would be a topic of far greater interest than the story LLorser LLitebrite repeated endlessly. Yakking on and on, LLorser would brag, at any given opportunity, about his exposure of the infiltrators from Lawyertown. Lefty hoped Liver's unexpected appearance, properly handled, of course, could shut LLorser LLitebrite up, for a while at least. He also hoped that Livers presence could somehow restore the lost fortunes of the town as well.

"Here's the old plantation," Lefty announced as they stopped before a three-foot-high gate set in a white picket fence that enclosed the front yard of a whitewashed, two-story wood-frame house. All the houses on the block looked identical to the Littleleathers' home. Side by side, they appeared as if designed by an architect equipped with an enormous cookie cutter. Reaching out, Lefty swung the gate back. He guided Oliver down the walkway, his arm firmly around the visitor's shoulders.

Lilies of the valley grew along each side of the wide stairway that led to the wraparound porch. A plump woman appeared at the front door. She came out onto the porch to meet them. Her short brown hair, puffy cheeks, long-toothed smile, and cozy apron greeted Oliver like a breath of fresh air.

"Oh, Lefty, you've brought a guest," she whined in a high-pitched voice that he knew as well as he did his mother's. "I wish I'd known. I hope there's enough to eat. There's only lamb chops, Tapplesauce, and lettuce salad. We also have loads of leftovers."

"This here's my wife, Lo-Rain," Lefty informed Oliver, who half-dragged himself up the steps to meet her. Uncomfortable and stiff, like the television character she resembled, stood Edith, Archie Bunker's television wife in *All in the Family,* How often had Oliver watched that pained face in reruns on the tube and laughed at her foibles? She reminded him of his mother. Each was absent-minded, a dingbat, actually. But each of them possessed a heart of gold, and they both defended their children at all costs against intolerable husbands. No one in all of L Land could have made Oliver more comfortable than Edith Bunker, except his own mother.

"Lo-Rain, this here boy ain't 'l'omputed like me and you," Lefty informed her. "Now, I know you're gonna think I'm foolin' or talkin' crazy. But for once I'm not. Somehow he fell down with all them dead letters they've got over at Lettering Heights. You know that eyesore mountain they're always complaining about? Well, this here boy fell from LTV Land. He got lost and ended up here. Can you believe that? Name's Liver Landwich, and he's staying a spell until we can help him find his way home."

Lo-Rain seemed skeptical.

"I see you lookin' funny at me, Lo-Rain. But sure as shootin' it's on the up and up. Already the young 'l'elia's performed lots of LTV tricks. Fainted dead away, he did, and let little raindrops fall right out of both eyes. Rained off the top of his head too. Think he needs some of your grub real bad though. You know how those LTV folks are always eating, and he's had no food since he came here. Can you rustle him up some grub?"

Oliver saw the familiar expression of compassion mixed with a look of confusion.

"Are you pulling another trick, Lefty Littleleather?" Lo-Rain asked, softening as she looked into Oliver's sweet blue eyes. "His color does look funny, skin, too, not like us. Why don't you help him into the living room, Lefty? Maybe he'd like a nice drink. I'll make a snack right away." Shaking her head in the dizzy fashion of the *All in the Family* character, Lo-Rain retreated down the hallway, leaving the door ajar. Lefty helped his weakened guest into the house.

A long hallway punctuated by a staircase at the back formed the entryway. The wide entrance to the dining room appeared on the left. Lefty helped Oliver into the living room on the right. Steered to an antique, high-backed couch covered in brown velvet with wide upholstered arms, Oliver sank down into the comfort of a soft cushion. His body settled as if it hadn't rested for years. Lefty crossed the room to an open rolltop desk that served as a makeshift bar.

"What would you like to wet your whistle?" the cowboy asked.

"Just a glass of water, please."

"Don't want a shot? Got some real fine drinking whiskey."

"Not now, thanks."

"How about some 'l'aspirilla then? That's what most of the kids drink around here. Mighty good sody pop."

"Sure," Oliver agreed.

Lefty handed him a glass filled with a brown liquid. One tilt of the glass, and Oliver emptied the contents. An aftertaste, like saltwater from the ocean, remained in his mouth.

A wooden coffee table separated two large matching armchairs across from the couch. Crocheted white headpieces adorned both chairs, and three other headpieces were spaced along the couch.

Before Lefty had a chance to sit or to down his shot of whiskey, Oliver placed his empty glass on a coaster on the table. Lefty tilted his head back to polish off the single shot. Then he took both empty glasses back to the bar. After placing Oliver's refilled glass on the coffee table, he finally seated himself in one of the stuffed chairs.

Somewhat refreshed, Oliver rubbed the arm of the couch. A glance at Watchim reminded him that back in Los Angeles, at one in the morning, he would usually be returning home from a Saturday night of hanging out.

"Sure happy to have you here, boy," boomed Lefty Little-leather. "Yessiree, you're going to be a big hit in this town. That's for sure. You feel well enough to answer some questions about LTV now?"

"I guess so … like what?"

"Mud in your eye," Lefty said, lifting the shot glass. Before Oliver had a chance to lift his glass from the table, Lefty downed the contents of his again and asked, "Can you tell me why people in LTV are always dying, then coming back to life?"

Oliver sipped the second 'l'aspirilla as he tried to understand the question.

"Take this 'l'elia I'm 'l'omputed after," Lefty continued. "This John Wayne 'l'elia. See him all the time on LTV. One minute he's some old cowboy like me. Another time I see him, he's just a young cowboy. Then he's some smart aleck flyboy, or he's working in an office, or something else again. It don't make a lick of sense to any of us.

"You know how much work we have trying to tell everyone who we are if we change looks? Took me a long time to figger which John Wayne to be. I decided on what folks call a grizzled look. Helps keep the town council in line, except, of course, for LLorser. Nobody keeps a double LL under control. There aren't many of them. But they're a wild bunch."

Though he had no idea how to respond, Oliver listened politely. All he could think about was whether Lefty would continue this train of talk until the snack arrived. Finally, Lo-Rain entered. She served him a white bread lamb sandwich on a plate.

"Thank you, ma'am," Oliver said, placing the plate in his lap. In violation of all he'd been taught, he attacked the sandwich in large bites, swallowing before he finished chewing. Amazement showed on both of his hosts' faces. Never had they seen anybody eat with such speed. Ls ate food only for the pleasure of eating. Therefore, they lacked any reason to consume a sandwich, or any other food, in such a manner.

"Guess the boy liked it," Lefty noted.

"I'm sorry to eat so fast," Oliver apologized as he finished the rest of his drink. "I've been on the road for hours. I developed a big appetite."

"Would you like another, Mr., is it Landwich?"

"Liver Landwich," Lefty interjected.

"Mr. Landwich? I'd be happy to make you another sandwich. But we'll be having dinner soon, if you can wait."

"I can wait, thank you, ma'am," Oliver answered. He was surprised to hear a slight Western twang creep into his inflections. "Just call me Liver."

"Liver here's gonna explain all about how they live on LTV, and why they do what they do, if you want to listen, Lo-Rain."

An addled shake of the head, and Lo-Rain took the empty plate. "That's all right, Lefty. I better get dinner finished. Mr. Landwich, Liver that is, looks very hungry. Why don't you call Laurie down, dear? She's in her room watching some program. I'm sure she'd like to meet our special guest."

"Sure thing," Lefty said. "Might be a good idea to make up the guest room when you can, Lo-Rain. Looks like Liver Landwich is set to stay a spell."

A bitter taste remained in Oliver's mouth and throat. It tasted similar to the paste used for collages that he had sampled out of curiosity in fourth grade. And worse, the sandwich hadn't satisfied his hunger. Too weak to stand, he thanked Lo-Rain warmly for the food before she departed.

Then the mayor stood up. "I'll round up that little filly of mine, Laurie Littleleather. Girl's the apple of my eye, Landwich. She'll be excited to meet a real live LTV person. What's that expression she and her friends use? It'll be super groovy and soooo cool." Lefty proceeded to the foot of the stairs to call his daughter.

Oliver examined the room, which was stuffed with furniture. A royal blue rug with a rectangular yellow pattern stretched from one end to the other. All four walls had been papered with a light-blue pattern of a sky with larks in flight. Turn-of-the-century furnishings reminded Oliver how antique furniture once filled the living room of his home. When he was a child, people would come from time to time to cart off different pieces his mother had sold out of necessity.

Most vivid was a memory of her sitting on the couch in tears when a prized display case departed. She'd hugged Oliver, then age six, to her and cried, "There goes a little part of my soul, dear Oliver, right out the door with that display case." How badly he wanted to bring back the piece of furniture. He'd pulled away to run to the window in hopes of spotting where the display case went. But the mysterious person who vanished with part of his mother's soul had driven away before Oliver had a chance to reclaim it. He was both concerned and angry.

In one corner of the Littleleathers' living room stood an antique pump organ close to the open rolltop desk on which Lefty kept his bar. Matching end tables flanked the couch. A combination display cabinet and storage drawers took up almost the entire wall next to the entryway. Someone had squeezed a cedar chest into the corner. Oliver liked the room. It made him feel comfortable and at home.

Horsin' Around

Laurie Littleleather was standing in her room watching one of her favorite LTV programs, 77 Sunset Strips when the sound of her father's loud voice boomed through the closed door. At first, she ignored him. But his persistence soon forced her to respond. Irritated, she opened the door and strolled to the top of the stairs.

She called down, not trying to hide her annoyance, "What is it, Father?"

"Come on down," Lefty insisted, sounding like a game show host. "There's a 'l'elia come to visit I want you to meet." Looking up the stairway, the mayor didn't have a clear view of her. "Come on down now. Sure as shootin', you're going to get a real surprise."

"All right. All right, already," she said, the reply of a rebellious teenager.

Alone and comfortable, Oliver began to regain his composure. How pleasant to be here among nice folks, even if they weren't real ones. What did it matter if nothing made sense anymore? Most things didn't make sense at home either. What better substitute mother could he have than the one in the kitchen making dinner? And Lefty, after a difficult start, proved far kinder than his own father, and friendlier.

Suddenly a loud clatter broke into his reverie, and the house began to shake as Laurie crashed down the stairs, taking them two at a time. "She must be built like a piano," Oliver thought. He was not interested in large girls.

Laurie burst into the room, paused in the doorway, then fixed an intense stare on Oliver, who stared back with his mouth open in astonishment. In front of him stood his favorite television celebrity of all time, a character he admired, probably even loved, more than either Edith Bunker or Grace Sandwich. Part in the hallway and part in the living room, snorting hot air that raised the hair on Oliver's arms, stood a gold-colored horse with a white mane, the one and only Mister Ed, the beloved talking horse. As Oliver gaped at the star of the early '60s' TV show, the hero of his youth, the horse wagged its tail in a friendly greeting.

"Laurie, this here is Mr. Liver Landwich." Lefty made the introduction despite Oliver's expression of shock. "He's come to visit us all the way from LTV land. This is my daughter, Laurie, Liver."

The horse looked identical to Mister Ed, though a colorized version of the horse he'd known only through Uncle Bobs black-and-white videos. Oliver had by now come to realize that what you see is not always what you get, but he never in his wildest imagination anticipated such close contact with the prized horse of his youth. "Oh, I used to love you so much, Mister Ed," Oliver blurted out. Pure and innocent, the words of one-time devotion floated through the air.

Oliver's cheeks blushed beet-red at his own unexpected utterance. His hand scratched the empty air beside Ed's nose in a futile gesture to rein in the words. To make a declaration of affection to someone he did not know, particularly a horse, violated several generations of Manners' etiquette. Oliver sighed. A slight bout of dizziness made him wonder if he might faint again.

Oliver's unbridled declaration of passion caught Laurie off guard. Tension tightened her stomach. An explosion of internal gases burst out from beneath her tail with such awesome force it produced a thunderous blast. Lefty, directly in its path, almost blew out of the room. The explosion even caused Lo-Rain to run in all the way from the kitchen.

A mighty skunklike stench overpowered the room. Oliver's face flushed as if struck by a sudden heat stroke. Despite all attempts to appear normal and polite, he could not hide his astonishment. Escape, groan, or die! Finally, he could hold his breath no longer. He tried breathing through his mouth.

Meanwhile, though observing his distress,* the family seemed unaware of what caused Oliver's problem. Even if Ls looked like humans that breathed, they couldn't breathe or smell at all. They did, however, continuously release a mild, odorous gas from their mouths, a fragrance that barely permeated the air around them. Like an old-fashioned incinerator, an L absorbed any substance that could fit down its throat. Whether it converted lead or lettuce, an invisible gas emerged in a manner Oliver or others might mistake for breathing. To state the process in simple terms: Ls were full of hot air. They needed release on a continuous basis. A human might notice the odor only on rare occasions. But, in a confined room with a large group of computed Ls, the air could at times outdo a pulp factory.

This particular blast was an occurrence that an L was unable to smell. However, Lo-Rain could not help but notice their guests discomfort and whispered something in her daughter's right ear. Also, when the mayor observed Oliver rolling his eyes while holding his breath and turning red in the face, he decided it best to head for the portable bar, hoping to wash away, with a few drinks, the horrible impression of a man dying. With his back toward the group, he downed a couple of quick shots from the whiskey bottle.

"How do you do?" Exhaling through his mouth, Oliver finally released the words he had meant to say to begin with.

"I guess you found my appearance a surprise. I'm sorry," the horse stated frankly. "Now you've turned a bright red color. Is that what they call a blush on LTV?"

Not wanting to explain the real reason behind his affliction, Oliver nodded in assent. As his discomfort waned, he reveled in the familiar and kind gravelly voice that so cleverly imitated Allan Lane, the voice of Mister Ed. Each word was formulated through the up-and-down movement of the large, flabby horse lips. Embarrassed, the boy managed to mumble an apology, as Laurie herself had done a moment ago.

Believing she'd cleared the air, Laurie explained her present appearance. "I don't always run around the house looking like a horse. There isn't much for us young Ls to do in liberal-town. Our moms and dads have their routines. But we kids like to groove, hang out, be cool. 'L'omputing ourselves after weird people on LTV is lots of fun. We have parties where we all come 'l'omputed as a new character and then take turns guessing who's who. One of my friends 'l'omputed herself as a cartoon character, Gerald McBoing Boing. Another one came once as Howdy Doody."

Since the crisis seemed to have passed, Lo-Rain returned to her work in the kitchen. As Lefty downed his quick shots at the bar, he also offered a silent thank you to Big Mac for making liquor available in L Land. Pouring from the bottle of 'l'aspirilla, he partially filled a shallow bowl for his daughter and a fresh glass for Oliver.

However, Oliver surprised Lefty when he declared that he needed a stronger drink, "If you don't mind, could I have a shot of whiskey?" Even Oliver was startled by his own request. Graduation night in high school three years ago had been the last time he'd drunk hard liquor. Since that time he'd had only a few beers, to celebrate his twenty-first birthday. Not surprisingly, he wanted to try it again.

"Now you're asking for a man's drink," Lefty responded, repeating what he'd heard on LTV. He poured himself another shot as well as one for the visitor. Laurie flicked her long tongue as daintily as she could between her big white teeth to sip the 'l'aspirilla from the bowl in front of her.

"Mud in your eye," the mayor toasted as he and the boy clinked glasses. Imitating his host, Oliver downed the contents in a single gulp. Expecting fire in his throat, he felt instead the now-familiar, slightly salty taste of 'l'aspirilla.

"Think I'll see how your ma is doing in the kitchen," Lefty informed Laurie, sashaying out the door.

The odor in the room soon vanished. Now alone, the horse and stranger measured each other face-to-face. A number of questions came to Oliver's mind. How, for example, could an animal as big as a horse move around this crowded house without creating havoc? No one he knew would allow a horse to run loose in the house even if it were a son or daughter. Despite Laurie's brief explanation, Oliver remained curious about what motivated a girl to become a horse.

"I don't understand any of it," Oliver finally confessed. "Why would anyone who lives in a house be a horse? What's all this business between Ls and 'l'omputed Ls? And why do people look exactly like people they're not?"

"I'm not just a horse," the deep voice of Laurie fired back. "I'm Mister Ed, the talking horse. That's a special horse around here. We can't just 'l'ompute ourselves to be any horse in L Land. If we could 'l'ompute horses, we'd ride them all over town. Did you see any horses when you arrived? Only llamas can be 'l'omputed, and there are very few of those because they're double LLs. Llamas, lions, leopards, lizards, lambs, that's it for L Land. You live with it or you don't."

"How about Legos?" Oliver asked.

"You know about Legos?" The horse sounded surprised. "You can have all of them you want. Just go to Lego 'L'avings and Loan and open an account. Then you can draw them out. You can buy what you want."

"You mean they just give money to anyone who wants it?"

"Sure, why shouldn't they? Isn't that what banks are for?"

Oliver's right foot tapped a steady beat on the blue carpet. "If you're restricted to things that start with L, how come you have houses? Houses begin with the letter H. Don't they? And towns with T?"

"So what?" Laurie snapped back. "Logs, you've heard of logs, right? Logs can be used to make boards to build houses. Lodges, laurel trees, lakes, lassos, lilies, and some things that start with other letters are here as well. We have lots of variety, though not as much as most of us would like. I guess you grow used to it. Ls like my parents, who have been back and forth from Word Central lots of times, don't seem to mind. I've watched all the things you have on LTV. So don't expect too much from us. We don't have so many wonderful choices. No cars, no beaches, no books, no music, or a lot of the other things you seem to take for granted. You can have anything you want there, can't you?"

Misunderstanding Oliver's hesitation, Laurie challenged him in a gruff manner. "Or don't you know? Maybe you're really from the town of Lyin'. Maybe that red face of yours was a trick. Sometimes my daddy plays stupid tricks like bringing home someone from Lyin' just for laughs. How do I know you're not one of them sent here to trick us?"

"What trick?" Oliver asked. How could anyone suggest he would want to blush on purpose? Tired of all the suspicions, he resented having to prove his identity all over again.

"I rain out of my eyes and head," he informed her. "Your dad said Ls can't do that."

"You did that?" Even though the horse had a hard time showing surprise on its long face, the deep voice resonated with incredulity.

"Ask Lefty if you don't believe me," Oliver said, confidently. He lifted his glass of 'l'aspirilla from the coffee table to take a sip. Laurie used her tongue to flick at the bowl again while she contemplated her next move.

"I believe you. You do, well, look different. I'm sorry if I sound difficult. You don't understand how often I've dreamed of meeting a real LTV person, but nobody took me seriously. My friends never thought it would happen," Laurie exclaimed before she paused for a moment.

Her horse head seemed to nod at the thought. "I can't believe you finally came. Though I did think you'd look more like that cute guy, Cookie, on *77 Sunset Strip*. He's so groovy. Or maybe one of those cute guys from *The Mod Squad*. I always had faith, though. I learned that from LTV. See, we Ls don't have much to dream about. Our lives are just brief interludes in between our real roles as letters in words. Only my friend, LLit-erally LLucid, the smartest double LL in liberaltown, thought my dream of meeting a real LTV person might come true some day. But he remembers different times in Letterland. I hope you'll meet him. I know he'd like to meet you."

Fascinated to encounter a horse with a dream, Oliver asked

what made her so eager to meet a person from LTV.

"LLiterally LLucid says, for some unknown reason, I'm different from the ordinary 'l'omputed Ls," she continued. "He calls me a little mistrike. He thinks it might be because I might have been an unusual L word in the past. Something like 'logogriph.' He said that if any letter ever met a real LTV person, it would be me."

"What's a logogriph?" Oliver asked.

"A kind of word riddle. LLiterally says that if you were the lead letter in a word like that over a long period of time, it could make you different. I can do lots of cool things. I 'l'ompute clothes for me and my friends. That's a special talent. Most Ls just copy what they see on LTV or they take Legos to buy clothes at the general store in town. I think making clothes is fun. Ever since we've been able to use temporary letters, I come up with little sayings. LLiterally writes them out for me because I don't spell too well. Then I 'l'ompute them onto the shirts or pants when I make them."

"What are temporary letters?" Oliver asked.

"Like those words Wavell the Shalles written on your shirt. Maybe they're temporary letters."

As the horse continued to speak, Oliver glanced down at the writing on his shirt, seeing for the first time the addition of the three little Ls. "When there's a surplus of letters waiting to be used in LTV land, we 'l'omputed Ls can use them. I think that writing with letters, even temporary ones, makes us more like LTV people. They have so many uses for letters: billboards, books, letters, magazines, newspapers, all that. Most Ls don't even learn to write because they don't have any reason to write. But, after we got to know him, LLiterally LLucid taught me and my friend Lucy how to put letters together to make the words."

Oliver dared not correct Mister Ed's English usage.

"I don't know why I've had so much longing to meet an LTV person. Maybe it's because there are so many things I don't understand. LLiterally's taught me lots about how LTV people live. If my dream ever came true, he said, I'd learn even more. To learn about LTV people or how to make clothes doesn't matter much to anyone but me. When Word Central calls, we must go. Then once again we'll be the lead L in some word written somewhere until that word is removed, or erased, or eliminated in some way. Then it's back to L Land again. So, does what we know really matter in the end? We come and go, come and go. But I enjoy learning even if there's no reason to learn. Does that sound silly?"

Oliver tried to imagine how a horse with four legs could sew. "I'd like to see some of the clothes you designed," he replied. He really didn't know what else to say.

"Sure, but I should 'l'ompute back to an LTV person first. I love Mister Ed. But none of my clothes fit him."

"I love him, too. I guess you know that," Oliver responded shyly. "I used to watch tapes of him when I was a boy. How did you know to make him a golden palomino?"

"I don't know." She went on lost in her own thoughts. "I just 'l'omputed him a little bit back. I couldn't make up my mind between that cute Cookie character or Mister Ed. It's harder to 'l'ompute into a horse. I've done it once before. For some reason, even though we have animals like lions and llamas, we can only 'l'ompute ourselves to be Mister Ed or a talking mule named Francis or the dog Lassie.

Surprised by how normal she sounded for a girl who could compute herself into a horse, Oliver asked, "Is LLiterally LLucid your boyfriend?" His own boldness startled him.

"Nay," she snorted with a little laugh. "He's the oldest and wisest double LL around. He was 'l'omputed long before LTV arrived. He works for Word Central. He told me he lived as a double letter as part of a word in an old book for hundreds of LTV years until they burned the book up. LLucid has been here from the time letters could travel freely from one letter state to the other. But he can't stand being around other Ls any more. So he hangs out on his own. Me and my friend Lucy like to go to the lake where her dad has a lodge. We stumbled across LLiterally once on a walk, and we became friends."

Though exhausted from his ongoing ordeal, Oliver couldn't stop conjuring up in his mind the endless possibilities offered by being able to compute oneself into different characters. Beneath that four-legged exterior and deep-throated voice, a young, perhaps even beautiful, girl existed. Was she his age? Did people even have ages in L Land?

"Who do you look like when you're not Mister Ed?" Oliver asked.

Before she could answer, Lefty popped into the doorway. "Your mama says grubs on in a bit. Maybe Liver would like to wash up a mite."

"I would," Oliver said.

"Just a moment, Daddy," snapped the wide horse lips. "We're talking about an important subject."

"Well, 'scuse me," Lefty said as he retreated.

Laurie, eager to make Oliver understand, continued in a voice as suggestive as a deep-throated horses could be. "I always 'l'ompute myself after one of those characters on LTV. We all change them around a lot. I can do one you'd enjoy. Is there another favorite you have? Maybe someone like Gidget?"

"You mean I can choose anyone?" Oliver drew a blank. After a long, silent pause, he rose to his feet, reached out, and stroked Mister Ed's head directly between its pointed ears where the mane fell over his forehead. "I'm pretty happy with you as you are, Mister Ed."

Laurie had difficulty looking up at Oliver. One big brown eye faced the blue wallpaper, the other looked out the window. Now, for the first time, Laurie had the slightest hint of how the touch of a real hand felt. Even without nerve endings or beginnings, Ls could mildly experience the sensation of touch. Every L she knew had cool, smooth, rubberlike skin. She found Oliver's gentle stroke soothing and warm. Oliver could sense by the way she moved her head that she liked his petting. He wondered what character he should suggest.

"Tell me which LTV person you'd like me to be. Is there someone you find beautiful? Anyone? As long as they're on LTV," she pleaded, her tone at odds with the gravelly sound of her voice.

Oliver, not in the mood for any more transformations, tried to change the subject. "Since I've come here," he said, "I've had some horrible tricks played on me. To touch your forehead, even though it's cold, makes me feel as if some things are real. I don't know why your coat is cold. But at least you seem genuine. Nothing else has seemed real so far. You all change and disappear so quickly. At home, people and places usually change gradually."

Laurie wondered if he might be pulling the wool over her eyes. "Hold on there," exploded the horse's deep voice. "I've seen lots of LTV people change more than we do. Once an L l'omputes, it doesn't change that often. My dad and mom have looked the same ever since I've known them. It's mostly us kids who change. But LTV people change the way they look all the time. Sometimes I see girls dressed in costumes with wide funny pants, and then these same girls are in long, full dresses. Sometimes I see the same person looking old, and another time young. They can dress funny and speak English that doesn't make any sense though I've heard some of the words before. One of our double LLs, LLorser LLitebrite, is 'l'omputed into a funny-looking fat man he saw on LTV, one with a long white beard. I think his name was Mr. King or Mr. Lear. Then I saw a movie called *The Third Man,* That same Mr. Lear was the third man. He looked different with no beard and no funny clothes. He'd even taken an L name, Mr. Lime.

"My friend Lucy 'l'omputed herself after a girl with thick, black eyebrows named Elizabeth Taylor. She looked real young when Lucy saw her. Then we saw Elizabeth at home looking lots older than when Lucy 'l'omputed her. I've watched a person be with one wife every week like Ricky is with Lucy, and someone else with different wives in different places at different times. How can you tell me everyone stays the same where you live?"

Oliver sighed. "Well, I never thought about it in those terms. When you put it that way, I see how you came to think like that."

Since arriving in Letterland only a few hours back, Oliver had been challenged by an odd-looking L, a lion in lamb's wool, a monitor, a president at the city limits, a dead man come back to life, and now a mixed-up horse. Was there no end? "Maybe I should go wash up," Oliver said. "Your parents might have dinner waiting."

Laurie slammed one hoof hard into the rug just a couple of inches from Oliver's left foot. "Stop that. I ask you to explain something serious, and you give me a silly response that has nothing to do with what I said." Turning away, Oliver walked across the room to stare out the window beside the rolltop desk.

"Isn't there anyone special you'd like me to be?" she persisted.

"Sure." Looking out the window, Oliver realized he had an answer. It popped into his head, then popped out. "Lysander."

"Who's that?"

"A girl I know," he answered. Instantly he realized what a lunatic response he'd come up with. Turning on one foot, he added regretfully, "She's a girl from home. But I think it wouldn't be a good idea to try to become her. Forget I said it."

Laurie, aware she'd hit on something, continued with enthusiasm, "Do you know her program call number? If you know that, I can bring her up fast. The process is pretty simple once I locate the right program."

"To change from Mister Ed to Lysander is a simple process?"

"More or less," she explained. "Though it's a little harder to 'l'ompute from a horse to a person. There's another step involved. It takes a bit longer because I have to 'l'ompute back to my L frame first. Is Lysander the girl on LTV you love most?"

"She's not on LTV."

The deep voice grew exasperated. "Well, if she isn't on LTV, how am I supposed to compute myself after her? I thought you were all on LTV. Where is she?"

"How do I know?" Oliver responded, surprised at his own testiness and bad manners. "I can't figure out how you do anything here. Towns appear and disappear. The countryside goes from color to black and white. Winter dumps on you without warning. Whiskey tastes like 'l'aspirilla. I haven't seen a hint of night since the moment I arrived. People look like celebrities but aren't. Nobody can explain any of it. You told me you could become any girl I wanted. That's the girl I want you to look like."

Laurie flicked her tail nervously as she kept her right eye fastened on the figure by the window. "I don't know what to say," she said. "You sound just like those LTV people who smile one minute and yell the next. I don't understand any of you, just like you don't understand any of us."

His voice mellowed. "I'm sorry. I'm so tired."

"Maybe your girl looks like someone on LTV," Laurie ventured in a conciliatory tone. "If she looks like someone on LTV, then I can 'l'ompute myself to look the same. Then every time you see me, you would be reminded of Lysander. Who is she anyway?"

"A girl in a class at my school. Here, I'll show you her photograph."

Oliver extracted Lysander's identification card as he crossed the room. He placed it a few inches away from Laurie's right eye.

"That's a real color photograph?" Laurie asked. "I've seen photographs on LTV lots of times. But we only recently got some programs in color. And we have no cameras or film here. You keep your pictures on fireplace mantles, or you take them out of wallets when you're far away from your loved ones, like you just did, don't you? Don't photographs sometimes show up in post offices to locate bad guys also?"

As Oliver nodded, she went on, "They don't do that in our post office. How groovy to see a real photograph at last. Of course, I've never tried to 'l'ompute from one since we don't have any. But I can try to make myself look like Lysander. If you tell me about her body, I'll try to 'l'ompute a similar one from LTV. That way I can place her head right on top of it."

Oliver began to squirm. Transposing Lysander's head to a TV person's body sounded ghoulish. "The only one who seems to have a figure like hers is Geena Davis, sort of tall and thin, but I think Lysander's much prettier," he asserted.

"Geena Davis? Who's she?" Laurie asked. "I've never heard of her."

"Do you know Cher?"

That name also drew a negative reply.

Puzzled, Oliver tried to come up with someone else. But his short list had been exhausted.

"Just describe how she looks. I'll find someone. There are thousands of LTV types, big, small, thin, fat, ugly, old, young. All I have to do is organize the features."

With great care, Oliver placed the identification card on the coffee table alongside the horses empty l'aspirilla bowl. In awkward strokes, he attempted to outline Lysander's thin frame, long, almost gangly legs, small round breasts, delicate shoulders, and a neck that looked as if it could serve as a model for a bust of Cleopatra. "She has a little black spot on her right shoulder," he continued. "And a few freckles on her face. Her skins tanned a little, about the same color as mine. She's radiant, full of life, bright-eyed, real smart." Despite all his words, the description somehow remained inadequate.

Twisting her long horse head sideways until one eye peered at the photograph on the table, Laurie examined the girl's face. Lysander's radiance didn't exactly jump from the laminated picture.

"You can't tell much from that picture," Oliver said. "She's so full of life when you're with her."

Oliver's heart began to beat with excitement as Laurie

continued to study the photograph. "You really think you can do this?"

The horse nodded. "I'm sorry, but it's hard to tell what's so special here," Laurie finally said. "Lysander looks pretty like lots of the LTV girls. I don't think it will be difficult to find one who looks almost like her, and then make a few little changes."

The suggestion she might look like so many other girls brought an involuntary frown to Oliver's face.

"She is very pretty," said Laurie. "Nice blue eyes, and that hair color, what is it?

"Chestnut."

"Oh, yes, chestnut. A nice chin, thin cheeks. She might be one of those LTV fashion models."

Oliver's face lit up. "Lysander could be a model. She could."

"I think I understand what she's like. If I 'l'ompute any of the features wrong, you can tell me and I'll correct them. Is that all right?"

Even though the whole idea seemed ludicrous to him, Oliver decided to go along with it. He had more to gain than to lose.

"There are just a few parts of the anatomy that confuse all of us around here," Laurie confided. "We kids talk about them a lot. On LTV, they never show people without clothes. My friends and I are really interested in figuring out people's actual shapes. We know women have what you call boobs or booboos. Isn't that right?"

"It's boobs. Boo-boos are mistakes," Oliver explained.

"Gidget movies show girls in bikinis hanging out in the sand next to the ocean. My friends and I have studied these girls, but none of us can exactly agree on how the girls look beneath their bikini bottoms. I see a little split at the top on the backside. There has to be something in front as well, or they wouldn't always cover up."

Anatomy discussions with the opposite sex ranked low on Oliver's list of favorite things to engage in. A discussion with a talking horse proved no easier.

"Men and women have hair down there," he informed her.

"The same kind?" Laurie asked.

"Well, I guess so. Women have a shape that looks like a triangle. Men just grow it around their you-know-whats."

"That's the point," Laurie said. "We don't know what's what down there. What are their you-know-whats?"

"You know, their things, their members."

Laurie cocked her horse head slightly to the right, regarding Oliver with a curious eye. "Members of what? Can't you show me what you're talking about?"

"No," he stammered.

"All right. Place that photograph between my teeth." When Oliver hesitated, Laurie continued, "I won't bite down. I need the picture to 'l'ompute from. I'm going to try to make the resemblance as accurate as I can. This is a new experience for me though. Don't expect the results to be perfect."

Oliver, who had less and less to say, could muster little beyond a bewildered look.

"You go to the bathroom in the hall to wash yourself," she suggested. "My mother's probably knocking herself out to make a fancy dinner. I'll come to the dining room when I'm finished 'l'omputing."

"Okay, I'll wait for you," he said.

As she held the card delicately between her long teeth, Laurie turned her rump 180 degrees in the hallway. She didn't knock over a thing. A final swish of the tail, and that was the last Oliver saw of Ed, though he heard the loud clatter all the way up the stairs.

Laurie's departure left him some regrets, however. He felt the pain of someone who has to let go of a childhood friend. As he stood alone in the hallway, Oliver wondered if he had made a good choice, trading Mister Ed for Lysander. He really did love the talking horse.

Laurie/Lysander

ysander/Laurie. Laurie/Lysander. As he washed away the sweat and grime in a sink filled with what felt like real water, Oliver's thoughts ping-ponged from Lysander to Laurie and back again. Could Mister Ed leave the room a horse and return as his beautiful Lysander?

Face shining clean but his hair still like a mop, Oliver passed through the hallway into the dining room, which was smaller than the living room but no less crowded. Flowered wallpaper covered all four walls. On the wall behind Lefty's chair hung a framed needlepoint message that read A huge crystal chandelier dangled low above the oversized oval table that dominated the room. Veiled by a tablecloth crocheted into the shape of a white diamond, the surface was cluttered with a large lead-glass centerpiece overflowing with lilacs.

The table was covered with platters and bowls of food. Each formal place setting presented a flower-patterned dinner plate, a salad bowl, a bread plate, silverware, drinking glasses in various sizes, and a silver-ringed white cloth napkin neatly fanning the middle of the plate. Eight high-backed chairs stood around the table. Little room remained for the cabinet and the sideboard that had been compressed into the corners.

Oliver had to squeeze in sideways past the sideboard to sit down in the chair Lefty pointed out to him. Oliver eyed the old-fashioned fixture overhead. Did it operate by electricity? Did it work at all? Did it matter anyhow? In the washroom, Watchim informed him that Los Angeles time had passed one o'clock in the morning. The date had advanced as it always did at midnight. Each glance at the timepiece comforted him like a mother, reminding him that all he held dear awaited his return. One day, soon he hoped, the date would register the day and hour he returned home to all he loved. Here, only daylight ruled. Either L Land suspended all planetary principles or he'd landed on the North Pole in the middle of summer.

"Please, make yourself comfortable," Lo-Rain urged, bringing in a basket of piping hot rolls. She sat down in the chair closest to the kitchen and passed a platter to Oliver. Lefty sat sideways with one booted leg crossed over the other. A bottle half-filled with whiskey stood next to his plate.

"I hope there are some dishes you like," Lo-Rain said to Oliver. "I wish I'd known you were coming. I could have gone to the store to buy licorice, lollipops, and others treats you LTV people seem to love. Next time I go, I'll find some special foods for you. Please, Liver, help yourself." She handed him the lamb chops and a bowl of vegetables. "These are leeks in Lefty's favorite cream sauce. That's lettuce salad, there are lentils in that bowl, and here are some fresh baked 'l'alt rolls."

While he took a serving of leeks, Oliver suggested graciously that they should wait for Laurie.

"No," Lefty answered. "She'll mosey in sometime soon. Told me she was headed off to fiddle with the 'l'omputing machine. Why in tarnation that little filly wants to change her looks before dinner is beyond me. That's okay though. I'm sick of listening to that darn horse banging around the house. That infernal animal eats like … you know what. Let's just eat and not worry a hoot about her. Laurie can take good care of herself. How about another shot of whiskey? Can I pour you one?"

"Sure thing," Oliver agreed.

While Lefty went for another shot glass, Oliver finally

finished filling his plate. "The food sure gives me an appetite, Mrs. Littleleather," Oliver exclaimed, waiting for his hosts to serve themselves.

Lefty insisted on pouring Oliver and himself a shot before they ate. The mayor stood up and came around so they could clink their glasses. Oliver raised his in tribute to the chef, who shook her head with dizzy embarrassment. "Mr. Liver certainly has lovely manners, Lefty," she pointed out.

"Mud in your eye," Lefty said, ignoring his wife.

"Mud in your eye," his guest responded, raising his glass to down the whiskey in a single gulp.

Lefty heaped item after item onto his plate: first a base of green leeks in white cream sauce, then a layer of brownish lentils, then lettuce over the lentils to provide a green bed for two large fried lamb chops. To finish the arrangement, Lefty swung his chair around and grabbed the yellow lemon pie Lo-Rain had left on the sideboard. He quartered it with his knife and removed a slice from the pie tin with a nearby spatula before he dropped the gooey mess directly on top of the lamb chops.

Used to Lefty's boorish behavior, Lo-Rain ignored her husband's table manners. By contrast, she helped herself to miniscule portions, each neatly spaced on her plate to prevent one from overlapping the next. "Please start eating, Liver," Lo-Rain insisted, as she completed her own serving. "You must be very hungry."

"Thank you, ma'am." Another check of Watchim revealed the precise Los Angeles time to be 1:37 a.m. Lefty stared at the watch as if he'd never seen one before. Oliver raised his arm to explain: "This is called a Chronosport watch. My mother bought it as a Christmas present last year. I wanted it because my hobby is geography. When I'm studying some part of the world, I can set the time for that specific zone."

"What do ya need that for?" Lefty asked as he examined the watch close up.

Oliver paused long enough to cut off a small bite of lamb. "I can also set the date, and it can display the time and the date at the same time. See, it tells me now that its 1:37 a.m. in Los Angeles. If you know the time here, I can set my other zone to correspond to it as well. It can keep the time in both places at once."

Lefty, in the process of mashing the lemon pie flat on top of the lamb chops, glanced at the wrist above his own left hand. "Looks to me like it's supper time, boy," he said, breaking into a loud guffaw. Cutting off a bite of pie-smeared lamb chop, he stuffed it into his mouth Old-West style. "Umm, heap good succotash," he mumbled.

Lo-Rain tried nervously to cover up for Lefty's rudeness. "People constantly talk about time when I watch LTV," she said flustered. "They act so busy. They always have someone to meet or someplace to go. They rush to work, to school, or to have lunch with a friend. Then they check their watches just as you did now. It must be a hard life. Why do LTV people measure time the way they do? No matter how much we like LTV, none of us is interested unless…"

Lefty interrupted her, "Unless you listen to that stupid double L, LLorser LLitebrite. A real varmint, that odd-talking 'l'elia. He tried to push us into making time regular here in liberaltown. But, for once, none of the council gave him the time of day."

His own comment brought another howl from the mayor, who speared a glob of food from his plate before he continued with his mouth full, "We don't really hanker to be that much like you LTV people. Sure as shootin' we like your looks, your dress, your towns, and we like how you play with your money. Ain't that enough? Why do we need your time, too? As the old poet said, "Ain't the time we got, all the time we got, whether we measure it or not?

"Here in Letterland, Word Central calls us 'cause our time has come up. That's what I told LLorser. Even Cyclops backed me up." He motioned toward Oliver with his fork as he continued, "You'll meet Cyclops. Hell of a guy, a real one-eyed eyesore. Cyclops told LLorser not to mess with our nontime. 'We have everything we want as long as we want it, until we don't have it no more. That's that,' he said. 'That's that. Why measure what don't need measuring?' First smart thing that ever popped out of his mouth."

The mayor loaded his fork again before he continued, "Well, LLorser about blew off he got so doggone mad. 'Measure for measure,' was all he could say. He's 'l'omputed himself in fancy dress like some 'l'elia he calls Shakespeare or Lear. Sometimes he starts talking real funny, and I don't get the gist of his lingo."

Lo-Rain cut in. "Lefty, give the boy a chance to eat. He's been patient listening to you."

"Sure boy, eat up," the mayor said.

Oliver lifted the fork, still holding his first bite of lamb to his mouth. To his disappointment, while it chewed just like lamb, the flavor did not differ from the sandwich he'd eaten earlier. A small bite of lentils produced an equally pasty glue taste in his mouth.

"'Time will tell,' is what LLorser yapped, stomping his feet around the saloon after we voted him down. 'As you like it. Think you can keep a tempest in a teapot? Someday you'll learn you can't avoid the moment in this hamlet. Something's rotten in the state of L Land.'

"Sure as shootin', when the legislature voted to reverse the capitol L in the town's name, LLorser blamed us. 'Those lawyers clock every minute,' he told us. 'They have divided their lives into the smallest fractions of time. That is organization. Might is right.' And when we refused to change it, he said, 'Your time has run out.' As if he knew. That oversized windbag should stuff it in his shirt," Lefty concluded.

Agitated, the mayor returned to the bottle and poured himself another stiff shot of whiskey. "Mighty fine vittles tonight, Lo-Rain," he said, trying to change the bothersome subject of LLorser to something more pleasant.

Sometime during the mayor's diatribe, Oliver had come to realize, much to his chagrin, that each dish Lo-Rain had prepared possessed the consistency of mealy dough. How could that be when it all looked so tempting? After the first three or four tastes, he could not force himself to swallow another bite.

"Perhaps LLorser is right, dear," Lo-Rain told her husband. "Maybe it is important to measure time. What do you think, Liver? Why do LTV people consider time so important?"

Too polite to reveal his distaste for the food, Oliver used the opportunity to put down his fork. "I'm sorry," he said, looking at his hostess. "I was enjoying the food so much I forgot what you asked me."

"He forgot to say what he heard," Lefty corrected.

Oliver played with his fork. How could his head and shoulders ache so much? His body began to sink in the chair. "I must be wearing out. I even forgot what I just said," he confessed.

"These LTV types get tired," Lefty explained to his wife. "Maybe we should show him the guest room to let him sleep it off."

"No," Oliver protested respectfully. "I want to stay here a while. I promised Laurie." Weary, the folds that kept his eyelids near half-mast began to droop.

"I promised Laurie," Laurie heard Oliver respond as she tiptoed through the hall to the dining room entry. His words sounded slurred. He sat directly facing the hallway in an ideal position to observe her grand entrance. Astute young Ls like Laurie had learned from LTV that timing, rather than time, was everything. She paused in the hallway as she heard her father's booming voice echo through the room. Out of sight, she listened to her father's endless complaints. She seldom heard her father talk about council matters or his hated adversary, LLorser LLitebrite.

When a moment of quiet followed one of Oliver's brief responses, she used the opportunity to set her plan into motion. A sudden leap brought her into everyone's sight. As she planted both feet in a solid stance, she spread her arms, palms uplifted, then spoke in a loud voice, "Ta da, announcing Lysander here."

Lo-Rain and Lefty, used to their daughter's shenanigans, failed to respond. By now immune to her erratic, crazy transformations, they saw this newly computed girl as yet another in an endless stream of identities: Laura Ingalls from *The Little House on the Prairie,* Betty Anderson from *Father Knows Best,* Lassie, Mister Ed. They had seen it all.

Now she appeared with long chestnut hair swinging over her shoulders and white pearly teeth. She jumped into the room dressed in a pink short-sleeved angora sweater with gold letters spelling #span_smallcaps LIESANDER!span across the chest. Black pedal pushers, penny loafers, and white socks transformed Laurie into a Polaroid moment of somewhat outdated collegiate wholesomeness.

"Dear, please, sit down," her mother urged. "The food is getting cold."

As Oliver stared, his eyes spun out of control. His head plunged in a sudden jerk, nose first, crashing forward with a loud thud against the plate, his right cheek squarely planted in the creamed leeks.

I'll Take Romance

Lefty suggested, "Liver may be dead. I seen this program once where an LTV 'I'elia said he'd rather be 'dead than red,' and Liver sure turned bright red-faced when you popped in, Laurie."

Laurie discounted her father's theory. "I don't think the 'I'elia meant that, Daddy. He probably meant "read" like in a book. Look at Liver's chest move up and down. You know, they say an LTV person's heart is beating when his chest moves. Don't you remember those doctor programs we watch sometimes? They say LTV people are dead once they stop breathing in and out. But then they usually come back again dressed like someone else."

"If he ain't dead, then I'll bet he's fainted dead away, just like he did on the sidewalk heading back to the old plantation," Lefty stated in a voice ringing with authority—the authority of a man who knew a faint when he saw one.

"I think he's fallen asleep," Laurie suggested.

"Maybe my dinner caused it," Lo-Rain worried, Oliver being her first and only LTV guest. "I hope I didn't poison him with some food he couldn't eat. You know, those people look kind of delicate. They're always talking about what they can and can't eat. I just hope I didn't do something wrong."

"Now, Lo-Rain, you're always so dadblame worried about the this and the that business. If he's dead we'll just bury him on the lone prairie or in the backyard like they do in the West … and we won't tell a soul he ever came through town."

"He's not dead, Daddy," his daughter insisted. "Watch his

chest. See how it moves up and down. Besides, if you're dead, your body is supposed to be cold."

"Are we cold?" her mother asked.

As so often happened, Laurie's parents bugged her no end. Shrugging her shoulders, she said, "I don't know if we're cold or hot. But next to Liver we're cold. I could tell that for sure when he stroked my head while I was Mister Ed. Let's carry him to his room. We can take his clothes off to feel if his body is hot or cold."

Lefty dragged Oliver to the unused guest room in the back of the house, with Lo-Rain and Laurie trailing behind, where they laid him out on top of the neatly made bed. Working together, they removed Oliver's Nikes, socks, T-shirt, and pants. Finally, they slipped down his jockey shorts. Lefty let out a hot-air whistle through his teeth when he saw the appendage lying on its side between Oliver's thighs.

"What do you think it is, dear?" Lo-Rain asked.

"Don't know," Lefty said, bending over the bed to examine it close up. "Ugly little varmint, ain't it?"

"I don't think so, Daddy. It's cute. See how it looks like a tired little man resting on his side."

"Maybe the poor boy has a tumor," Lo-Rain suggested. "There was this doctor program I saw once where this 'l'ella had a growth on his neck. They called that a tumor."

"I'm sure its supposed to be there," Laurie corrected, remembering well Oliver's comment about his you-know-what. "Lets see if his body feels warmer or colder than ours."

Drawing air in through his mouth, Oliver let out a sudden guttural sound.

"What was that snort?" Lefty demanded. "Sounded like a lamb bellowing." While his eyes never left Oliver's member, which flopped like a seasick sailor, Lefty edged closer to the boys head.

"That snorts a snore, Daddy. Don't you remember seeing LTV people make that sound when they sleep? They joke a lot about snoring."

"You always think you know it all, don't you?" Lefty snapped. His hand descended cautiously to press flat against the boy's chest. Under his cool hand, the body felt hot. Summoning enough courage, he moved his hand over the odd-looking appendage.

"Boy's hotter than a smoking pistol," Lefty announced.

"Why don't you two leave?" Laurie suggested. "I'll stay here to keep an eye on Liver until he wakes up. LTV people are different from us in a lot of their ways. I've watched them real carefully."

"Are you sure you can take care of him, dear?" her mother asked. "We'll be happy to help."

"No, it's fine, Mom. You go ahead."

"I better figure out what to say to the council about this here problem," Lefty said. "I'm gonna call a meeting pronto to give a report before Lexi starts running his mouth about the visitor. Next thing I know that fat graybeard, LLorser LLitebrite, will be banging on my door wanting to know all the facts. This whole thing's gonna be a big pain in the butt." Before they exited, the mayor paused at the door. Turning back to face his daughter, he asked, "Who is this gal you computed yourself after, Laurie? I ain't never seen her before."

"You haven't seen everybody, remember?"

"You sure make a pretty little gal," Lefty said, holding the door open for his wife.

Laurie moved a chair from the corner of the room and placed it beside the bed near Oliver's head. She sat close enough to touch his sleeping face. She remembered that LLit-erally LLucid once told her that if you stretch yourself beyond your reach, you'll find something special.

She let her finger probe inside his ear. Her fingers ran up and down the stubble along one cheek. What caused the roughness? Ls either computed a full beard or they kept a clean-shaven face that remained cool, smooth, and rubbery to the touch. Placing her ear next to Oliver's chest, she heard the rhythmic beat of his heart. Why did an LTV person's chest feel solid when the skin below the rib cage bounced back? She pushed her fingers against his stomach. How different his skin, with its hairs and little pores, felt next to her own of thinly stretched rubber.

The girl petted one of Oliver's thighs. Thrilled by the warmth of his flesh, she turned to the mysterious object that fascinated her most of all. Just as Lefty had earlier, the girl began a scrupulous inspection. She used two fingers to grip Oliver's member by its tip. Her sparkling eyes probed the flabby exterior from top to bottom. A few inches long, only its rounded tip felt firm to the touch. A small slit had been cut through the middle of the tip. *Why would anyone cut it open?* she wondered. Below the long object was a round sack containing two balls; above was a thick, short curl of dark hair, just as he'd told her. What possible use could such a little thing have?

As she attempted to grip the entire 'l'ella to give it a pull, the member expanded. Wide-eyed, she watched as it transformed into a tall and firm tower. A pout crossed her face. What had caused this sudden change? Two of her fingers did a slow descent along each side of the hardened, reddish surface.

A desire to snuggle beside Oliver's warm body suddenly stirred in Laurie. She'd seen boys and girls snuggling close on LTV. The more she looked at him, the more she wanted to feel his body touch her own. Longing made her wonder how it would feel to lie down beside him. In neat and orderly fashion, she removed every piece of her clothing. She folded the lot, then placed the stack on top of the dresser. After a moment's hesitation, she stretched out next to him, her body as close to his as possible.

To lie in his arms, as the girls did in the *Gidget* luau scene, seemed a grand idea. Turning toward him, she burrowed in. She caressed his handsome face with her left hand. Then she patted his firm stomach and tugged at the cluster of hair in the center of his chest. Finally, she toyed with the little you-know-what, which had deflated while she had undressed. When it stood at attention again, she giggled.

As if rising through a pool of clear, deep water, Oliver headed toward the light, moving through alternating layers of hot and cold until he broke the surface. Awake, his eyes remained closed. Conscious first of his erection, his instincts told him this differed from the one he felt when he awoke each morning. A cool hand had wrapped itself around this erection. Always slow to wake up, especially after such a short nap, he forced his brain to focus. But all that penetrated his fuzzy mind was the ridiculous notion that he'd grown a third hand.

Blinking, he saw the white ceiling overhead. This nightmarish adventure was not a dream. Where was he? His brain tried to recall his last waking memories. As he turned his head, a cheerful voice greeted him, "I thought you might be stirring after your little nap."

His body stiffened. Who was this girl who looked so much like his Lysander? She spoke with a different voice than Lysander, and her naked body felt cool to the touch. But most incomprehensible of all, she pressed herself against him, her fingers curled around his member in a firm grip.

"We moved you into our guest room because you fell asleep on your plate," Laurie explained. "You sure were heavy. Daddy could hardly pull you up on the bed." She removed her left hand from his erect penis to touch the long hair that curled around his neck.

"I don't believe this," Oliver whispered to himself.

Hadn't the lion warned him of a town that would worship his erection? The memory startled him. The thought fit a dream more than the real world. Then, like a surfer's wave, the truth crashed down over him: a talking horse, famous people, the Littleleathers' home. Lysander, last seen on an ID card, now lay naked beside him. An urge to close his eyes suddenly overwhelmed him.

"Liver, what exactly is your you-know-what you got down there used for?"

Aware of Oliver's hesitation, Laurie became impatient. Despite her cold exterior, she'd warmed to the idea of playing around with him as she'd seen boys and girls do on LTV. She raised her head to plant a long kiss flush on his warm lips. Sweat formed across Oliver's forehead from the intense and unexpected contact. His heart thumped against his chest. His arm freed up, he reached around to embrace her, drawing her small round breasts close to his chest.

Scattered moments of past panic attacks flashed by: un-consummated desire, a serendipitous night of heavy kissing at a party, a stranger's touch in a crowded elevator, a backrub by a teenage friend during an algebra study session, roughhousing in boyish play with a neighbor girl. No past encounter had been flesh to flesh like this.

Well, if not exactly flesh to flesh, then flesh to rubber, but it would have to do. A more-experienced lover might turn away from this unlikely love object, but Oliver had nothing to compare his experience with. He saw before him the image of his dream girl, Lysander. Caught up in the excitement of the moment, he even tolerated the smell and taste of the light gaseous substance that slowly escaped from Laurie's nose and mouth.

"Liver, you're such a good kisser," Laurie said, as if she knew. Meanwhile, Oliver broke away, trying to swallow the lingering taste in his mouth.

His hand explored the silkiness of her hair, the rubbery sameness of her cheek, shoulders, breast, neck, and arms. Her skin had the texture of an expensive doll. A kiss on her soft lips raised his member by degree. "I'm going to do it," he whispered. Though her skin remained cool, her every move indicated to Oliver that she desired him as much as he desired her.

"I better get a rubber," he stated abruptly, unaware of the irony in his words. Mostly, he tried to get a grip on himself. Drenched in his own sweat, Oliver rolled over before sitting up. A quick survey of the room revealed his pants on the desk. A bout of optimism had caused him to store a single Trojan inside his wallet four years earlier. Now the moment he'd longed for awaited him.

Once he stood, he remained frozen in place as bright outdoor light flooded the room like midday. His you-know-what drooped like a hanged man plunged through a trapdoor. Watchim, still on his wrist, caught his attention. Currently 3:30 a.m. the digital display informed him. He sagged onto the edge of the bed.

"What's wrong, Liver?" Laurie asked as she noted the deflated member resting against his right leg. How could she ever know the little 'l'ellas use when it went up and down as fast as a yoyo?

"No good," Oliver moaned. "I've dreamed about this moment for years. When I copy a map every part has to be right. When I make love for the first time, I don't want to do so in the middle of the day in a room filled with bright sunlight like some whorehouse. That wouldn't be respectful."

"Well, I think it's okay," Laurie reassured him. "I just want to know what to do and how to do it." Her attention continued to focus on the little member. "I've watched them kiss on the beach and all. Sometimes they kiss in the sunshine. I've seen that lots of time on LTV."

"That's just kissing," Oliver said dejectedly. "Kissing's okay." Sweat continued to roll down his cheeks, dripping onto his naked chest and down onto the floor.

Laurie could not resist scooping up a fingerful of sweat to sample, as her father had earlier. She noted the mild 'l'alt taste. "Help me understand, Liver. What would make you happy?"

Hunched over, he twisted his shoulders and neck downward, lowering his head to less than a foot from her face. He took one of her hands between his two and spoke in a voice barely above a whisper. "Promise, if I tell you, you wont laugh at me."

Laurie adopted a solemn expression, one she'd seen LTV people use in church. "I'd never laugh or tell anyone, if that's what you want," she agreed. "So help me God."

He hesitated for a second. Then, buoyed by her sincerity, he slowly revealed his dream to another person for the very first time: "I want our first lovemaking to be beautiful, something neither of us will ever forget," he began. Eyes computed green when they should have been blue followed his lips as they formed each word. "The pitcher and washbasin, the wallpaper, the throw rug, even the dresser and wood desk," he continued, "That's all perfect. If there only were a fireplace, I could imagine this room as a cozy cabin somewhere in the countryside. You're beautiful, too, as beautiful as I knew you'd be." Laurie didn't say a word.

"One part of my dream, though, is still missing. Moonlight. I call moonlight God's milk in the sky. I've thought a lot about the moon and the best way for it to appear at the moment of lovemaking. Once in a while, the moon sat above my house hanging as big as a ball illuminating the sky like a giant street lamp. At those times I imagined an eerie glow would enter my room. Wow, I get goose bumps when I remember." He reached out his arm, and Laurie's hand caressed the strange little bumps that ran from shoulder to wrist.

"Moonlight across a dark room makes skin look as rich as fresh poured cream," he went on in a dreamy voice. "The light becomes the soft glow of a lit candle. That's what I imagine as the perfect way to make love for the first time. On a night bathed in moonlight." His voice grew louder. "I'm sure I must be crazy. That's why I've told nobody. Who thinks like this anymore? Today, they do it in airplane bathrooms, supermarkets, even in alleys. Nobody cares about the details anymore. I've waited a long time to find someone special like you. Maybe I'm really stupid to want each part of my dream so perfect."

Laurie wrapped her arms around Oliver before she pulled herself up to plant a kiss in the middle of his cheek. "That's so beautiful, Liver, more beautiful than any words those LTV lovers ever said. Sometimes on LTV they say that dreams can come true. Tell me, if I could make the moon come into the room the way you like, would your little 'l'elia want to grow big again?"

"Can you change day to night, too?" he asked.

"Sure, that's easy as pie. We keep daylight because we can see easier."

"Well," he confessed, "I know growing hard is easy, too."

"That's groovy then." She bounced off the bed with a burst of enthusiasm. "You put on your little rubber doodad, and I'll whip up some pretty little moonlight."

Oliver's eyes followed her as she disappeared through the doorway. As she walked away, he noticed for the first time that her rounded buttocks separated only at the top and that her breasts, round as oranges, lacked any nipples. But these minor anatomical deficiencies didn't concern him under the circumstances. He retrieved his pants to remove his wallet. He fished through the contents until he located the packaged rubber. He tore open the protective cover and held the circular object in the palm of his hand.

Oliver agonized as he crossed the hardwood floor to the window that faced the backyard. Outside, he saw an identical two-story wood-frame house on a lot behind the Little-leathers'. Unable to stop thinking, he gazed absently through the window at the few flowers planted in a corner of the dirt-packed backyard. His heart pounded from fear he would mess up; he would somehow die before he knew the pleasure of lovemaking and the passion of love.

Outside, light remained. The sky remained the same monotonous blue color he'd seen since his arrival in liberaltown.

Before his eyes, as sudden as the flick of a light switch, the world turned dark. Little stars twinkled in the heavens. A bright full moon, fair and round, shone directly above the neighbor's house. Beams of soft light poured in through the window, filling the room with magic.

The light transformed and illuminated Oliver's skin. His heart pounded once more against his chest. Errant fairies danced across his body as he stretched out on his back on the bed to await his Lysander.

As Oliver lay quietly like a character in his own dream, Laurie entered the room, bursting across the floor through a beam of moonlight. An apparition in white, she appeared to levitate into his arms. Her cool body, settling in beside him, seemed to ask, "Is this what you want?"

"You're a wonder," he said, each word accented with a soft kiss. "Yes, this is exactly what I want."

"This is just so cool," she told him. "I can't wait to find out what we're going to do."

"You won't have to wait long," he promised, quieting any further talk with a lingering kiss.

Public Policy Meets Private Parts

Lefty Littleleather sat alone at his favorite poker table inside the Lucky Lady, the only authentic-looking saloon in liberaltown. Swinging wooden doors opened into a large rectangular room with coarse planked floor and walls. Behind a polished wooden bar hung a long rectangular mirror. Several sets of turn-of-the-century chairs and round tables filled one side of the room, while three poker tables occupied the other.

His long legs resting across the table, Lefty tilted back on the wooden chair. From time to time, he tossed down a shot of whiskey from a bottle, by now half-empty, as he awaited the arrival of the other members of the town council. Behind the bar stood LooLoo, the jovial, round-faced bartender. LooLoo wiped each shot glass sparkling clean with a towel after a careful wash and rinse. Dressed in his finest apron, he proudly scrutinized the glasses he'd placed in a line below the large mirror.

An LTV monitor sat on a wall stand in a corner above the bar for the pleasure of the patrons. After he finished cleaning up or washing his beloved glasses, LooLoo spent his free time watching Westerns or series like *Cheyenne, Have Gun Will Travel, Gunsmoke,* or *Wyatt Earp* that depicted life in Western bars.

Now and then, computed Ls would drift into the Lucky Lady to socialize over a glass of lemonade or a shot of whiskey. But business remained slow most of the time, as locals preferred to meet at the soda fountain down the street. LooLoo was delighted that the town council always held its meetings in his saloon.

When a customer arrived, he would slam a bottle of whiskey down on the bar. After he filled the shot glass, he would watch the customer raise it to his lips to down the contents. He would adjust his head slightly to catch the noise of the little gulp sliding down the customer's throat. He could listen to the delicate sound over and over again. If the customer decided to pay, LooLoo would gain added satisfaction by the sound of his own hand slapping the bar to return Legos in change.

Lefty planted his feet on the floor as he sat forward to shuffle a deck of cards. LooLoo had cut razor-thin wood shavings and numbered each suit one through thirteen and laminated them in Lucite. The cards were far from perfect, but they suited Lefty just fine.

Ls enjoyed a good game of poker, though they made up their own rules. Patrons, including the mayor, played the game with great enthusiasm at the Lucky Lady. Once a game started, a big crowd of spectators soon assembled. Loafers such as Lew, Lowen, and Larry would gather to watch the locals slap down cards, call each other, raise bets, toss Legos into the pot with abandon, puff on lettuce cigarettes, and blow smoke out through their nostrils. Unlike the grizzled cowboys on the LTV screen, computed Ls rotated pots so each one got a chance to win a hand. If a player ran out of Legos, he had only to run to the bank to get all he wanted at no charge. And since the bank never closed, money always remained at hand.

Today the poker tables remained empty except for the one occupied by the mayor. The LTV monitor remained off. LooLoo closed his bar to the public until the council meeting ended. These meetings were serious business. With townspeople barred, the large room looked empty.

"Where is Ludis Limpy Limedime?" Lefty asked with irritation in his voice. He had dispatched Limpy, nicknamed because of his floppy foot, ages ago to round up the council for this special meeting. A young L, Limpy fell head over heels in love with Chester, Marshal Dillon's original sidekick on *Gun-smoke*^ whereupon he computed himself as the Dennis Weaver character. As the mayor's sidekick and chief errand boy, he incorporated the limp that Weaver perfected, thus earning his nickname, Limpy.

The sound of a choppy pattern of thumps along the sidewalk telegraphed the return of Limpy. He pushed open the saloon doors and, with halting steps, he crossed the room to where the mayor sat with a deck of cards in his hands. Limpy noticed right away the mayor's grim expression.

"They should all be here real soon, Marshal," came the hurried message. Limpy exhaled hard after the exhausting tour about town. Dressed in simple Western garb and computed with long sideburns that ended just above his earlobes, he steadied himself as he spoke, holding onto the poker table with one hand. "They all should be comin' sometime soon, Marshal," he repeated again in a drawl.

Irked at being called marshal, the mayor nevertheless held his tongue. He'd learned to tolerate Limpy's eccentricities. Limpy performed faithfully and with enthusiasm.

"How about a drink, Limpy? You earned it," LooLoo said, planting a bottle of whiskey on the bar. Next came the sound of a shot glass hitting wood. LooLoo raised the bottle, and carefully poured out the drink. Then he moved his head forward to listen closely as Limpy downed the contents in a single gulp.

"Good to have a shot of rotgut in the old craw, huh?" Lefty called out with his back to the bar. He liked to sit where he could keep an eye on the entrance at all times.

"Won't you tell us what this special meeting is about,

Marshal?" Limpy asked, exchanging a wink with his friend LooLoo. "You know I won't tell anyone."

The mayor spoke without turning around, "I know that. But you'll hear soon enough. Tell me, did it appear Llorser would come fast or slow?"

"Slow this time," Limpy answered. "He didn't even have his robe or crown on yet."

"And did you spot that ridiculous young L he's been dragging around with him lately?"

"Sure thing, Marshal. Saw him in his jester's suit right there in the library. Sitting in the corner strumming that lute was what he was doin' while Llorser said, I'll be along as soon as I don my kingly garments,' or some such hogwash. Strutted around like a peacock, he did."

"Which is exactly what the varmint is," the mayor agreed. "Now I just know he's gonna give me all kinds of misery over this here situation, sure as shootin', you wait and see."

Just as Lefty spoke, Lexi Lenticular materialized in the flesh, lickety-split, in front of the bar beside Limpy. He used the same trick to arrive that he'd performed earlier to disappear in front of Oliver at the crossbar when he had been in a hurry to inform the mayor about the stranger's impending arrival. Eager to grab onto any excuse to depart from his lonely outpost, Lexi usually arrived first at these council meetings.

"Howdy, Lefty. Howdy, Limpy," Lexi called out in good spirits, punctuating his cheerful greeting with a wave of his hand. LooLoo plopped the bottle down in front of him. "Hey, hoo, how youyou, LooLoo?" Lexi exclaimed, still wearing the ten-gallon hat that looked even more out of place on his head inside the bar than it had at the crossbar.

"How's that young Liver Landwich doing?" Lexi asked, downing a quick shot while he tried to ignore the snickering his colleagues directed at his hat.

"Well as can be expected," Lefty answered, matter of factly.

Lexi turned his attention to Limpy. "Strangest thing happened at the gate. Haven't seen nothing like it in all my gate-tending days. Young 'Telia comes up to the gate for no reason at all. Then …"

"Say, Lexi," the mayor interrupted as he twisted his neck around to face the council member. "Come on over here. I want to talk with you about an important job that'll get you off the gate for a while. Sit down here beside me on this here chair."

Fortunately for Lefty, neither Limpy nor LooLoo questioned the gatekeeper's story since they were used to hearing Lexi tell all kinds of tall tales and other nonsense.

"Howdy doody," Lexi said to the mayor.

Lefty ignored him, talking more to himself now. "Seems like ever since Word Central let us use temporary letters, we got a chance to write out one hundred percent pure official town documents like they use on LTV. We're gonna have to have a meeting soon about how to write this and that. Now, if we write and print up what we talk over in our meetings, then we gotta find a way to circulate the documents around town so people can read what we wrote. We gotta find a way to read what we write to all those folks who don't know how to read. Right? You see?"

"How," Lexi interjected, Indian style.

"Yeah, so if you see how, tell me, dadburn it. We gotta find a place that can print it up, and we gotta have something to say to print up."

At that moment, two more council members appeared through the swinging doors. Lexi and Lefty both looked up and greeted them warmly. The mayor's conversation had served its purpose, to divert Lexis attention from the subject of Livers unexpected arrival into liberaltown.

Arm in arm, the two council members entered to the sound of doors swinging behind them. As they approached the bar to receive the traditional whiskey bottle, they greeted the others present. Lindsay Luckgut, on the left, sported thick, light-brown hair, part of which swept across her forehead while the rest she'd piled high over the top of her head. A solidly built woman of about forty, she wore a modest print dress cut below the knees. Though liberaltown had no schools, Lindsay had decided to become a schoolteacher in looks if not in action. Long ago, she had computed herself as Eve Arden in the role of Connie Brooks in *Our Miss Brooks*. She sipped the shot glass served by LooLoo in ladylike fashion.

On Lindsay Luckgut's right arm was Larry Languishes who had arrived fresh from his fifteen minutes of local fame as talk of the town. After a long spell as Ricky Ricardo/Desi Arnaz, he'd made a sudden drastic switch to become Lucy/Lucille Ball. This transformation of Larry's had resulted in quite a commotion at the last council meeting. Lefty recalled how everyone had been dismayed because a blond-haired Lucy showed up for the meeting rather than a dark-haired Ricky Ricardo. LLorser LLitebrite pronounced the switch a trick.

"So quick bright things come to confusion," LLorser LLitebrite proclaimed in kingly fashion. And he spoke truth. For Larry's wife, Lana, had long ago computed herself as Lucy Ricardo.

Therefore, LLorser refused to believe Larry had recomputed himself as a second Lucy. He could not imagine a blond and a redheaded Lucy living in the same household.

LLorser insisted Larry had sent his wife, Lana, in his place to the council meeting as a joke. LLorser argued that Lana had merely computed her hair color from red to blond to confuse the council. Larry, however, explained that he had changed to Lucy. His blond hair color allowed their daughter and others to more easily identify the two Lucys. To prove his identity, Larry went home and returned with Lana. There they stood, a blond and a red-headed Lucy in the middle of the Lucky Lady Saloon. Forced in the end to relent, LLorser had proclaimed, in as kingly a fashion as a retreat allowed, that the blond Larry could take his lawful council seat.

As the mayor watched Larry, still computed as the blond Lucy, down a drink at the bar, he understood why LLorser and the other members of the council drove him nuts. As a group, he considered them a bunch of numbskulls without a lick of sense.

In short order, every one of the council members meandered into the meeting. Lance LaRue arrived next, dressed in black pants, black books, and a black cowboy shirt with a polka-dot-scarf tie held by a cow-skull clasp. He looked like the popular cowboy Hopalong Cassidy portrayed by Bill Boyd. Then came Cyclops, the one-eyed giant, computed somewhat shorter by mistake by Lomash Loghog, whom everyone around town called Crazy Lomash. How Lomash first came to join the council remained a mystery to all except LLorser LLitebrite, who declared that the mayor brought him on board because Crazy Lomash, an inveterate bickerer, always sided with the mayor in the final vote.

Known as a loose pistol, Crazy Lomash once arrived at a meeting computed as Frances, the talking mule, and wearing a special pair of sunglasses. Not able to see clearly through the dark glasses, he made a sudden turn of his rump between table and bar and knocked off several of LooLoos precious shot glasses.

Now, computed as a shortened giant Cyclops, one-eyed Lomash struggled with depth perception. This handicap made picking up a shot glass a tricky feat. So when LooLoo poured a drink, he placed the glass in Lomash's hand rather than risk yet another loss.

Next entered the one and only noncomputed L council member, the pie-tin face character known as Lillbzellmet, who sported an Ls traditional shape. At first, acting like a tourist, it separated the swinging doors just slightly to peek inside; then a small suspended monitor appeared through the doors, followed by Lillbzellmet itself. Its rapid hockey stick movements whirled like a chainsaw kicking up sawdust across the wooden floor. LooLoo ignored the latest arrival: noncomputed Ls never pretended to eat or drink.

Lillbzellmet proceeded directly to the open spot reserved for it at the table. As the L rotated in place, the support tubing parallel to its metal body shifted forward to secure its neck about a foot back from the table. LLorser once suggested this position in order not to have the monitor interfere with anyone's line of vision. With the support firmly locked into position, Lillbzellmet suspended its rotating motion.

Now peace and quiet settled over the saloon. Without greeting those present, the pie-tin head stared straight ahead. To its consternation, this placed Lillbzellmet directly opposite the recently seated Lomash, whose one eye, at this very moment, attempted for the umpteenth time to locate his shot glass and bottle. Finally, Lindsay took pity on him and poured him another drink.

With the appearance of LLorser LLitebrite, the council would be complete. As they waited for his arrival, the council members chatted away cozily among themselves. LooLoo leaned against the bar, taking pleasure in the company. Much of the talk centered, in a somewhat circular manner, around the purpose of this unexpected meeting. Since they had met quite recently, they were all, except for Lexi, curious as to why Lefty had Limpy summon them so soon again.

Lexi wanted very much to be the first to tell his fellow council members about his recent encounter, but as he began to speak, the mayor always managed to change the subject.

While they sat talking, musical sounds began to drift into the saloon from the street. The group grew silent. A young jester dressed in a brightly colored outfit entered the saloon playing his lute. In a final touch, his head was crowned by a large foolscap without bells.

"All bow, the king appears," the jester announced. He made a graceful move to one side before he swept the upper part of his body into a prolonged bow, letting pass LLorser Llitebrite, dressed to the hilt as a king. Though unattended by an entourage, the mighty king made a grand entrance into the Lucky Lady. Behind him, the saloon doors swung furiously back and forth on their hinges. Once inside, he paused deliberately. Face-to-face with the council, he viewed the group with the disdain of a true royal.

A full, unkempt beard and long, partially curly hair framed the distinctive features of Orson Welles. A magnificent six-pointed golden crown adorned his head. Just below the regal face, a circular Elizabethan collar severed the head from the body. A thick velvety robe, black and ornamental, draped itself in dramatic fashion over his body, secured in place by a heavy clasp just below the collar. Before the king took his appointed chair at the table, he directed a question to the mayor: "What dost thou profess? What woulds't thou have with us?"

"How 'bout spoutin' some plain old-fashioned Hollywood lingo, kingo?" Lefty responded. His voice echoed the chill of his glare.

Accompanied by a processional from the lute, LLorser walked stiffly on his thick legs past the waiting council to the bar. LooLoo set a bottle and a glass before him with a happy plop. LLorser poured himself a shot and consumed the liquid slowly before he offered a scornful response to the mayor's ignorant remark: "Why, pardner, I just finished punching some heifers over by the library, and thought I'd mosey on over to find out why our dumb, cowpoke mayor is calling yet another useless council meeting so soon after the last. Methinks the mayor loves to waste my precious time."

"Good. Sit that fat ass of yours down in any chair big enough, and you'll find out what this is about just like the rest of 'em," the mayor responded in an exasperated tone.

Shot glass and whiskey bottle in hand, the king squeezed his full-figured, weary shape into his designated chair at the table and covered his bloated knees with a sweep of the robe. With a glance in the direction of the saloon ceiling, the king soliloquized: "O, let me not be mad, not mad, sweet heaven. Keep me in temper; I would not be mad."

"Meeting's called to order," Lefty began after noting that each member had emptied his or her glass. "LLorser, get that fool with his lute out of here right now. You know council meetings are closed to local folks."

"Pray tell, what of those knaves?" LLorser asked, pointing one chunky, bejeweled finger in the direction of Limpy and LooLoo.

"Behave yourself, LLorser. You know they're not the same," Lindsay cut in. "Those two have always been at the meetings. We don't even know which fool is behind that ridiculous jester costume. If he came to my school dressed like that, I'd have him expelled. I'd expel you, too. You always enjoy creating trouble, don't you, LLorser?"

"King Lear to you, serpent-fanged wench," Llorser hissed. He pointed a beefy finger directly toward Lindsay. "She hath tied sharp-toothed unkindness, like a vulture, here."

"Climb down from your high horse so we can get started," Lefty demanded.

LLorser folded his arms regally across his chest and shifted his huge bulk to the back of his chair.

"All in favor of letting that 'l'omputed fool of LLorser's stay in the Lucky Lady for the meeting, raise a hand," the mayor said.

LLorser's hand went up, fortune's lone flower blowing in the wind.

"He's out of here, LLorser."

"Begone, fool. Know you serve me well."

"I'll speak a prophesy ere I go," answered the fool, striking the strings of the lute for emphasis.

"Get your ass out of here pronto," Lefty threatened, rising to his full height to make his point.

The fool rushed off, leaving behind the creaking sound of swinging doors.

"Now down to business," the mayor said. "A 'l'elia came some time recent to Lexi at the gate. Claimed to have come from

LTV land. Lexi did a good job questioning the boy. Then he did his vanishing act to tell me about the boy's arrival before the stranger found his way into town. Naturally, I put the boy hard to the test when he finally arrived. Truth be told, a number of things happened to convince me this here boys the genuine LTV article. Right now he's at my house sleeping. That's something no letter does, I might add. But I wanted to let the council know the situation first before the town finds out. So I called this meeting dadburn fast."

"What do you plan to do with him, Lefty?" Larry asked.

"Let him stay with us until we can help him find his way back home," Lefty answered. "What else could we do, being decent folk?"

Lomash had wisely held his glass in his hand to avoid groping for it during the meeting. Now he set the glass back down on what he figured to be the table. With a crash, the glass shattered into small fragments all across LooLoo's floor. Ignoring the smashed glass, the cyclops asked, "Does he fly?"

"Damn it, Lomash," the bartender interrupted. "I lost four glasses to that mule routine of yours. Now you come here 'l'omputed like a one-eyed idiot. If you can't see straight, don't drink. I've got only eighty-four antique shot glasses left, thanks to you."

Like a frustrated mother, poor LooLoo stood hands on hips bemoaning the wasted glass on his floor. With his one and only bewildered eye staring back at Lefty, Lomash managed to ignore the unhappy bartender.

"What kind of stupid question is that, Lomash?" Lefty demanded.

"A smart stupid one. I saw one of them fly once on LTV," Lomash answered in defense of himself "He wore one of those capes like LLorser, and he flew with his hands and arms straight out in front. A big *S* covered the front of his shirt. I thought maybe he flew here."

"Well, use your head, Lomash. That's what Big Mac gave you one for. Why would an S fly to L Land? Don't you think a flying S would have flown direct to S Land if he'd come from LTV?" The mayor seemed pleased with his own sound reasoning.

"Maybe he is from S Land," Lexi suggested. To nobody's surprise, Lexi seemed to support Lomash's bizarre notion of a flying S. Lexi suddenly remembered that Oliver had said his name was Sandwich when he first approached the gate. "I told him we ate sandwiches here, and he didn't even laugh," Lexi concluded, proud of his recall.

"This here 'I'elia's from LTV and nowhere else, sure as 'I,' " Lefty insisted, fiddling with the playing cards as he spoke. "And sure as 'I,' he didn't fly in. Did he?" Annoyed by the continued challenges, the mayor grew as hot as an internal combustion engine. Short bursts of vapor poured through his nose from the buildup of pressure.

"I think we should be careful with him, Mayor," Lance suggested while he nervously toyed with the cow-skull clasp on his tie. "You know we've already had our capital L reversed, liberaltown's as branded as a little dogie on the range. Strange things have happened since then. Look at how many 'I'omputed Ls left town without saying goodbye. Then, this 'I'elia comes out of the blue claiming to be from LTV Land. Seems mighty suspicious to me."

"How do you know the boy didn't come flying in?" Crazy Lomash persisted, in line with his one-track vision.

"I say the boys true blue," Lefty raised his voice. "I watched raindrops fall from both eyes. Rolled right off the middle of his forehead too. Saw him drop like a sack of lemons smack dab in the middle of the sidewalk in a dead faint. Couldn't talk or nothin' at all. Up real close, I saw how his skin had tiny little holes and hairs. Ugly as sin that skin is. But that ain't all…"

Just before he could reveal his final proof, the mayor heard his words cut off at the pass by LLorser LLitebrite: "How know you this? Nothing will come of nothing. Speak again."

"If you don't cut that claptrap jawing of yours out, …" the mayor threatened.

"You'll do what, sniveling knave?" LLorser LLitebrite sputtered. "You'll blunder as you did before. Is there a person on this council who doesn't remember Lurie Lure, the spy from Lawyertown? We all remember how you as our mayor offered to share inside information—even promised him an office, you did. That is, until I uncovered the truth and exposed him for the scoundrel he was. Won't Lurie Lure have to dwell in the town of Limbo until the time he's called by Word Central to fill some dark word? He is doomed to end his days restricted to words like lie, loser, or licentious. Of that I am certain. I warn you, Littleleather." At this point, LLorser resumed his quasi-Elizabethan rhetoric. "Mend your speech, lest you mar your fortunes."

LLorser raised his empty shot glass as if to challenge the mayor in a toast. "To your health and to your wisdom," he added as he gulped down his drink. Then, tossing the entire glass into his mouth, he began to chew.

LooLoo covered his ears to silence the dreaded sound of glass being crunched between teeth. LLorser wasn't Lomax, and the bartender dared not confront him. Nobody but Lefty ever opposed his bullying tactics. "Eighty-three," the bartender counted in a whisper.

Once LLorser's act of showboating had ended, the mayor tried to continue the meeting with some semblance of dignity. Already he'd lost control, and they'd yet to resolve a thing about Liver. With an unsteady hand, he poured another shot of whiskey, downed it in a gulp, and tried one final explanation. "This situation ain't the same as that Lawyertown one," he proclaimed. "The boy's come here from LTV. I've never been so certain about anything. And he's been sleeping the longest time right in my guest bedroom. Saw him myself before I came over here. Laurie had to make day into night for him before he could go to sleep."

Suddenly the doors swung open and the fool rushed in. He'd followed the meeting as he stood beside the saloon door. Now he confronted the council to give a warning: "He's mad that trusts in the tameness of a wolf, a horse's health, a boy's love, or a whore's oath." Then he whipped around the room in a wild fashion, one hand on his foolscap as it almost tumbled off his head, then rushed through the double doors before the mayor could give him the boot.

"LooLoo, you and Limpy take a shotgun and stand guard at the door. If that fool comes through again, shoot the sidewinder," the mayor demanded.

During the activity with the fool, LooLoo occupied himself gathering the pieces of his beloved glass from beneath Lo-mash's chair. On his knees, he paused to look up at the mayor. Both of them knew the truth: no shotgun, rifle, handgun, or any other weapon of destruction existed in L Land.

"I'll pull out my lasso. But that's about the best I can do, Lefty," said Limpy, as he ducked behind the bar to display the long rope.

When the meeting first started, Lefty intended to reveal his news about the discovery of Oliver's astounding appendage. But discouraged by the suspicious attacks on his every word, he began to lose interest. None of the council appreciated his analysis and acute vision. Upset, he experienced the lightheaded sensation of his hot air evaporating after all his internal matter converted to gas.

"I wanted this to be a good meeting," he explained in a deep voice filled with sulkiness.

Around the table all eyes, except those of Lillbzellmet's and Lomash's, focused on the mayor. LLorser and Lefty often clashed, but none of the council members remembered hearing the mayor sound so resigned in the past.

"I wanted to share my excitement of this find. I am one hundred percent all-American convinced this 'l'elia sleeping in my guest room is the genuine article, a real LTV critter. Now I figger this might give us something special in liberal-town if we're smart. Anyway, this ain't any fun anymore 'cause none of you believes this young 'l'elia is the real thing. I'll tell you this though. Right down there, where the legs spread apart, the boy has a peculiar-looking thing, kind of like a tiny, ugly sidewinder. This thing sags to one side like it's sleeping. Right below, there's a round sack with lots of curly hair all around. Never saw nothin' like what this 'l'ellas got before. I don't know what he does with that ugly sidewinder."

"Since you will not suffer my fool gladly," LLorser responded, "then I'll tell you what wisdom he has taught me." He reached up to adjust his shiny crown before he recited: "'Have more than thou showest. Speak less than thou knowest. Lend less than thou owest. Ride more than thou goest.'

"Its fine advice my fool gives you, Littleleather," the king said, pointing his finger in the air and dropping all linguistic pretensions. "If you spent more time heeding the words of my fool, and less time riding your high horse, you might find you know far less than you assume. No doubt this lad is some kind of government spy from G Land or maybe even from our own L Land government.

"Perhaps he has been sent to check on us. Perhaps the blasted legislature is ready to take over our town and ship the lot of us out to Word Central. Did you ever think about the possibility of mass extermination? What are we? A defenseless town full of Ls and double Ls, that's what we are.

"Maybe you don't understand that those letters from G Land, the center of government, can move from A to Z. Particular postal routing codes allow them to travel, on special business, through the post offices in each letterland. How would we know the truth?" LLorser looked to his left toward Lillbzellmet, whose pie-tin face, still stuck in the same position, stared directly into Lomash's one eye.

"Take our friend Lillbzellmet. Who knows whether some G Land agent has taken its place to learn how we deal with our non-'l'omputed population? How would we know? Our distinguished non-'l'omputed L representative could just as easily be a spy, since all non-'l'omputed Ls look and act the same."

All eyes now turned to Lillbzellmet. The pale, sunny-side-up orbs in the middle of its pie tin showed no reaction. Caught off guard, the noncomputed L could only sputter the classic curse: "Lullxiclepcicalsesosasllllweaaalll, alalalalalala."

Howls of laughter shook the room. A loud snort came from LLorser, while Lefty tried to contain himself. In the end, even Lefty had to give up and laugh.

"We now have temporary letters available to use for writing," LLorser continued after the meeting settled down. "I have been doing a study that I call "L'omputing the Mind of the LTV Creature.' We all know the habits of these strange creatures. Some of them jump about like fleas on a dog, changing identity over and over again.

"LTV people probably don't exist at all," LLorser went on, since no one could stop him once he got started. "I suspect they are only bits of fluff created by Big Mac for our amusement. They are only models for us to mimic until we assume our positions as letters fixed in words where we remain until we return. No, these creatures the mayor speaks about with such conviction do not exist at all. They are no more important in Big Macs scheme than a comma or a period is in a sentence. Believe me, council members, I have been right before, and as a double L, I always remain an L ahead."

LLorser, deeply moved by his own profundity, paused for a moment before he droned on. "Think of your future, council members. You will one day become immortalized as the lead letter in an important l word, while those LTV people with their lofty sentiments will vanish as soon as they change into a new identity, with no thoughts or ideas at all."

Intimidated into silence, the council members couldn't contradict LLorser's claims of superior wisdom and experience. Lefty, for his part, jumped out of his seat to pace back and forth across the sawdust floor of the saloon. Granted LLorser spent more time in the library than all of liberaltown combined, Lefty knew for a fact that if he only had a gun, he'd shoot that low-down varmint dead as a doornail.

"You're full of hot 'l'air," came an unexpected, flat-toned voice vibrating across the room. Awestruck, all heads turned toward Lillbzellmet. Never before, throughout the long unrecorded history of council meetings, had the noncomputed L spoken. Retracting its support clamp to an upright position, Lillbzellmet ordered the monitor to make a right turn. Loud noises ensued as the hockey stick whisked back and forth along the wood floor until the support clamp had reset.

Lillbzellmet confronted LLorser face-to-face and spat its words out between its slit lips. "You think you're so smart, Mr. Double L, because you've visited so many lands, met different letters, and read so much. You sure talk so nobody knows what the 'l' you're saying. I don't know if that means you're smart. But if all you say is true, how come you never told us about any LTV person who kept a little snake down where the legs grow apart?"

LLorser, stunned by the words emanating from the mouth of a noncomputed L, tried to maintain his superior demeanor. At the bar, Limpy and LooLoo shook their heads. An appearance by Big Mac himself could not have produced a greater shock than the words flowing from the mouth of Lillbzellmet. Even the fool, banished to the sidewalk, could not keep from sticking his head through the swinging doors. The impact of the words struck them so much harder because the pie-tin face had spoken out against the king himself.

LLorser, mouth slightly agape, kept his silence. Why hadn't he, a powerful double L, been aware of the little thing between the legs of Tellas from LTV? How could he have memorized so many lines and yet have no knowledge of such a small anatomical fact? His mouth opened, as if to respond, but not a word emerged.

"I say that the mayor knows what he's saying," continued Lillbzellmet. "Let him show us this creature. Only then can the council decide what proper action to take."

"Hear, hear," cried Larry, patting his blond Lucy head.

"A fine idea," shouted Lindsay. She enjoyed this moment of

LLorser's comeuppance.

"I'm not sure I see any reason for that," complained Lomash, who wished to move about town as little as possible in his one-eyed state.

"Stop being so damn short-sighted, Lomash," Lefty complained. The mayor felt swell now. Gas fumes once more flowed through his nostrils.

A long stare-down ensued between Lillbzellmet and LLorser, the latter finally tilting his head back in a sudden gesture, as if to appeal to the gods above. "You heavens," he said to the ceiling, rolling the last word over his tongue. "You heavens, give me the patience, patience I need. You see me here, you gods, a poor old man, as full of grief as age, wretched in both."

LLorser moved his head forward to stare into the pie-shaped face partially obscured by the monitor before him. "You are right, Lillbzellmet. Wise you were to strip away the arrogance of power and smite my foolish pride a telling blow. How dare I assume, even for an instant, that the wisdom gathered through my many LL word experiences should offer more to any of you than words uttered by a pie-faced non-'l'omputed fool? Here I stand, crown in hand, tongue in cheek, seeking forgiveness for my flagrant sins." With rising resonance he concluded in a theatrical flurry, "Pray, do not mock me. I am a very foolish old man."

Moved by the seeming humility of LLorser's speech, the council members of liberaltown quickly accepted his apology. They thought they heard him acknowledge publicly, for the very first time, his own frailty, his humble revelation of the powerlessness that all letters deny but feel deep inside. The council members knew that they as computed single Ls would eventually become a lead 1 in a word.

But noncomputed Ls like Lillbzellmet, and double Ls like LLorser, shared the same fate. They could be assigned to any location within a word.

In a somber state, they listened as the mayor invited each of them to join him on a group trip to the Littleleather house. "You can see this Liver and judge for yourselves where he's from and what he's doing here," Lefty suggested graciously.

And so, in an overwhelming "yea" vote, the town council decided to pay a call on the sleeping Oliver.

Oliver Makes a Splash

Lorser, determined to prove Oliver a fraud, made an attempt to snap off the young visitor's erect member. His sudden tug caused Oliver to sit up in bed. The pain forced him to open his *eyes*. Clear as day, hunched over, less than a foot from his face, stood a fat man with wild eyes and a gold crown, and sure enough, he yanked at Oliver's member again. Crouched behind the crowned hulk, an honest-to-god cyclops aimed his one blue eye intensely upon the procedure in progress.

Another fierce pull, and Oliver squealed like a pig. Some strangely menacing words stabbed his sleepy brain: "By Juno, I shall expose thee, cursed knave." Helpless, after hours of accumulation, Oliver suddenly lost all control of his bladder. A stream of yellow liquid, violently unleashed, shot straight through the air in the direction of his assailant.

The first powerful barrage caught the king flush in his right eye. Though temporarily blinded, LLorser continued to tug at Oliver's penis, using a firm two-handed grip, much the way a firefighter holds a nozzle. With a slight shift, the stream changed course. As the fluid hit with magnum force against his kingly forehead, the liquid cascaded like rain down LLorser's face. Instantly, he let go to cover both eyes.

Like a berserk garden hose, Oliver's member began to water the room indiscriminately. Lomash, still huddled behind the king, caught a shot squarely in his only eye. Limpy and LooLoo, both of whom had been invited to come along for the inspection, found themselves in the line of fire. Lindsay, too stunned to duck in time, received a direct hit on her forehead below her Miss Brooks sweep of hair. Lance, Lillbzell-met, and the blond Larry shared enough spray to experience a quick, communal shower. Lexi ended up with his own private river spinning around the rim of his ten-gallon hat. Only the mayor, a few steps from the bed, remained out of range and bone dry.

Laurie and her mother showed up late during the demonstration. They stopped short inside the bedroom door far out of Oliver's reach. Lefty, vindicated, gave them the "Duke" smile he'd practiced so often in the mirror. A happy grunt escaped his lips as LLorser backpedaled to the window. With one hand LLorser began to wipe his drenched face while with the other he clung to his kingly crown, now slipped down across his left ear.

Laughter erupted from the group. In spite of their soaked condition, all the council members except Lillbzellmet found the incident hilarious. Poor Lillbzellmet reacted with panic to the liquid that rolled down its unprotected metal pie-tin head. Unlike computed Ls, whose bodies were protected by a rubbery skin, this L had no cover whatsoever over its vulnerable metal frame.

As the fluid dripped down the length of its thin body, it retracted its support bar in near hysteria, jerking around so fast the monitor almost decapitated Larry. Disoriented by the urine in its colorless orbs, the noncomputed L began to spin around in a circle. When its hockey-stick joint made a loud scraping sound over the wooden floor, everyone turned their attention from Oliver's member to the sight of a noncomputed L in distress, a rare spectacle indeed.

Faster and faster, the hockey stick whirled until its monitor and its L frame lost balance. Falling like a snapped stop sign, Lillbzellmet crashed to the floor. In a pitiful monotone it released the soulful sound of the mournful L chant, "lalala-lalalalalalalala."

Utterly insensitive to the fate of the pitiful Lillbzellmet, most of the council members howled with laughter again. None could remember this much fun and excitement in a long time. Not since LLorser uncovered the spy from Lawyertown had anyone enjoyed himself so thoroughly. Laughter among the Ls had become a rare event ever since the legislature's unreasonable demand that the capital L in the towns name face left. Though they had resisted the law by using a small l, many residents felt targeted. They feared the passage of such an irrational law offered the beginning of the end for their town and its way of life.

Only Lindsay leapt into action. A Miss Brooks teacher in spirit if not in occupation, she immediately realized the liquid could rust a noncomputed L in no time. And she knew the face of a rusting L: a slow and painful deterioration that would eventually render it useless to Word Central. Defective Ls were carted off near the town of Limbo to a scrap heap the size of Lettering Heights.

Lindsay grabbed a folded towel from atop the dresser. With no time to spare, she rushed to the aid of the fallen Lill-bzellmet. As she wiped away the drops of liquid from its pie-tin head and metal body, it continued chanting its pathetic "lalalas."

Meanwhile, with the contents of his bladder dispersed, Oliver wished he could just disappear off the face of L Land. His member had returned to normal size. Exhausted from the ordeal, it flopped over for a little rest. With his eyes closed, Oliver silently recited, one by one, the list of magical words he remembered from a book on conjuring his mother had given him on his ninth birthday. But the words had no effect whatsoever. Surrounded by screwballs crazier than any he'd seen in Los Angeles, Oliver remained on display, stark naked in Lefty and Lo-Rain's guest room in liberaltown.

Oliver covered his genitals with both hands when he began to detect a vile, gaslike odor emanating from the excited Ls. He opened his eyes to look up and out the window just long enough to see a sliver of blue sky behind the obese, black-robed man holding on to the golden crown pressed against his left ear. The man, in a sudden move, let in the light behind him as he advanced in a threatening manner. In response, Oliver pressed his hands even harder against his sore genitalia.

The mayor pushed his way through the council members who had spread out across the room. Standing between Oliver's bed and LLorser, he moved to stop the king in his tracks. "Next time, when I share something I hope some big-mouth fancy-talking LL will take notice," he warned him.

"Have you folks seen enough?" Laurie interrupted as respectfully as she could. She did not allow herself to be too forceful. The council, after all, represented the only authority in liberaltown.

"I demand to know how you perform such a trick," LLorser said, reaching up once again to adjust his tilted crown.

"What trick?" Oliver responded in a barely audible voice as he continued to look away.

"Your sorcerer's trick of making rain. How else should we know if you are a fair-weather friend or foul? To quote my wise fool: 'That sir which serves and seeks for gain, and follows but for form, will pack when it begins to rain, and leave thee in a storm …'"

"I beg your pardon," Oliver said in a voice dropped so low he could barely hear himself speak.

"Don't pay him no mind," Lefty cut in. "He's just fancy talking 'cause he knows you're the genuine article."

"From where exactly do you hail, brother?" the king asked.

"LA, that is, Los Angeles."

"And do all your brothers there behave as you?"

"I beg your pardon."

"Do they all rain from a pipe as you do?"

"I'm terribly sorry," Oliver mumbled. "I had an accident. I couldn't control myself." He didn't dare face any of the council members. Words stuck in his throat. "Of course, well, usually we use, you know, toilets."

"Know? How should I know, scurrilous knave? Nor do I know your true intent or the stories spun that you invent. If I knew, I would have no reason to inquire of one who rains as he desires." LLorser concluded his speech still holding fast to his crown.

For an instant, Oliver recalled the rhyming lion. This plump king might be another of his disguises. "I didn't desire that," Oliver protested.

A heavy sweat broke out across Oliver's forehead. "See, rains out of his head too," Lefty boomed like a carnival barker hustling his act. Two fingers scooped up a bit of the forehead moisture, and the mayor waved his fingers around for all to see.

"I'm so sorry. If I can do anything, I would be glad to make up for what happened," Oliver murmured. He stared, as if conversing with his big toe. "The whole thing is a blur. Please, forgive me if you can."

"Is he praying like they do in church?" LooLoo asked Limpy.

"Beats me," his friend said.

LLorser used one hand to steady his bulk against the headboard of the bed as he questioned the visitor. Now he raised his huge frame to face the other council members. "I proclaim that this visitor exhibits qualities identical to LTV creatures. I hereby pronounce him authentic," he declared in true royal fashion.

LLorser looked straight at Oliver. "Knave, hear me. As members of the town council, we will discover whether you are a fair-weather friend or foul-weather foe. Woe to you if you have come to deceive us. I decree you shall not leave liberaltown until such a time as you receive permission. We will discuss your status at the next meeting." Before another word could be spoken, LLorser vanished from sight.

"Big deal," the mayor said after he'd left.

"I hate to see how those double Ls take off like that," Limpy whispered to LooLoo.

"Guess I gotta get back to work," Lexi said. He'd overheard Limpy's comment, and for an odd reason known only to himself, Lexi took the words to mean that he should leave, too.

At the moment Lexi vanished from the room, Oliver glimpsed at the gatekeeper long enough to see waves of fluid crash ferociously over the rim of his ten-gallon hat. The ten-gallon river splashed a long, wet trail on the floor behind him as he faded into the distance.

"Bunch of show-offs," Lefty declared.

"Why don't the rest of you come into the dining room?" asked Lo-Rain, always hospitable. "I have a lovely lemon pie and some lemonade ready."

Before she could finish, Lexi popped back to the very spot he'd just left behind. He sounded out of gas. "Got halfway back to the gate and thought I heard someone mention a lemon pie."

"Mighty big ears you've got, Lexi," the mayor chuckled.

Lo-Rain led the group through the door. As they departed

single file, they babbled with great excitement. Only Laurie remained standing. When all were gone, she shut the door firmly behind them. "Those people are just so awful," she pouted.

"I can't tell you how sick this makes me," Oliver answered.

"Why? Are you sick? You should be well. You were groovy, Liver. Maybe you don't think so, but you proved exactly what Daddy hoped you would. You showed them how different LTV creatures are and that you are for real. Even that fat LLorser finally shut his mouth. You were wonderful."

Laurie wanted to cheer him up. But she didn't know how to make him feel better. "Do you like this outfit?" she asked, turning around slowly like a model to reveal black pedal pushers and a white T-shirt similar to the one Oliver wore when he first arrived, #span_smallcaps LAURIEANDR!span had been misspelled in gold letters across the chest. "I designed these clothes myself, and I wrote that new name you gave me in the moonlight."

"They're very pretty," Oliver agreed. "But you should spell your name #span_smallcaps L A U R I A N D E R!span. I gave you that name because somehow the name fits. I don't even know why exactly. You look like Lysander, and you act like Laurie. I guess you are my Lauriander now."

Lauriander flashed a big smile. "I like being Lauriander."

Drained, Oliver glanced at Watchim again. "I wonder how long I slept," he said out loud to change the subject. The hands showed the Los Angeles time to be a little past eleven on Sunday morning. "I guess I slept a lot. I see bright daylight outside."

"The council asked me to 'l'ompute light again when they came," Lauriander explained. "Ls don't like the dark very much. Do you want me to 'l'ompute the sky back to moonlight for you?"

When he didn't answer, she pulled her T-shirt up over her head. Sitting on the edge of the bed, she slipped off her shoes, socks, and pants. Lauriander couldn't wait to reveal her little surprise, which she hoped would cheer him up.

"I feel sick inside," Oliver complained. "I don't know how I could have lost control like that… and in front of all those people."

She turned to kiss his cheek. Her small, firm breasts brushed against his arm. "Don't look so unhappy, Liver. It's all right. I told you I can bring the moon back for you."

"Not now. This is supposed to be daytime. Shouldn't we change the sheets in case they're wet or something?"

She responded by pushing him flat against the bed. She sat down on his stomach. She bent forward to plant a long kiss on his tight lips.

"Look," she blurted with the enthusiasm of a child. As she leaned back, she spread her legs to display a rather startling change to her anatomy. In the moonlight, Oliver thought the mood perfect, only to discover a shocking revelation that quickly deflated his "first-time" experience. Lauriander lacked the necessary opening to "first-time" with. Now he could see for himself that she had followed to the letter his meager instructions culled from his imagination, questionable magazines, occasional gropings in the dark, and scant attention paid during sex education classes.

He dared not ask how she had accomplished the feat. The humiliation he had experienced before the town council played on his mind. Things couldn't get any worse. He decided he no longer cared whether the "first time" came in day or night. The moonlight idea had gone nowhere. Mired in madcap events, he suspected his chances of ever returning home would diminish with each passing day.

But opportunity existed, literally in front of his nose, a chance to make love, and if not in Brentwood, then here and now. And while he'd made love to Lysander only in his dreams, his own new, beautiful Lauriander appeared eager and willing. Lauriander had somehow computed some semblance of the right equipment just for him. That she cared for him mattered most. So, without further ado, he took her in his arms and did what he had dreamed about doing for a long, long time.

A Few Surprises

ost in thought and ankle deep in water, Oliver sat down to sponge himself in the claw-footed bathtub. He had tried the ornate faucets to find them bone dry. Oliver had taken a bowl of lukewarm water from the wash-stand to pour into the tub. A good, hot soak became yet another unfulfilled Letterland dream.

Earlier, in a slightly blue mood, Oliver had cuddled in the afterglow of lovemaking while at the same time experiencing the letdown of too-high expectations. Much as he thought the experience had been nice, the moment seemed a bit overrated. Of course, he kept that sentiment hidden from Lauriander. After all, he could barely admit the truth to himself.

Lauriander, on the other hand, couldn't wait to share her wonderful experiences. She happily anticipated getting together with her friends soon. She looked forward to disclosing her newly acquired know-how about the little thing between Oliver's legs that went up and down and in and out like magic. Also, she knew from past experience that her own newfangled equipment would soon be the talk of the town. No doubt about that.

"Liver, do all you people do what we just did?" she'd asked soon after they'd finished making love. "We never see anyone do that on LTV."

Spent, Oliver flopped onto his back beside her.

"What?"

As she squeezed against him, he held her tight with one arm. "Do all LTV people do what we did?" she repeated.

"That's a private matter that's shared between two people.

They don't show real lovemaking on TV, except of course on cable, which you don't get here," Oliver explained. He reached up with his free hand to stroke her hair.

"I've seen them," she went on. "They lie in bed like we do, but never without wearing some clothes. That's why I didn't know about these pretty little nipples here," she said, pointing to her own newly formed nipples at the end of her computed breasts. Do you like them?"

"Yes," Oliver answered, amazed by her ability to make quick anatomical adjustments to her body. He hesitated for a moment, as if he had a sudden thought. "Where I live, people change their bodies a lot too: new noses, new ears, new teeth, new knees, new boobs, just like that. One day, one of my mother's friends showed up with a completely new face. Her eyes had even changed from green to a scary turquoise color with the help of contact lenses." As he spoke, the difference between his present and past life seemed to blur. A terrifying thought flashed, then vanished. In that instant, Oliver questioned whether the world he knew was any more real than L Land.

With his revelation beyond her grasp, Lauriander changed the subject to something tangible. "Did you notice what else I did?" Bursting with joy, she sprang from the bed to reveal her newly computed buns, shaped like two half-moons. A full split ran up between them.

As his eyes followed the movement of her sweet, round bottom, Oliver smiled. Lauriander knew from his contented expression she must have computed herself well. She couldn't be happier. All Lauriander wanted was for her Liver to feel good.

"Do you think that when all those people leave, we might

find something to eat?" Oliver asked. "I'm starving, as if I haven't eaten for days. In Los Angeles, we'd be eating Sunday brunch," he added. Though hardly eager for the taste of Lo-Rain's salty food, Oliver felt his stomach growl ferociously at the very thought of food.

Lauriander laughed and bent down to give him a hug. "You LTV boys. All you think about is food."

But Oliver had thought about more than food, like having a good hot soak before lunch. Instead, he had to settle for this lukewarm bowl of water taken from the washstand.

"How come you have water to wash with and not in the bath pipes?" he asked.

Lauriander could only shrug her shoulders. "Mama buys this clear liquid at the store. I think she poured some for you because she knew you LTV people wash in it."

Oliver went no further in his questioning. Despite his nagging hunger pangs, he'd wanted to have his daily bath before he did anything else. He had to make do with what he had.

Lauriander hung back as she watched him struggle with the pitiful amount of water he'd poured in the tub. Oliver was not in the least amused by his plight. Soon the bottom of the tub resembled a mud puddle.

"This is pitiful," he said, staring down at the puddle. "I just don't understand why you don't pipe in water."

"We don't take baths. We don't need water for anything. A lot of the fixtures in the house aren't used at all. They're just here because we've seen them used on LTV. Even though we don't need to eat, we have kitchens. We have beds in our bedrooms, too. But we don't have to sleep, ever," Lauriander reminded him. "We just want everything to look the right way"

Oliver reacted as if hearing the words for the first time. "You don't have to eat, or sleep, or bathe? I guess you don't have to use the toilet either," he said in a sarcastic voice, already resigned to the answer. He attempted to control his pressing needs, but the pressure he felt reminded him he would have to act quickly.

"I don't know. Come on, Liver. If you're finished, I've got a present for you in my room."

With a disgusted glance at the murky water, Oliver climbed out of the tub. After drying off, he quickly slipped on his pants. He opened the toilet seat and found only an empty space beneath. He dared not relieve himself there. He wanted to find a roll of toilet paper, but found none in the bathroom. "Shshshit, I have to go outside without any paper," he said, bolting for the door. Lauriander looked after him with surprise as he rushed down the stairs toward the backyard in search of a tree.

Without a tree or even a bush, Oliver had to relieve himself out in the open for all to see. He felt humiliated and embarrassed. In the Sandwich household, respect for privacy remained holier than cleanliness. In liberaltown, he had no privacy whatsoever. And to add insult to injury, he could barely clean himself for lack of water.

He returned to the bathroom to finish up his attempts at hygiene. Then he went into Lauriander's room. As miserable as ever, he asked himself why his life in Letterland had become so complicated. He looked around Lauriander's room; she had a small desk, a white dresser with a mirror mounted above, and a single bed with white and pink fluffy pillows strewn on top of the quilted bedspread. The decor seemed snatched from a bedroom in an Ozzie and Harriet sitcom.

Lauriander had laid out a white T-shirt on the middle of the bed. #span_smallcaps LIVERR!span read across it in gold letters. "I hope I spelled your name right," she said. "As I told you, I'm not so good at spelling. We've only had temporary letters for a little while here. LLiterally LLucid's still teaching me how to use them."

Oliver appreciated her efforts to make him happy and thanked her, leaving out any mention of her spelling. "How did you make the shirt so fast?"

"Easy as pie. I just 'l'omputed your name in lambscotton."

He pulled the shirt over his head. To his surprise, it fit well. He crossed the room to kiss her on the cheek. "Thanks again. I'm starving. Do you think you could get dressed now too?" She had been walking around the house without a stitch, no doubt to show off her latest computer corrections.

Lauriander, delighted with her *success,* chose a full, pink, felt skirt decorated with a black poodle with a pink rhinestone collar around its neck. She tucked in a tight black sweater at the waist. Before they went down to the kitchen, she spun her skirt high above her legs, showing off her white panties.

"Liver's mighty hungry, Mama," Lauriander said as they entered the kitchen. "Should I make him some food?"

"I'll make him a snack, dear," Lo-Rain responded. She didn't like anyone messing in her kitchen.

"I can wait until lunch if you're planning to eat soon," Oliver suggested politely, even though Watchim showed the time as early afternoon and he soon expected to die of hunger.

"I better make you something. I don't want to see you faint," Lo-Rain answered as she headed for the large, old-fashioned wooden icebox. "Would you like a sandwich like the one I made when you arrived?"

Lauriander and Oliver sat down at the kitchen table while Lo-Rain scurried around the kitchen to prepare the food. "Would you like a little extra 'l'alt on this?" Lo-Rain asked.

"What's 'l'alt?"

Lauriander picked up a silver Taltshaker from the table. "'L'alt's all we taste when we eat food." She sprinkled a few grains into Oliver's outstretched hand.

"Wow, that stuff's strong. No thanks. Why do you call it 'l'alt when it tastes like salt?" he asked, rejecting the offer as diplomatically as possible.

"I don't know. 'L'alt's always been 'l'alt to us," Lauriander answered.

Oliver took only small, measured bites of the lamb sandwich. Though he certainly didn't like the pasty sensation any better, he found he could tolerate the sandwich easier than the lamb at dinner. The 'l'applesauce contained only a trace of 'l'alt, though the taste proved far from flavorful.

Revived for the moment, Oliver finally began to focus on Lauriander, who had been pushing for a walk into town. She couldn't wait to show him the stores on Main Street. Most of all, she wanted to take him to visit LLiterally LLucid. She felt sure Oliver would like to meet the longest living and most interesting LL in L Land. But to her disappointment, Oliver wanted to stay home to watch LTV in her room.

They flopped down on her bed. "What do you want to watch?" Lauriander asked. "We can just see what's on. Or, if you tell me what you like, I can call up the number." Seated on its own stand, the monitor resembled a computer screen about the size of the television in his parents bedroom.

Oliver shrugged his shoulders. What they watched didn't matter much to him at this point. His hunger pangs already began to return, as if he hadn't eaten at all. Lauriander flipped on the screen. An old Ed Sullivan program called *Toast of the Town* appeared. The segment featured, of all possible guests, Orson Welles dressed in rags as King Lear, doing an excerpt from the Shakespeare play he had performed in his television debut on CBS.

Lauriander giggled. "LLorser LLitebrite's on LTV. Just look at him."

Next to Ed Sullivan stood the great actor as Lear, complete with wild hair, a scruffy beard, and tattered clothes. When performing, Orson had boomed his words in true Shakespearian fashion. But now, talking with Sullivan, he reverted to his everyday sonorous voice. Lauriander, smiling, took it all in. The 1950s were no different to her than Shakespeare's time.

"He is so funny to listen to," Lauriander observed. "LLorser speaks in the same strange way."

"That's Old English," Oliver informed her. He knew trying to explain the concept of Old and Modern English to her was most likely useless, but he couldn't help himself. As he tried to explain the differences, he wondered if he understood them himself.

Oliver's explanations made Lauriander restless. "Let's go for a walk," she suggested. She stood up and fluffed out the folds of her skirt. "Maybe we should go visit Lucy or some of my other friends. Do you mind?"

Oliver stretched out on the bed. "Go ahead. I can't believe

I'm so hungry again. I don't know what's wrong with me. I'm tired too. I might even take a little nap," he said, yawning.

After Lauriander left, Oliver stared at the colored pennants tacked onto the wall, and then he watched a bit more of *Toast of the Town*. The irony was not lost on Oliver. He might have just as easily been watching this program sitting next to Uncle Bob. Instead, he found himself in a place where the people looked as if they came directly off the screen from those old programs. Worst of all, now that life around him imitated television, he couldn't really enjoy life or the TV shows.

He closed his eyes and dozed off into a fitful sleep. He thought he had nodded off for only a short moment when loud, girlish laughter from the floor below awoke him. A movie in color now played on the monitor. Oliver sat up on the side of the bed. He rubbed his eyes. His stomach ached with hunger pangs. Not wanting to move, he ran his pocket comb through his tangled hair. But curiosity finally got the better of him, and he headed down the stairs.

In the living room, he encountered a group of young girls giggling and chatting among themselves. "Oh, Liver," Lauriander said, bouncing excitedly out of her chair. She gave him a little hug. "Everybody, this is Liver. Liver, these are my friends," she exclaimed as she introduced Lauren, Linda, Lucy, Lydia, and Lucinda in breakneck order.

Encouraged to pull up a chair, Oliver squelched his reluctance and joined the group. Lauren was clearly a member of the Mickey Mouse Club. A blond-haired girl around twelve, she'd spelled her name across the chest of her white turtleneck shirt. On her head sat a little beanie with mouse ears. An emblem was sewn right in front of her hat.

Linda resembled a youthful Sandra Dee in the film *Gidget*.

Lucy, Lauriander's best friend, resembled a sexy version of a teenage Elizabeth Taylor, with black hair, thick black eyebrows, violet eyes, and a perfect little nose.

In gingham dresses, Lydia and Lucinda had computed themselves after the set of twins, both played by Hayley Mills, in *The Parent Trap*. Oliver looked from one to the other and couldn't tell the difference.

The girls offered him lemonade and 'l'alt cookies. All eyes followed his every move. When he drank lemonade, they watched. When he ate a cookie, they watched. When he ate another cookie, followed by another, they watched in amazement. The expression on his face as he nibbled at his strongly 'l'alt-laced cookies made them giggle. A scratch at his nose intrigued them. As he began to feel like a goldfish in a bowl, Oliver squirmed in his chair.

Lucy broke the silence first. "My daddy told me about you, Liver. He came to visit with the council when you splashed all that water on them."

"Liver was so cool," Lauriander explained, looking possessively at her beau. "Right off he showed them how a real LTV person acts. You should have seen LLorser LLitebrite's face when Liver shot him right in the eye." All the girls giggled while Oliver's back pressed into his chair and his face turned a bright red.

The girls tittered at his sudden change of color.

One of the twins took a sip of her lemonade. Then she went right to the subject closest to her heart: "One thing I can't understand is how you LTV people have babies. Here Word Central just 'l'omputes a bunch of Ls when we need more. You've seen them. They look just like capital letter Ls. But you don't 'l'ompute yours, do you?"

"Only about one percent of us can 'l'ompute like LTV people," Lauriander informed him proudly. "LLiterally LLucid told me so."

"Oh, that LLiterally LLucid thinks he knows everything," Lydia snapped, irritated by the interruption.

"Shut up, Lydia," her twin, Lucinda, said, cutting her short. "You know how much Laurie and Lucy like him."

"My name is Lauriander," the young hostess corrected.

More giggles.

"You have cute little babies in LTV, don't you?" Lucy continued, following up on Lydia's question. "We don't have anyone who looks like a baby here. Someone told me he tried to 'l'ompute himself into a baby once. He couldn't move around very well, and he spoke funny."

"Who was that?" Lydia wanted to know.

"Men don't have babies," Oliver corrected, still stuck on Lucy's last question. "Women have them."

"Who was that who was a baby once?" Lydia persisted.

"How many babies can you 'l'ompute at once?" Lucinda asked, continuing to ignore her twin.

"I don't understand 'l'ompute," Oliver answered, totally confused. He basically understood what they meant by now, but his hunger had led to an irritation with all their nonsense.

The Ls all exchanged glances. Lucy set her glass on the table. "See, Liver, we just 'l'ompute the person we want to be from LTV. Then we print ourselves out. And we can add or change parts. Laurie,

I mean Lauriander, showed you how she did that, right? But when we first return from Word Central, we look like little or big Ls, not babies, and there are a whole lot of us at once."

"But only one percent can 'l'ompute to look like people?" Oliver asked incredulously. *Why in the world only one percent?* he wondered to himself.

"There aren't many like us," Lydia said.

"I still don't understand this baby business," Lucy persisted.

"When a woman gets pregnant, she carries a baby in her stomach for nine months before the birth," Oliver explained, in spite of his hunger.

"You mean that's what all those fat women on LTV are doing?"

"Not all of the fat ones have babies. Some are just fat. Some are pregnant, though, and look fat."

"Do a lot of babies get 'l'omputed from the fat stomach at the same time?" Linda asked.

The questions arrived too fast for Oliver to handle. He began to sound as frustrated as he felt. "No, usually only one. A baby is born alive, not 'l'omputed. Sometimes there are two. Those are twins. All babies come out through the vagina."

"Where I put my slit?" Lauriander asked.

Oliver flushed as he nodded.

"Wow, that's so cool," Lauren the Mouseketeer said.

"I think that's a stupid idea," Lydia said. "All that work to make one little LTV person. Big Mac's smarter to 'l'ompute a thousand Ls all at once."

The most outspoken of the group, Lydia continued brazenly. "Lauriander showed us her new slit. She said you have some little pipe you call a member that grows all big and hard. We all want to see how you do that."

Oliver shook his head in a rapid movement. He turned the color of autumn leaves once again.

"Liver, everyone's going to want to see your member," Lauriander said. "All those council folks have been talking. A couple of the council men are already trying to 'l'ompute one that looks just like yours."

"That's right," Lucy agreed. "My daddy said he would too if he hadn't already 'l'omputed himself into Lucy Ricardo."

Only good manners prevented Oliver from walking out of the room. Instead, he examined the larks on the wallpaper. Lauriander, sensitive to his moods by now, tried to help him out. "You know, Livers not like us. Maybe he's not feeling so well right now. That's why he doesn't want to talk anymore."

"I don't see why he's such an uptight dude," Lydia pouted, tossing out a popular 60s' expression.

"Shut up," her twin told her.

"Would you excuse me?" Oliver asked as he stood up, slightly dizzy. Lauriander followed her unsteady lover all the way into his room. As he undressed, he asked her to change day to night. For a moment he sat, in his underwear, on the edge of the bed. "Oh, I'm so hungry," he moaned, then toppled over and closed his eyes.

Lauriander computed darkness right away, even before she returned to her friends. They complained bitterly about the sudden darkness. With no need to sleep, darkness provided nothing more than an irritant. But Lauriander wouldn't budge. She would do anything to please her Liver. The girls decided to move over to Lucy's house to continue the visit. Lauriander refused to go. Instead, she checked on Liver. He'd already fallen fast asleep.

Lauriander understood he would sleep a long time. She departed for the computing room. She intended to compute herself to LLiterally LLucid's Lodge for a short visit while Oliver slept his life away. She needed LLiterally's advice, for the realization had hit her that her life now had a deeper meaning. She would care for and protect her strange and wonderful lover.

A New Dimension

efty squeezed into his easy chair. "Finally, some peace and quiet in this here house," the mayor bellowed after Lauriander as she went into the computing room.

Lefty had had just about enough of all the commotion stirred up by Oliver's arrival. But just as he planted his big boots on the coffee table to enjoy a shot of whiskey, someone knocked on the front door.

"Who in the 'l' can that be?" the irritated mayor asked as his wife bustled across the room to open the door. There, on the front porch, stood neighbors Lucky Looper and his wife, Lilly. Lo-Rain, caught off guard, invited them in to join Lefty while she hurried to the kitchen to make everyone a cup of tea.

"How come its all dark around here?" Lucky wanted to know.

Lefty ignored him. "How about a shot?" Lefty offered, after he'd seated his guests on the living room couch. "And maybe a 'l'aspirilla for the little lady?" Lefty definitely was not a tea person.

"Thanks, Lefty," Lilly answered in her sweet, sultry, baby-doll voice. The voice came with the look, for Lilly numbered one among many computed Marilyn's running around liberal-town. Lucky had computed himself into a dapper, thin Frankie, the crooner-actor who once had his own television program.

Lucky even tried once to sing like the LTV Frankie at the Lucky Lady Saloon. But he couldn't keep a tune if his life depended on it. Lucky's dismal performance occurred after he'd downed several shots of whiskey, which he pretended affected him in a similar way to humans. LooLoo, afraid of losing his few remaining customers, refused ever after to give Lucky another drink. No matter how many Legos Lucky tried to seduce him with, LooLoo refused. He'd made up his mind.

Lefty had no hesitation serving Lucky a drink. Lucky didn't sing during social calls. Lefty returned with two filled shot glasses, one of which Lucky grabbed. He came straight to the point of his visit. "Saw your friend LooLoo down at the Lucky Lady," Lucky began. "LooLoo said you had a new 'l'elia in town staying here with you. Lilly and me thought as neighbors we'd be neighborly and meet the young man."

"So what is he to you?" Lefty asked in a suspicious voice. "Liver's asleep right now, according to my little Laurie. You know, these LTV 'l'ellas are a mite peculiar. Seems like they sleep all the time. Carried Liver to bed once and found he weighed as much as five Ls stacked straight up. But he's not worth a can of beans if he has to keep his eyes open."

"I want to see that big long pipe he's got sticking out," Lucky said. "I plan to 'l'ompute one myself. Up until now, LTV had me believing their water only came out of a sink or garden hose. But I heard his pipe shoots water, too. Sounds like you can have a lot of fun with one of those attachments he's got. LooLoo claims he saw that pipe get hard as a rock."

"That LooLoo's got a mighty big mouth," Lefty growled.

At this point Lo-Rain entered with a tray bearing cups of hot tea for Lilly and herself. Lilly turned to her and asked, "Have you made one of the new slits yet, Lo-Rain? They're going to be all the rage."

Lo-Rain gave a slight shake of her head, and answered with a bit of embarrassment. "No. Laurie showed me the one she made for herself. She said I should 'l'ompute one, but I don't think that's for me. Maybe only the young people should have them."

"Well, we're young," Lucky said, patting his wife's knee. "And we're going to have us some fun."

"I already made a slit, Lo-Rain," Lilly confessed, staring directly at her. "Maybe I should have waited. I hope I 'l'omputed the direction right. Did Laurie's go from side to side or front to back?"

"When Laurie showed me hers," Lo-Rain confided, pausing to sip her cup of tea, "she said front to back is what Liver told her."

"Darn," Lilly griped. "And did she 'l'ompute the slit down where the two legs come apart?"

Lo-Rain thought a moment. "Maybe more towards the front, somewhere down around there. But I don't want to talk about it any more, Lilly."

Lucky polished off his drink. He repeated his earlier question. "Say, why's the place so dark, Lefty? If you ask me, this looks like a pool hall with the lights out. When we came up the walk, I could barely see the porch."

"Liver likes the house dark when he's sleeping," Lefty explained as he went to get the bottle to pour himself and Lucky another drink.

"Well," the guest requested, "if you don't mind, I'd like to have some daylight so I can have myself a good look at his pipe."

"All right," the mayor agreed warily, leaving to make the change.

"Come along and see for yourself, then," Lefty said once daylight had returned. Lucky and Lilly scooted ahead down the hallway with the mayor reluctantly trailing his eager neighbors to the guest room. Lo-Rain flitted along behind the group.

"Liver, Liver, wake up. Folks here want to meet you." The mayor's voice pierced the quiet of the room. Aroused from a deep sleep for the second time in two nights, Oliver heard the voice like an echo in his ear. He simultaneously covered his genitals and opened his eyes.

At the far end of the bed, Oliver saw a voluptuous pair of partly exposed breasts dangle menacingly forward to obscure his vision of Lucky. He spotted Lo-Rain and the mayor on one side of the bed. Before he had time to think, his member rose up and pointed straight toward Lilly from beneath the sheet.

"Wow! Is that the one?" Lucky asked the Littleleathers as he jumped out from behind his wife. He reached out to yank the sheet away.

"Frank! What are you doing here?" Oliver's startled voice confronted Lucky as he bent over him.

"That's something, don't you think, honey?" Lilly asked, blinking her big blue eyes sweetly at her husband.

"That pipes a lollapalooza," Lucky said, brimming with admiration. "I'm gonna 'l'ompute myself one even bigger. Mine's going to stick out so far Lilly will have to be across the room."

"That Lucky is so thoughtful," Lilly responded, fluttering with delight.

Lucky grabbed hold of Oliver's member just for a second. He quickly let go. "That pipes hot as blazes. How does he do that?"

As Oliver squirmed around, Lefty took pity on him. Besides, his guest might decide to shower the room again. So the mayor voiced his concerns. "All right now. You two had enough gawking? You go do some more sleeping, Liver. We'll leave you be."

Oliver tried to go back to sleep, but the bright daylight interfered. Watchim showed the Los Angeles time to be almost six on Monday morning. Oliver had always been a sound sleeper, but this constant shift from night to day destroyed his rhythm. He looked around for Lauriander. He remembered she had been in his room before he dropped off to sleep.

Just as he wondered where she might have disappeared to, Lauriander skipped into the room. She held a box of cornflakes in one hand. The moment she saw Oliver awake but huddled beneath the sheet with his face still bright red from embarrassment, she put the box of cereal down. As she sat beside him on the bed in order to hold his hand, she tried to make him speak to her. His expression resembled a confused puppy who didn't know how to please his master.

"I'm so happy," she told him. "I just came back from 'l'omputing a visit to LLiterally LLucid. He gave me a lot of food to bring back from his dimension. He told me that you can eat our food, but you won't be filled up. But LLiterally has real LTV food. He gave me enough to last for a time. I brought you all kinds of cans and such. He wants to meet you. He invited us to dinner, and then we can get bring home more food for you."

She handed over the box of cornflakes. Oliver examined the familiar package for a moment before he excitedly tore open the lid to take out a handful of cereal. Much to his surprise, these cornflakes tasted like the real thing. He swallowed the dry food as fast as he could chew until the sharp pain eased in his belly.

When Oliver stopped munching, seemingly satisfied,

Lauriander began to run her fingers through his long hair, making him inclined to recite his woeful tale of Lucky and Lilly's visit. Finally, she did the only thing she knew would make him truly feel better. She changed day back to night, undressed, and crawled into bed with him.

Around noon, Oliver woke up again, his ferocious appetite renewed. Food had begun to consume his every waking thought. "Lauriander, let's see what else you brought for me to eat. I can tell you I'm going to go nuts if I have to eat any more of your mother's food. That taste is like paste to me. A few bites and I want to throw up." He spat out the words while his hands gestured wildly in the air.

"Whenever you're ready we can leave," she said, stroking his arm. "LLiterally LLucid's excited about our coming. I didn't tell you. He's a cook. He used to have a restaurant."

"Why did you wait so long to tell me?" Oliver snapped in an irritated voice. Nobody understood him here. Not even Lauriander, though she tried.

"When should I have told you?"

Oliver didn't answer.

"We'll bring LLiterally some of Mama's Tapplesauce. He loves that more than anything. This visit is a special occasion. Even though he's been all over Letterland, and often in LTV land as an LL placed in words, you'll be the first LTV person he's ever met. I made you a nice suit to wear. I know how you all like to dress up for important occasions."

Oliver remained silent a moment. "Everyone talks about LLiterally LLucid," he finally said. "When I came off that mountain of letters, an L mentioned him and a lion did, too."

Lauriander looked astonished. "You met a real lion from Lyin'? Nobody knows what those lions know because they don't know themselves what they know. They eat limes and live in rhyme time. They're really weird."

"No kidding," he said in an ironic tone.

Lauriander, oblivious to sarcasm, continued to portray LLiterally LLucid in the best of lights. "He remembers far back when letters could travel from one land to another," she merrily went on. "In those times they had no LTV. LLiterally knows more about everything than anyone in all of L Land. At least I think he does. But he says how much he knows doesn't matter. Underneath he's just another LL, and one day when his job at Word Central is done, he'll return to your world as just another double consonant, whatever that means."

"All right," Oliver said with a burst of sudden enthusiasm. He hopped out of bed to get dressed. "Let's meet this LLucid character. If he has real food and he knows so much, he might know a way I can get back home."

Oliver followed Lauriander to her room. In the closet hung the strangest suit he'd ever seen. The white jacket had no collar and no lapels. A row of gold buttons extended from top to bottom in front. Beside the suit hung a white shirt and a colorful tie, cut like an L. Stacked up on her dresser were ten pairs of underwear, each one identical to the pair Oliver wore when he arrived. A pair of black socks and black patent leather shoes, the same size as Oliver's Nikes, stood on the floor nearby waiting for him.

"You made all this for me?" he asked. Even though he thought the clothes looked ridiculous, her efforts touched him.

"Designing clothes is fun. I just study what I see on LTV. I try to make them my way. It's really not so hard. Try them on. Style, that's what counts," she said with conviction.

Oliver, dressing himself in the white Nehru suit and black shoes, crossed the room to examine himself in the rectangular mirror above the dresser. He now noticed that the mirror actually resembled one of those rectangular flat plasma screens his mother had wanted to buy for the house.

"How do I see myself in this?" he asked Lauriander.

"Just press the button."

Oliver hesitated. "What does that do?"

"It's a leerer. It's cool. Its better than your mirrors."

Oliver pushed the button. A mirror of sorts, he first saw himself reflected as a stiff young man in a buttoned-up white suit. Then, layer after layer stripped away until Oliver saw his own naked body, then an X-ray of his own internal organs and skeletal structure, and finally nothing at all. After a brief pause, the machine automatically reversed the process. Again, Oliver saw himself reflected as fully dressed in his white suit.

"JJJJJesus."

Oliver sat down in a chair. He covered his face in both hands. How could he continue like this? He felt sick to his stomach.

Lauriander emerged from the closet dressed in a pale blue miniskirt and high, spiked heels. A blue beret sat tilted to one side on her head, covering part of her flowing chestnut hair, and a small black purse hung over her shoulder. She walked past him to the leerer and pushed the button. Oliver watched as her fully clothed reflection disappeared to an outline of an L-shaped metal frame, then to nothing at all. An instant later the process reversed. By then, Oliver had closed his eyes.

"Lets split," Lauriander said, taking his hand to pull him up from the chair. "We'll stop at the kitchen to get the 'l'applesauce before we 'l'ompute ourselves to the lodge."

After they took the container of 'l'applesauce, Lauriander led him into a small room directly behind the kitchen. Compared to the rest of the house, the computing room seemed quite sparse. A desk as large as a draftsman's flat table held a square, old-fashioned computer. Several buttons and dials were visible across the front of the machine. On the wall above the desk, a big display screen resembled the leerer in Lauriander's room. White walls and a bare hardwood floor contributed to the austerity of the room. A circle had been painted in the middle of the floor near the desk.

Lauriander activated the machine. In the middle of the computing room, a beam of light began to pulsate in colors. Oliver was reminded of the monitors he encountered along the road. A steady stream of circular light ran from the ceiling through the center of the circle.

"Go stand in the light," Lauriander instructed.

Oliver took two steps forward, then hesitated. "What's it for?"

"That's how we 'l'ompute ourselves to other places or change what we look like. I'll direct you to the lodge. Then I'll 'l'ompute myself after you. From there we'll go to LLiterally LLucid's house. We can't 'l'ompute directly into his dimension."

She made the process sound so simple that he almost believed her. Oliver approached the light. Then he turned to face her before entering the circle. "How do you know I'll be safe?"

Her expression went blank and her eyes moved toward the ceiling. "What's wrong? Just get in the circle. We do this all the time," she said.

Oliver approached the light. He hesitated for a moment before he extended a hand into the beam like a swimmer testing the temperature of the water before diving in.

"Nothing's going to happen," Lauriander reassured him.

He stepped inside the circle. He turned to face her again.

"Are you all right?" she asked.

He shook his head. "I don't feel a thing."

Lauriander began to adjust the controls. A large image of Oliver impaled by a light beam appeared on the screen above. "When I 'l'ompute you to the lodge, you'll land next to the big wooden table," she informed him. "I'll be along soon after. So move out of the spot, will you?"

Oliver pictured himself flying through space and landing next to a wooden table in some faraway lodge.

"All right," Lauriander said. "Count out loud until you reach three."

"One, two … three." The pulsating beam widened to embrace Oliver. In his white suit and shiny black shoes, he sagged like a tired dandy on his way to the gambling tables.

No Greater Love

Life went on … sort of. To her surprise, Grace Sandwich woke up the Sunday morning after her son's disappearance. Monday, Tuesday, Wednesday, Thursday, and Friday rolled around as well. Intent on maintaining a routine, she showered upon rising each morning, dressed in a plain dress or in one of her two jogging suits, made Fred's breakfast, and saw him off.

That first week, Fred went to work as if nothing unusual had happened. Fred came home. A friend called. Grace visited the doctor for sleep medication. She visited the community college to reassure herself that Oliver had not attended classes. She mixed the salad with vinegar, forgetting the oil. She overcooked the steaks.

Oprah, Jerry, Montel—each helped to keep her going. She spent hours in Oliver's room. She wandered in at random times throughout the day. Sometimes she sat on the chair to stare at his bed where the creases still remained from the last time he lay there. Other times she sat gazing at his desk. She could sit, thoughtless, for an hour or two or longer. Not even the ring of the phone would break the spell.

During those first days, she had come to accept Fred's theory. Oliver left home. He'd return one day. He'd write or call. "You can't cling all your life," Fred told her. "The kid couldn't breathe around you." Even the police detective, when she called to file a missing person's report, had reassured her he would return sooner or later. "Kidnapping a twenty-one-year-old man would be highly unusual," he explained. "Most people eventually come back home."

For two weeks, Grace left Oliver's room intact. Maps to be traced lay across the desk. The English literature book on the floor stayed open on the first page of a short story by Hemingway. An empty water glass sat on the night table.

By the end of the second week, Grace had begun to return to her own room rather than haunt Oliver's. After making breakfast and straightening up, she spent the day in bed, not only with her talk show friends, but also with a long list of soap characters. Yet, despite the constant babble of voices, her days had never been so quiet.

One morning, without warning, she decided to clean Oliver's room. Out came the vacuum, a duster, a spray bottle of 409, and a roll of paper towels. She pulled off the sheets, changed them, organized the tracings of the Soviet Republics, and placed them with the maps in a desk drawer. Closing up the literature book, she fitted it between a biology and psychology text on the top shelf of the small bookcase.

In the midst of her cleaning, she stopped. In the top desk drawer, Grace discovered Oliver's bankbook. The Wells Fargo savings account showed a balance of $1,643. She inspected the bankbook like a detective sniffing out the scene of the crime. Did Oliver have another account with savings from his job at the Leanmeaneating Machine? If not, and if he had left home voluntarily, why wouldn't he have taken his bankbook with him?

She placed the savings book on top of the desk as Exhibit A. No matter how hard she tried, she couldn't get his savings out of her mind. Wheels spun in her head. One eye twitched. Her hand ran through her gray hair.

Before lunch, still in her red jogging suit, she visited the Brentwood branch of the Wells Fargo bank. She spoke with the manager, a pleasant woman near her own age, who sympathized with her dilemma and checked, against the rules, Oliver's account. "Yes, Mrs. Sandwich," she said when she looked up from the computer.

"Every cent is still here."

At that moment, like a phoenix rising, Grace went to work, newly determined. Oliver hadn't left to seek his fortune. Foul play, as she first suspected, had snatched her son from her. Somewhere out there, someone held Oliver against his will.

Grace marched to the police station straight from the bank. Inside, she located the detective she had spoken with earlier. He looked a lot like Fred, though taller and thinner. "I'm sure he just took off," the sleepy detective explained. "That happens a lot more than you think. We are looking into the case. Don't worry"

"What about the bankbook?"

"Well, when they decide to go, they just go. They crack. Most of the time it's impulse, a break with the past. They don't want to take anything. They're not rational. Your son will get tired and be home soon," the detective said in a benign voice.

Unconvinced, Grace went for lunch at the Montana Aveenue restaurant she had often frequented with Oliver. Alone at the table, she decided that, despite the lack of support, she had a duty to perform. She owed that much to her son. She finished her lo-carb turkey burger plate and returned home.

A busy afternoon followed. Grace carefully printed out a notice similar to the one she'd conceived that first night of Oliver's disappearance. She pasted a small ID picture at the top. As soon as she finished, she drove to the local Kinko's to have a hundred copies made. Home again, she plotted out where she needed to post them. The very first notice went up on the side of the mailbox at the corner.

Over the next two or three days, the entire neighborhood learned that Oliver had vanished. They could read the details on the flyers Grace posted on trees, telephone poles, even trash cans.

Systematically, as a follow-up, Grace visited each house within a two-block radius of hers. In a polite but persistent manner, she asked all her neighbors if they had noticed anything suspicious occur lately, or if they remembered seeing anyone lurking about in the neighborhood a couple of weeks earlier. She handed each occupant a flyer and asked him or her to call if something should turn up.

Another three weeks passed, June days with no answers. Grace expanded her search. She filled each day going from door to door and doing research on missing persons at the new branch of the Brentwood library. She kept in touch with Lieutenant Pearson of the LAPD.

One afternoon late in June, the first break came. Grace heard a sharp knock on the door. The unexpected sound caught her right in the middle of a program about three transvestite husbands and the wives who tolerated them. A red-haired boy of about fourteen stood on the porch.

"Are you Mrs. Sandwich?" he asked.

"Yes." Her voice sounded dull.

"I, uh, saw one of those notices you tacked up, the one about your missing kid."

"Please, come in," Grace said, suddenly awake. "Come into the kitchen where we can talk. Can I get you something to drink? A Diet Coke, perhaps?"

"No thanks," the boy said. He appeared nervous as he followed her through the hall into the kitchen. She offered him a seat at the kitchen table.

"I'm going to have a cup of coffee. I'm afraid I've become an addict since Oliver disappeared."

The boy stared at a picture of two kittens at play above the month of June on the wall calendar.

"Just where did you see Oliver?" Grace asked after she'd poured the coffee and sat down across from him.

"Right at the corner. He tried to stuff a long ladder into the big corner mailbox. I helped him so he could stick the end part inside. Anyway, that's it," the boy finished.

"That's what?"

"That's all I know. I just thought you'd want to know. By the way, you didn't say. But is there any kind of reward?"

Grace cast a cold stare in the boy's direction. "I'm sure I can give you something. What did he do after you helped him?" she asked.

The boy responded with a shrug of his shoulders. "I don't know. I just left."

Grace thought a moment. Fred had complained of a missing ladder soon after Oliver vanished. Of course, he'd held the Mexican gardener responsible. She excused herself, left the kitchen, and returned with a twenty. "Thank you," she said. "I'd like your name and number in case the detective wants to talk with you."

The boy's eyes widened. "Really?" he asked.

"He's only a missing person's detective," she explained.

The boy snatched the twenty from her hand. He took off down the hallway and out the front door. By the time Grace reached the porch, she spotted him almost a block away.

Grace stood hands on hips, staring down the street in the direction the boy ran. She could see him pass the corner mailbox. An idea began to form in her mind.

Lliterally Amazed

Lo-Rains Tapplesauce in hand, they walked arm in arm through town, down Main Street and past the city limits: Oliver in his white suit and tennis shoes, Lauriander in her pale blue miniskirt. Before he'd achieved a complete meltdown, Lauriander had yanked Oliver out of the pulsating beam. She expressed great surprise at his resistance to the computing machine, yet another proof that Oliver differed from her and the other folks in L Land.

About an hour's hike out from liberaltown, they stopped alongside a dusty dirt road that ran forever through a flat black-and-white landscape. Lauriander's fashionable high heels made her wobble as she walked, forcing her to keep a grip on Oliver's arm for support. When she could take the awkwardness no more, she halted to take off her shoes. Even barefoot, she remained in charge of the situation. She undid the clasp of her purse to extract a miniature monitor the size of a Palm Pilot, flipping it open to stare at the keyboard.

"The lodge is right around here somewhere," she said. "Let me scan for it." Several dials and buttons of Lilliputian size protruded slightly below the screen. Oliver could barely decipher them. Lauriander turned one knob, and a 360-degree view of their surroundings displayed on the monitor. "Oh, the lodge is over there," she pointed.

With a click of the button, they found themselves surrounded by lush-colored woods of brown and green. Before them stood a building made of rough-hewn boards. Directly from the dirt road, they entered a rich forest of laurel trees, wild lingonberries, and lilac.

"I can smell the country here," Oliver said as he bent down over the lilacs.

Naturally, with no nose for such things, Lauriander didn't make time to stop and smell the flowers. She pointed to the building. "That is the lodge Lucy and I stay in sometimes. We would have been 'l'omputed there, if you could be 'l'omputed. The lodge belongs to Larry, her father. Let's go on now. We still have a distance to walk before we reach LLiterally LLucid's dimension."

Through the woods, Oliver trailed behind Lauriander. For another hour, they walked past laurel tree after laurel tree. Oliver became convinced they'd passed the same spot three different times.

"We've arrived at his dimension," Lauriander finally informed him. In the forest of laurel trees stood a single flowering oleander. "Stand next to it," Lauriander told Oliver. "But be careful. LLiterally says oleander's poisonous for you." Once more, Lauriander removed the small monitor and clicked a button.

A forest with a different growth surrounded them. Oliver scanned the view. The woodsy area looked more like a postcard from California than a place in L Land. Evergreens, redwoods, junipers, thick ferns, and a carpet of needles with a strong musty odor stretched as far as the eye could see.

"His house is right over here," Lauriander said. Almost immediately, they entered a clearing where at the center a large cabin stood, overgrown with clusters of blooming flowers and exotic plants. Trees ripe with fruit grew all around.

With smoke curling from the chimney, the exterior resembled the lodge they had just passed. Formed by rough cuts of logs, the structure had a square, rugged shape. Along the width of the cabin ran a front porch, upon which two empty rocking chairs stood to one side of the front door.

"Do you think he's home?" Oliver asked. "We took so long to walk here."

"How long is long?" Lauriander asked inquisitively.

Oliver looked to Watchim for the answer. "Over two hours. You could drive from one end of Los Angeles to the other in that time."

Lauriander smiled. "You can't live in LTV time here, Liver. We've arrived the same as when we left. If we'd 'l'omputed ourselves to the lodge, we wouldn't have arrived any sooner than we did by walking. But don't worry, LLiterally almost never leaves his dimension anymore. He says he can't stand being in the new L world."

"I wouldn't leave either if I lived here," Oliver said, even though he still didn't get the thing about time being timeless.

"Thank you, young man," chirped the high-pitched voice of a diminutive figure. LLiterally LLucid had made a sudden appearance on the porch. A boy, tousle-haired and freckle-faced like Huck Finn, greeted them. He could be no more than nine or ten years old. With his turned-up nose, thin eyebrows, and small chin, he resembled any Little League ballplayer from Anywhere, U.S.A.

They walked up onto the porch. "This is LLiterally LLucid, Liver," Lauriander introduced them.

"Very nice to meet you," Oliver said, his voice betraying his surprise. "Lauriander's told me so much about you."

"Welcome to my small dimension," LLiterally responded. His smile indicated genuine pleasure at meeting his visitor. "I think you'll find many of the plants and trees familiar here. LLiterally pointed out a few of his favorites. "You see across there pink fuchsias, yellow marigolds, pansies, wild carnations, chrysanthemums, and in that corner is my rose garden."

Past the garden, a square plot of land had been planted with bushes that overflowed with white, red, and pink roses. One bush even bloomed with green roses. Oliver had never seen green roses before.

"My mother has a rose garden in her backyard," Oliver said. "Hers doesn't look anything like yours though." He tried hard to act as if he weren't speaking to a child.

"Come in, come in," LLiterally insisted, leading them through the open front door, his body moving slightly off the ground as if undeterred by gravity.

In contrast to the exterior, the room that Oliver entered imitated the fashionable New York apartments he had seen in old movies. The walls were finished in cream-colored, textured silk. Every piece of furniture conveyed a modern and simple design. Vases with fresh-cut flowers, tall teakwood bookcases, and an austere marble fireplace helped to create the perfect ambiance of elegance and good taste. On the mantle stood several candlesticks of various sizes and shapes. A single small painting of a landscape hung on the wall behind them.

Above a black leather couch hung three paintings. The first canvas portrayed two giant aspirins, the second showed an Ajax can painted on a white background, and the third portrayed the Little Lulu cartoon character with a big bow in her frizzy hair. Oliver wondered why the words #span_smallcaps A WISE OLD AAL!span had been written in block letters at the bottom of the last painting. The juxtaposition made no sense to him, but he decided not to ask.

He didn't want to appear stupid.

At the back of the room hung three wall clocks. One, like Oliver's own Watchim, showed Los Angeles time, exactly 3:54 p.m. The next had no hands, and the third had hands that rotated so rapidly no time could be read.

The polished, dark wooden floors were partially covered by two different-size rugs, each a gray rectangle with a single black line an inch wide forming a second inner rectangle. Perfect order prevailed. Every object looked in place. A book on the coffee table lay at the correct angle so as not to disturb the symmetry of the room. LLiterally had positioned his metal lights over the couch and easy chair to render maximum mood and effect.

"I love to come here," Lauriander gushed. "LLiterallys furnished his home with so many wonderful things he's 'l'omputed or brought back from visits to other letter lands. When I come here, I always learn so much about what life used to be like."

LLucid smiled. "Laurie, or should I say Lauriander, told me that you found the cuisine in L Land unsatisfactory. While I do not have the good fortune to share your sense of taste, I do have unlimited access to a supply of food and drink others in L Land do not have. I can cook any meal you desire. I fancy myself something of a chef. I have studied with the great master, Chef Cooseen himself, in C Land, where the cooks and capitalists live. I'll be delighted to eliminate the 'l'alt that accents our food. We use an abundance of 'l'alt because that is all we can taste."

"That would be great. Thank you," Oliver managed to say. "And thanks for the cornflakes Lauriander brought back. They saved my life." Impressed by his surroundings, Oliver spoke softly to his host, whose appearance still baffled him. He had seen interiors such as LLucid's in magazines, but never in real life. He couldn't imagine how such a young child would own such a beautiful house.

"I'll be back," LLiterally LLucid said before he vanished from sight. An instant later, he reappeared in the same spot with half a raw onion in his hand. "Kindly do me a favor and smell this," LLucid requested as he thrust the onion under Oliver's nose. The burning sensation caused Oliver to blink while tears welled up in his eyes.

"Then all I've heard is true," the boy said, loudly enough for the others to hear when in fact he spoke only to himself. He pulled the onion away. "Chef Cooseen told me that any human would cry if he had an onion placed under his nose. A wise old chef, that one. He and my dear friend LLalchemist, the figure in the painting behind you, were the wisest of the wise."

Blurry-eyed, Oliver wiped away the tears with the back of his hand. He wondered if this might be some boys-will-be-boys trick or an L Land game. Whatever the intent, the sharp scent of the onion brought back a touch of home that tugged at his soul.

"Please, ignore my dreadful manners. I just had to satisfy myself," LLucid said, trying to placate Oliver. "Sit down, both of you. What may I offer you to drink? There is wine, beer, spirits of your choice, soft drinks. State your preference. I am a bartender of some modest ability."

"He's made me some funny-looking drinks," Lauriander said. "Of course, they all taste the same to me."

"I'll have a Coke, please," Oliver requested, still smarting from his encounter with the onion.

"A young man with simple tastes," LLiterally LLucid observed. "Lauriander, may I make you one of my most recent experiments? This drink is currently very popular in Livers homeland."

LLucid vanished again. Oliver stared at the spot where he'd stood.

"How does he do that?"

Lauriander shrugged her shoulders. "Just an advantage of being a LL. They don't have to 'l'ompute themselves to move around L Land. They just wish themselves there. Each time I want to go somewhere fast, I have to 'l'ompute myself, as we tried to do to you."

"Well, I have to walk everywhere," Oliver reminded her.

"But at home, you have trains and planes and automobiles. All those cars we see on LTV look like so much fun. They race against each other sometimes. And you can fly in the sky, skate, sit in wheelchairs, ride bicycles. Have you ever used any of them?"

Before Oliver could answer, LLiterally reappeared on the same spot with a tray in his hands. He'd balanced on the tray a large glass of Coke on ice and two iced margaritas with 'l'alt and lime around the edge of each glass.

"Thank you," Oliver said. LLiterally disappeared with the empty tray and returned in a flash, this time holding bowls of chips and guacamole dip in his small hands. "I thought I might try to make this as well, to go with the drinks," he told them as he placed the bowls on the coffee table in front of them. He sat down in his chair to watch.

Oliver dipped a chip into the guacamole—a crunch, instantly followed by the delicate flavor of slightly spiced avocado. The combination provided the perfect taste. He sipped at the Coke. Suddenly, he realized his great thirst. He had to use restraint to control his desire to gulp down the Coke. After a second sip, he reached for another chip. He felt much better now that he had the opportunity to consume real food and drink.

"Why and how do you have so many different foods?" Oliver asked.

"I have learned some helpful secrets in the time I've been an LL. For three hundred years of your time, I sat in a book as the double l in the Old English word *literally*. You know, there are Ls that have dreams, just like some of your kind have dreams. And my dream as a young LL was to form part of an important sentence in an important text. Of course, we don't have control over such things. However, I found the good fortune to be the double l in a very fine sentence in a 1593 book by an obscure author named Richard Harvey."

His confession surprised Lauriander. "What sentence?" she asked.

LLiterally laughed. He spoke in a tone surprisingly rich for someone his size. "As written, the sentence read, 'And yet I tell you, methinkes you are very bookishly and literally wise.'"

"See, that's Old English," Oliver told Lauriander, glad for the chance to elaborate on the difference between Old and Modern English.

"Yes," LLiterally agreed. "And I thought I would never escape my past. But, to my good fortune, after three hundred years passed without a single person perusing the book's contents, someone tossed the tome onto a bonfire, and automatically I returned to Word Central a far wiser LL."

"Is that why you took the name LLiterally?" Lauriander asked.

Oliver, though following the conversation, turned his attention to the guacamole and chips.

"Yes, the name fit," LLiterally answered. "After my return to Letterland, I traveled to many of the other lands of letters. In fact, I seldom stayed home. This happened, of course, in the days before LTV changed everything. I dwelled for a long time in C Land, working in the cafe of the famed Chef Cooseen. Back in those days some letters still cared about nuance. Cooseen had a reputation for being the only chef that could bring subtle tastes to his 'l'alt-accented dishes. Computed letters from every land waited in long lines to eat there. I visited A Land many times also, though the place proved little to my liking. I obtained these paintings you see from art dealers who ruled the land. However, this portrait came as a gift from my friend. I visited D Land, where design ruled everything that mattered there." LLiterally LLucid concluded his explanation with a whimsical look on his face.

"Can you teach Lauriander those secrets?" Oliver asked, downing the last chip. He realized skills of this sort could come in handy. When Oliver paid attention, he could be quite sensible. And since his arrival in L Land, he had begun to understand the value of listening. How he wished he had paid more attention to his mother.

"He's a clever 'l'ellow, isn't he?" LLiterally smiled.

LLiterallys question gave Oliver an opening to ask one of his own without sounding rude. "Why do you use words like *'l'ellow* and *'l'alt* and *'l'omputer* instead of just regular words, since you obviously know them?"

"As you may have noticed, we don't really appropriate many," LLiterally explained before he took the empty chip bowl, disappeared, and returned an instant later with the bowl filled again to the top. "Ls, as you may have noticed by now, exhibit certain L-word characteristics. We are basically a languorous people here. We are loving, likeable, lethargic, literal, and loyal, and sometimes a little lackadaisical. We are subject to longing. Be on your guard and remember the letter of the land will always be the indicator." He watched Oliver gorge himself with more chips.

"Do save room for dinner," LLiterally suggested, sitting down once more. "I know you humans have bigger eyes than stomachs."

Oliver nodded. In spite of the fact that the taste of real food of any type so comforted him, he had difficulty controlling himself, he remained eager to learn why there seemed to be no rhyme or reason to life in L Land.

"To answer your earlier question, there are certain words that have evolved here in L Land just as they have in your land. There are no hard-and-fast rules. Through usage, similar I believe to the etymology of language in your world, words have come to stand for certain things. For example, 'l'alt is a special kind of salt used by Ls. Computers are our versions of your computer, and 'l'orecation is the process that transforms Ls who are sent to Word Central to be used in a word in your world. The explanation is really quite simple. Why is a "tomato" called a tomato, or a "banana" a banana? I remember that a clever fellow of yours once said, 'What's in a name? That which we call a rose by any other name would smell as sweet.'"

"Can anyone be 'l'orecated?" Oliver asked, turning the conversation away from Shakespeare, whose writings had caused him hours of torture through his high school days.

"Unfortunately, yes. 'l'orecation is like a magnet that draws letters into a central processing plant based upon calculated need.

Even computed Ls such as Lauriander and me will one day again be 'l'orecated. As your people say, 'it goes with the territory.'"

Oliver found these thoughts chilling. "Then you're no better off than we are."

"Well, at least we know we're headed toward a word. Sometimes, we even know which word. But do you know where you go when your life ends?"

"I see," said Oliver, not wanting to go there.

Lauriander, too, wanted to steer clear of this uncomfortable subject. She turned her attention to Oliver. "LLiterally's tried to teach me a lot," she explained. "I have no real talents. I am only good at making clothes."

"And what may I offer you for dinner?" LLiterally asked, bouncing up from the chair so fast his head almost hit the ceiling.

"More than anything I could eat a hamburger with French fries and a salad with Thousand Island dressing and a big piece of apple pie with ice cream," Oliver responded, close to drooling in anticipation.

"Your wish is my command," LLiterally assured Oliver as he snatched his empty glass from the table and disappeared once again.

Oliver shook his head. "He's amazing, the way he appears and disappears," Oliver told Lauriander. "Though he speaks and acts like an adult, his appearance makes me think he's just a little boy. "

"He lives in a different dimension," Lauriander explained. "He's never told me why he 'l'computed himself to look like this. I guess I never asked. "

LLiterally appeared again, now wearing a formal light-blue poplin suit and a white shirt closed at the neck by a narrow yellow banana-shaped tie. Oliver decided the tie must have been a gift from Lauriander. He preferred the L-shaped tie she'd made for him.

LLucid seated them at the elegantly appointed table. A white Irish linen tablecloth covered the round surface. The three settings each consisted of a cream-colored fine Meissen plate with a gold LL embossed in the center, heavy Waterford crystal water glasses and wineglasses, and Tasman House silverware in the Queen's pattern. Fine linen napkins with an LL monogram had been folded into a fan shape and placed at the center of each plate.

Being polite, Oliver praised the table as he sat down. "This looks really terrific. My mom's dinner parties never looked so fancy." As he spoke, he thought to himself that he would have traded this exotic moment for a night on the couch at home with a plate of leftover pizza and a Coke.

"I used to do a lot of entertaining in the days when letters could move about freely," his pleased host replied.

After seating them, LLucid vanished once more. Oliver speculated, "He vanishes so fast. I wonder if he had to make himself as small as a boy to vanish quicker."

"I don't think there's anything he has to do," Lauriander answered, following Oliver's lead and placing her napkin in her lap. "There's nothing any L or LL has to do."

LLiterally reappeared almost instantly. "Excuse my delay," he said. "For our honored guest." He handed Oliver a plate with a perfectly grilled hamburger on an open bun. "Allow me to serve you." Next came a platter with garnish of lettuce, tomato, onion, and pickles, and finally a plate of steak fries. Then LLucid placed a three-piece condiment container with separate sections for catsup, mustard, and mayonnaise beside the plate.

For Lauriander and himself, LLiterally LLucid brought an array of bowls containing couscous, a souplike liquid with chickpeas and vegetables, as well as a platter of lamb, chicken, and sausage. "Couscous Royale became a specialty of Chef Cooseen's," LLiterally explained as he served Lauriander a helping of couscous followed by a scoop of the liquid on top. Before he sat down, LLiterally poured each of them a glass of red wine. Then he raised his own glass in a toast. "To opportunity, the mother of all pleasure," he said, pushing his glass forward.

Oliver watched LLiterally LLucid take a small sip and roll the liquid around in his mouth before he swallowed, as if imitating a true wine connoisseur. Oliver had a hard time reconciling the picture before him of a small boy dressed in a poplin suit and a yellow banana tie holding a crystal wineglass in his hand in a most dignified manner, sipping a wine he could only pretend to taste. As a matter of fact, LLiterally LLucid appeared to look quite silly to him at that moment.

"Can you really taste that?" Oliver asked in a surprisingly rude tone. Without waiting for an answer, Oliver bit into the hamburger.

LLiterally dabbed his mouth slowly with the linen napkin before responding. "As you know, we can taste only 'l'alt. But we can feel texture. Though lamb and chicken taste like 'l'alt, each has a different texture when I chew. I have been attempting to teach Laurie—Lauriander—that the presentation, style, texture, even the gesture, are as important as taste. You, Liver, may think you can taste. But in point of fact, you can't experience what a wine connoisseur tastes any more than I can."

"I can't?" Oliver asked. He tried to converse between bites of the divinely scrumptious hamburger.

"Of course not," LLucid stated categorically. "Do you have

experience enough to know why that wine you are drinking actually tastes good or bad?"

The question puzzled his guest. Oliver thought for a while before he responded, "Sure. I know the wine tastes good going down. What else do I have to know? The wine has a nice taste."

"But my question is, why do you know the wine tastes good? How many different types of wine have you sampled?"

"I don't know."

"Five or ten, perhaps? You're very young."

"Maybe, but I know what tastes good and what doesn't."

"If you had tasted a thousand wines, would you have formed a better idea of why one wine tastes better than another?"

"I wouldn't," Lauriander said. "To me they'd all taste like 1 alt.

Oliver laughed, not answering his host's question immediately. He couldn't decide whether LLucid wanted to show him up.

"Do you believe someone who has tasted five kinds of wine has knowledge equal to someone who has tasted a thousand?" LLucid asked again.

LLiterally had stopped eating his couscous to stare straight at the young man across the table. Oliver continued to eat in silence. Though he wanted to change the subject, politeness required a response.

"I think so. Maybe the person who has tasted only five kinds of wine is young like me, and so he has better taste buds than the person who has tasted a thousand wines," he finally answered. "I've read that your taste buds can get dulled when you're older."

LLiterally nodded his head in an approving manner. "Now, that's clever," LLiterally LLucid told Lauriander. He looked back to Oliver. "I am quite certain you're wrong. But I have no way to disprove you. If what you say is true, young people in your land have better taste buds but less knowledge than older tasters. If true, your process of aging has an impact on taste. Of course, taste as a concept is all a subjective conjecture. But, I still contend that the person who has tasted a thousand wines has learned more about the subtleties of taste than someone who has tasted only five, despite the dulling of his taste buds." He glared at Oliver, who, nodding his head in accord, didn't know whether he agreed or not. LLiterally LLucid had lost the young man about halfway through his hamburger.

LLucid, who appeared to be more interested in talking than eating, continued. "I suppose one might apply the same argument to vocal ranges. Certainly the range of a voice does vary from person to person. That is clear enough. All right then, young Liver, drink and eat hardy. Real food can only do you good. And so can food for thought." LLucid smiled mischievously at him. "There's apple pie waiting for you. Fresh baked by yours truly."

Oliver felt a sense of relief to learn that LLucid had ended whatever lesson he had in mind. The rest of the meal, consumed without discussion, proved tasty and agreeable. Apple pie with delicious vanilla ice cream and coffee followed. Oliver found the glass of port LLucid poured for him delightful if a bit sweet. Over coffee, LLiterally pressed Oliver to talk about himself.

"I miss my home," Oliver said. "I've been away before, but never like this. I have to find a way to return." He'd just finished his long story of his arrival to L Land.

"We shall do all in our power to send you home," LLiterally promised. "Be careful though. You know about LLorser LLitebrite. He can be a powerful obstacle. He's only one of many that can jeopardize the possibility of your return. I must be honest with you, Liver. There is a chance you may never return to your home. Since none of your species has visited before, we have no way of knowing if you can return. But as long as you are here, Lauriander can receive all the food needed to provide you with a steady diet. And you are welcome to visit me anytime. I always enjoy cooking a meal. I wish I could take you on a tour of the grounds. Certain events have occurred that require my immediate attention. Perhaps, next time you come, I can show you around."

The host stood up, as did Oliver and Lauriander. Then he vanished for an instant, returning with a shopping bag filled with food for Oliver to take with him.

"This has been a wonderful day," Oliver said, taking the heavy bag from LLucid's small hand. "I really enjoyed being here. Thanks so much for everything." He extended his free hand for a proper handshake. "I hope you're wrong about my chances of returning home." He looked into LLiterally LLucid's brown eyes as if seeking an answer there.

"One more thing, Mr. LLucid. I wondered if I might borrow one of your books. You have a nice library. I can't find any books in Lauriander's house. If I have to stay here for a while, I would like a book or two to read. Perhaps you have a book about L Land. You know, something to pass the time."

LLiterally LLucid walked over to his bookcase. "Each book here is a treasure. They came from B Land long ago, when letters and books were abundant. One day, there were no more books to be had. Big Mac, in his infinite wisdom, had replaced them with LTV.

"I keep hearing about Big Mac. Who exactly is Big Mac?" Oliver asked.

"We don't know for certain," LLiterally LLucid answered. "We think of him as the first creator of all letters, and therefore all words. Without him, we would not exist. But none of us has ever seen him. We try to understand his ways. For example, he replaced books with LTV. I believe he did this for our benefit, and his action meant to conserve letters. After all, you may assume that there are an infinite number of letters available, but just as you have learned that there is a limit to the universe, I can assure you there is a finite end to the letters that form words. I have been fortunate to retain some vestiges of the old Letterland world. In return, I have promised to restrict the use of these books to my dimension. However, you are welcome to come here to read any time you desire."

Oliver thought about the long walk necessary to reach LLiterally's dimension, and decided not to pursue the issue. "I guess that closes the book on that subject," Oliver said in an attempt to be humorous. Right then, Oliver saw LLiterally LLucid shrink from a boy into a tiny, aged man who looked like one of the seven dwarfs in the fairy tale. In spite of the pleasant evening, a sudden cold fear squeezed Oliver's heart as he saw LLucid, shriveled and old, fade slowly from sight with a coy smile stretched across his puckish face.

A Period of Adjustment

Life had become a struggle. Just as his mother struggled to discover the truth of Oliver's disappearance, so her son struggled to keep himself mentally balanced in his new, unfathomable world. Watchim had become his compass and Lauriander his comfort. The sports chronometer watch allowed Oliver to maintain the cycle of day and night. Though the climate never changed, he could count the days as June faded into July, and July led into August.

Every night at eight o'clock, Watchim time, day ended and night began at the Littleleather house. No matter the demands put upon Oliver during the day, he refused to relinquish his routine. Each morning, as close to eight as possible, night ended and day began. When Watchim told Oliver evening arrived in Los Angeles, darkness engulfed the Little-leather house from the inside of the white picket fence to the solid wood barrier that divided the lot with the property behind. All the other liberaltown residents kept their houses bathed in sparkling daylight at every moment of their timeless existence.

Lauriander insisted on fulfilling Oliver's demands. She forced her parents to comply with his schedule. "I want him to be happy here with us," she explained to her father one evening some time after Oliver's arrival. Oliver had just fallen asleep. Lauriander stopped in the living room to say goodbye on her way to the computing room to compute herself off to visit a friend.

Lefty seemed to be in a terrible mood. Straightaway, he complained about all the bullying he endured at the Lucky Lady before he came home. "They all hoot hoot me," he grumbled. "Call me the night owl. Ask me if I can see in the dark."

"Daddy, you know Livers all up and down lately," Lauriander reminded him. "Think positive thoughts. You know we're the envy of the town because he's staying here. They're jealous so they tease you. Try to be more patient. I'm sure that after a time Liver won't need to be alone with me or sleep so much. He'll be more like us. Then maybe we can have daylight all the time.

"Look at the people still lined up outside just waiting for the chance to meet Liver and talk with him. I haven't seen Mom so happy in a long time. She is constantly baking 'l'alt cookies, making lemonade, and brewing tea for her guests. You know how much she loves to entertain."

Lefty, shot glass in hand, couldn't deny the truth. He shook his head and ran his hand through his full head of brown hair. "I just can't figger why anyone wants to turn light to dark," he commented. "Seems to me those curtains you made keep his room dark enough for you two. But if I say a word, he yammers, 'midnight sun, midnight sun.' Sometimes I can't make heads or tails out of what that greenhorn is blab-bin' about."

Lauriander gave her father an affectionate hug. "Come on, Daddy. Don't be an old bear. You know you love having Liver here. And you know how happy he makes me. I'm Lauriander now, and I'll remain Lauriander forever. I can't explain why. But I'm just crazy nuts about Liver."

Lefty patted her hand before he walked across the room to the rolltop desk to pour himself another drink. He stopped at the window to stare out at the visitors who stood lined up in front of the house in the darkness. "Damn, isn't there ever gonna be an end to those folks?" he asked, turning back to face his daughter. "I know you're right, Laurie. Nothin's better than seeing you and your ma happy. You got yourself the hottest game in town. Everyone is going plumb loco over what you did. Talk about grabbin a bull by its horns. Damndest thing I ever saw. Talk of the town is about Liver's big pipe. Every miss or missus here wishes she was you. All the men think I'm the only one who knows Livers secret of how his pipe grows hard. That's kinda fun, even if I'm in the dark about how that happens.

"Yeah, as dark as this here house," Lefty went on. "All I know is every blasted cowpoke in liberaltown is aiming to make his pipe stand up and dance, 'cept me and LLorser LLitebrite, of course. For once, the old geezer and I agree. We thought we had problems with the legislature, but that craziness is nothin' beside the fuss Liver's pipe is arousin' here among the locals."

Lauriander sat down on the couch and watched her father pace around the room in the moonlight. This moment appeared as good as any to discuss the nagging problem of Liver's state of mind. She felt helpless to alter the incessant attention bestowed on him that so affected Liver's mood. Every day that went by found him more and more despondent.

Lucky and Lilly, or Frankie and Marilyn as they computed themselves, had started the whole crazy situation off. Once word spread from the council about Oliver's pipe, most folks in liberaltown had set out to compute private parts. Female Ls, following the advice of Lilly after her visit, computed their slits from top to bottom in the correct location. Males, following Lucky's information, computed pipes in all sizes, from small to extra large. On the surface, the alterations looked more or less accurate. But, in fact, just like the liberaltown plumbing, nothing worked. Computed males soon learned, as LLorser had proved shortly after Oliver's arrival, there's more to a pipe than meets the eye.

Every attempt to make the newly computed pipes grow hard failed miserably. No computed L could make his pipe stand up straight or spray water.

When the men of liberaltown looked down and saw their little pipes dangling helplessly between their legs, they were forced to remember the old adage Lefty often quoted: "You can lead a horse to water, but you can't make him drink." The mayor used his favorite saying to describe the resistance he encountered at council meetings.

Until now, liberaltown had survived in what LLiterally had described as a languorous state that included a general acceptance of fate. After Oliver's arrival, the scales tipped. Emotions grew high and tension filled the air. Indeed, liberaltown held the heavy odor of a place that could explode at any moment. Luckily, no one could smell the danger.

Oliver had become an irritant, a fly in the ointment. His presence reminded each computed male that his pipe, no matter its size or shape, hung limp and more useless than a nose hair. And what they had to endure: Every woman in the town learned that Oliver and Lauriander really did the act. Every man found his woman constantly on top of him, ready to point a finger at each failure. Though the women didn't know exactly what they missed out on, they reminded their deflated partners constantly that Lauriander and Oliver shared what they could not. As domestic problems spread across town and the flow of visitors increased to the Little-leather home, Oliver found himself in a most delicate position. That all happened before he demanded a daily schedule.

At first, each time a visitor arrived, no matter the hour, the Littleleathers played the role of flattered hosts, rousing Oliver from a sound sleep. At one time or another, he would encounter Jackie Gleason, Milton Berle, Pat Boone, even Billy Graham clasping his hands in prayer upon seeing "the real thing." Oliver would awake, groggy and uncommunicative, half-covered by sheets, to find himself face-to-face with a young Carol Burnett, Gregory Peck dressed as Captain Ahab, or Alan Ladd in his buckskins as Shane.

In those first days, Oliver was peppered with every conceivable question about his life in LTV land. Over and over, he explained details of his daily routine. He attempted to explain the complexities of his own city. "Los Angeles is a lot bigger than liberaltown," he told them. "Day and night the city's a very busy place because everyone has a lot to do there."

But the Ls couldn't get his descriptions through their noggins. The only world they knew came filtered through LTV.

They imagined what they saw on the screen to be like their own Letterland home, an equally flat, two-dimensional place that could be shifted from black and white to color at the push of a button. Some even admitted they expected an LTV person to look as flat as a noncomputed L, since that's how they appeared on the monitor.

On the other hand, Oliver wondered why computed Ls didn't look like two-dimensional cutouts of the characters they computed themselves after, since they received the transmissions on a flat screen. One day he asked Lauriander that very question.

"I don't know why we are the way we are any more than I know why you are the way you are," she responded matter of factly.

And that put an end to that.

Ultimately, the queries about Oliver's life in Los Angeles, no matter how elaborate, proved a smoke screen, a mere bagatelle. In the end, the visitor would always come to the most burning question: "Do those men on LTV all have pipes that get as big and hard as yours?"

A few days after the visit to LLiterally LLucid, a computed version of Milton Berle introduced as Lyle Lumbar, disturbed his sleep. Lyle asked the question Oliver hated hearing the most, especially at two in the morning when awakened by an inquiring mind. Lefty and Lo-Rain stood nearby, beaming like two kids. He couldn't let them down.

"All of our pipes, yes, they get hard, but not all the time," Oliver managed to respond.

"Well, how come I can't get mine hard then?" Lyle complained. "That babe of mine you see here, Luscious Linda, is driving me nuts. Ain't that right, you beautiful babe?" He emphasized the question by hugging the unresponsive platinum blond in a short skirt standing next to him. She had clearly lost patience with Lyle's inability to raise the flag. She looked as sour as a pickle.

Oliver shrugged his shoulders.

But the visitors proved persistent. Now, Luscious Linda, a Jayne Mansfield big-boobed look-alike, took control. Sick and tired of Lyle's wimpy attitude, she, like the other computed females, longed to know the truth about the exact workings of Oliver's pipe. Like all computed Ls, Linda had heard the in-and-out rumors. Perhaps more persistent than any previous visitor, she seemed determined to see Oliver's pipe swing into action.

In her eagerness to uncover the truth, Luscious Linda pulled back the sheet to have a good look for herself. She reached over to slide down Oliver's underwear, then quick as a wink, hiked up her skirt and plopped herself down across his legs to grip his startled member. As her cold hands took hold, Oliver saw his member swell up to full size. Linda tried to mount him, but in an automatic response, he doubled his legs, knocking her off balance and flat onto the floor. Everyone laughed except poor Oliver, who pulled the sheet all the way up over his head.

As much as he respected his hosts, the strain of these unexpected encounters became almost unbearable. A less-polite person would have rebelled much sooner. How was he supposed to respond when the Littleleathers stood alongside their guests smiling like a pair of proud owners of a Kentucky stud horse? Only the image of his stern grandmother Manners made Oliver hold his tongue.

Several sleepless nights resulted during this first phase of Oliver's life in liberaltown. Finally, after one particularly trying day, Lauriander came into Oliver's room to find him bawling on the bed like a child. "I want to go home. I miss my home. Home, home." At first she stood back, startled by the outburst.

After she recovered somewhat, Lauriander came forward to sit beside him on the bed. As she held him, trying to comfort him, he looked up through tear-stained eyes and muttered again, "Last night I had a dream. I dreamt we drove through the streets of Los Angeles in my own car. You were sitting beside me. We were on our way to the Leanmeaneating Machine to meet my friends. The dream seemed so real I could feel the vibration of the car. I want to go home. I want to bring you home with me. I want us to live a normal life in Los Angeles. I hate this crazy place. I never know what to do here."

She slipped into bed beside him. She cuddled up to him while one hand stroked his cheek. She whispered, as she'd seen mother's do to crying babies on LTV. For the moment, she managed to calm him down, but she knew she needed to do more than console him to solve his problems.

That same night, after Oliver drifted off to sleep, she told her parents that Oliver needed to have rest and privacy. From then on, they restricted visiting hours to the twelve hours of daylight each Watchim day.

Since liberaltown did not go by minutes, hours, or days, no one there had ever set any restrictions on time. Stores always remained open. Ls felt free to drop in on each other whenever they wished. Just as visitors ridiculed the darkness surrounding the Littleleathers' house, these new visiting hours drew resentment. As hosts, the Littleleathers felt equally uncomfortable with the restrictions. They didn't like to appear more important than other folks in town. But they had no choice in the matter. Lauriander had put her foot down in her support of Oliver's quirky needs.

With visiting hours now restricted to daylight, the line of visitors grew longer and longer. The citizens of liberaltown had no schedules and nothing better to do. They stood in a line that extended down the walkway, out the sidewalk, down one block, and around the corner. Ls waited day after Watchim day for an opportunity to visit with the mysterious and exciting stranger.

The endless barrage of visitors forced the Littleleathers to entertain in groups of five. Lo-Rain spent considerable time making and serving refreshments. On top of it all, each group of visitors lingered in Oliver's presence, and the hosts always felt compelled to engage each group in small talk for a time prior to bringing on the main show. These sessions occupied the majority of Oliver's waking hours.

Now that Lauriander knew she held a special place in Oliver's heart, she became an even more ferocious protector. After Oliver's near-breakdown about too many visitors, Lauriander had come to understand that he couldn't express in public the frustration he felt inside. Only when they were alone would he complain to her. She tried to intervene when a visit dragged on too long or if she saw him getting tired and in need of a break. She discussed the situation with LLiterally LLucid, who explained she had begun to think less like an L and more like an LTV person.

The young man staying in the Littleleather house began to experience odd mood swings. While the Littleleathers never tired of entertaining, the daily grind left Oliver exhausted. After first being forced to answer repetitious questions, he then experienced the continual embarrassment of exposing himself before curious eyes day after day. As the well-trained guest, he could not refuse. Even his new schedule proved more than he could bear. Each visit followed the one before in a never-ending peepshow. Oliver and his pipe had become the most amazing freak show in all of Letterland.

Oliver became convinced he was losing his mind. In between visits, he would sometimes curl up and babble to his Watchim. Lauriander, seeing her beloved in such a state, began to worry for the first time in her life. So, after yet another urgent plea by Lauriander, visiting hours were reduced to four a day. This restored some sanity to Oliver's miserable life.

Townspeople quickly became irritated. Even with endless time on their hands, they tired of standing in such a slow-moving line. Eventually they began to drift away. Also, by now most folks had had a good look for themselves. And since Oliver refused to demonstrate either the up-and-down motions or the in-and-out motions, scant reasons remained to continue their visits. Lauriander's efforts effectively brought an end to the lineup. So now only a few hangers-on and some who had inexplicably returned for a second visit remained outside the house, forming a small line down the walkway.

But though the line thinned out, the bittersweet relationship between Oliver and liberaltown's residents remained tense.

Undercurrents of gossip surfaced about Oliver and Lauriander. Bits and pieces were revealed to her during visits with her friends. Her closest pal, Lucy, shared with her the mood in town during a visit one night long after Oliver's arrival.

As they baked 'Talt cookies together in Lucy's kitchen, Lauriander's friend mentioned that she had overheard the funniest comment when she went to the shop on Main Street. "I heard Lil Lonebone and Larcy Lassiter talking about you. They know we're friends, but they didn't even lower their voices when they saw me in line. Lil wondered whose slit Liver would use if, for some reason, you were sent off to Word Central."

Most young Ls seldom discussed Word Central openly. Lauriander, stunned, sat down in a kitchen chair after Lucy relayed the information.

"I don't know what to say," Lauriander murmured in a weak voice. "Why would I be sent to Word Central?"

"You need to understand what's going on, Lauriander," Lucy said. "Some girls are just not cool because they're so jealous. Lots of them are unhappy about you and Liver. They think you keep secrets. They claim you control Liver's pipe. They think you want to keep him for yourself. They feel that anyone who wants to give Livers pipe a try should be able to do so."

With her eyes focused on the kitchen floor, Lauriander emphasized her words by pulling her checkered dress over her knees: "Liver's told me lots of times he wouldn't want that. He hates all the attention he gets. One time he said that he didn't know why anyone in LTV wanted to be famous if what he had here was fame. 'People only come after you because you have something they want. As soon as that changes, they go after someone else. They'll forget you in no

194

time,' he told me."

"But he's got what they want," Lucy exclaimed. "We're all dying to know what you two do together with his hard pipe."

The words struck Lauriander hard. "You, too, Lucy?"

"Sure. You wouldn't care if he wanted to show me, would you?

Lauriander reached out to touch her friend's cool hand. "Why would I?" she asked, bewildered. "Of course not. I'd share him with anyone, if he'd let me." She paused a moment. "You know you're my best friend in all Letterland except, of course, for Liver and LLiterally LLucid."

When Lauriander came home again, she felt overwhelmed by this new dilemma that followed on top of Oliver's deteriorating condition. Oliver only wanted to be left alone or to spend time with her. Lucy's words convinced Lauriander that by staying with Oliver, she'd let her friends down. Desperate to share her concerns with somebody, she located her father sitting in his favorite chair in the living room. "Daddy, yesterday Liver stared out the window at the people still waiting outside. And do you know what he said?"

The mayor shook his head. "How would I know what he said?"

"He said, 'I can't believe Bobby Kennedy, Roy Rogers, Natalie Wood, and all those other famous faces are waiting in line just to meet me. Bad enough they're not really the people they look like—and what's worse, it's not really me they want to meet. All they want to do is to stand and stare at my stupid pecker."

"What the hell's a pecker?" Lefty interrupted.

"That's his pipe, Daddy. Liver told me there are lots of

different names LTV folks call a pipe, like a prick, dick, cock, penis, pecker, maybe a decker. Some people even call a pipe a Willie Johnson, like the name for a boy."

"Those LTV folks don't make a lick of sense, if you ask me. Why have so many different names for one little dangly thing no bigger than a finger? You might as well call a sidewinder a jumping jack. No wonder they use up so many of our letters. Seems to me excess is what LTV is all about. But dadburnit, they have just one name for big things like arms and legs, don't they?"

Lauriander didn't respond to her father's observation. She continued with her own thoughts. "Sometimes Liver just lies in bed and moans after he wakes up. He tells me I'm the only reason he can stand being here. He doesn't want anyone else to touch him. If he didn't have me, he says he'd run away. He gets all worked up, and I don't know what to do for him."

"Probably acts like we do when our engine gets too overheated," Lefty suggested. "How about bringing him a good shot of whiskey when he gets like that, girl?"

"No, that won't work. I've tried."

"What do you want me to do?" Lefty asked.

"I just thought there might be some way to stop the visitors. Or maybe Liver and I could go somewhere quiet for a while, like to Lucy's lodge in the country," she suggested.

"Don't know if you can do that," Lefty said. "That damn LLorser's always on my tail about not letting Liver leave town. Always wants to know his whereabouts and what he's up to. Seems some of them townsfolk have gone to LLorser to complain about Liver."

Lauriander looked concerned. "Complain about what?"

Lefty headed to the bar to pour himself a stiff one.

"All kinds of stupid stuff. I can't figure why our folks act more stupid than those folks on LTV. They never know when to let sleeping dogs lie, even if we don't have any lying dogs that sleep."

"What's going on?" Lauriander asked anxiously.

"Just that some folks think maybe Liver's going to destroy the town if he stays on here. Especially since word slipped out that some members of the legislature are planning to visit here sometime or other."

"They are?"

"Now don't go talkin' around about it, not even to Liver. Seems the legislature heard talk about his coming here, and they want him to show off all the things he can do. I didn't want to tell you, Laurie, but I guess I just did. None of us knows exactly when they'll be here or what this means. But LLorser LLitebrite's going to use it against us, sure as shootin'."

Lauriander sat quietly on the couch thinking for a while. She had thought to visit LLiterally LLucid to discuss the situation. Lefty, seeing her so quiet, suspected he had said too much. Finally, she stood up and informed him she had decided to stay home. "I don't feel like a visit with anyone right now," she told him before she went up to her room.

Alone on her bed, Lauriander contemplated Oliver's future and her own, even if she didn't clearly understand the concept of a future. If something should happen to Oliver, what would she do? She wouldn't be able to go on without him. She knew that for sure.

Dangers and Deletions

efty never could say no to Lauriander, even when she took the form of Mister Ed and stomped around the house. Looking into the *eyes* of his little girl, his L heart just melted. So, observing Lauriander's distress, Lefty overcame his misgivings about LLorser LLitebrites ferocious temper and sharp tongue. In the end, he gave in. The mayor permitted his daughter to go off with Oliver to the country, but not to Lucy's place. He feared their being discovered there and instead sent them to a different lodge by a lake he knew about inside the border of LLiterally LLucid's dimension. They collected a supply of food and left by the back way to walk there.

Thus Oliver got the break from liberaltown he desperately needed. After some time without prying eyes, he began to feel more like his old self. The air, the country smell, and most of all the freedom from visitors made him a new person. He felt almost human again.

Oliver taught Lauriander to swim. All the times she'd visited the lake before, she'd never thought to enter the water. First, she and Oliver paddled around in the lake. Then he showed her how to water fight. They splashed and laughed like schoolchildren. Oliver taught her the crawl, breaststroke, backstroke, and butterfly. Fortunately, computed Ls, protected by their rubbery skin, did not rust like noncomputed ones when they encountered water. Once Lauriander mastered a stroke, she instantly surpassed her teacher. Under water, she proved unbeatable. With no need for air and unlimited endurance, she could stay down forever.

The first time that Lauriander stayed under water by herself, she didn't surface for three whole Los Angeles minutes. Not aware of her limitless capacity, Oliver had gone crazy with fear. He'd even dived in to look for the body. But once he realized her ability, he lay by the shore on his back with both hands cupping his head. He casually bobbed his right foot up and down over his left knee. Chewing on a piece of grass, he waited for his true love to emerge in her own good time. Happy as punch, with not a worry in the world, he looked up at the still clouds frozen like chunks of ice in the blue sky and a sun that never moved through the heavens or caused a sunburn.

August had come to Los Angeles during these days Oliver and Lauriander spent at the cabin in play and fun. Oliver thought about home every day, but during the three months he'd spent in L Land the sharp edges of his memory had faded. His future remained in limbo. LLiterally LLucid remained his only hope.

So when Lauriander asked if she could invite LLiterally LLucid to visit them for only a short while, Oliver had no objection. He felt ready for company again, and besides, they were down to the last of the real food. So he welcomed a visit from the double L.

LLucid came skipping through the forest like an Easter bunny. He carried with him several books for Oliver to enjoy, along with a stack of ham sandwiches. Before saying hello, LLucid pulled out a small monitor from the pocket of his white sailor jumpsuit and clicked it. Crash! Crunch! -A huge oak tree, complete with a swing, stood in the middle of the garden, surrounded by small, pathetic laurel shrubs.

LLucid, still looking like a young boy, jumped on the swing that hung off a high branch of the oak tree. Ordinarily planted in LLucid's backyard near his home, the grand oak now stood firmly rooted into the ground by the lake. LLucid swung back and forth, back and forth. A low groan from the rope that stretched over the branch followed each shift of the swing. The boy laughed with childish delight as he propelled himself higher and higher.

Oliver stared wide-eyed at the performance. The thought that a boy could fiddle with Mother Nature stunned him. Once again, he had to come to terms with L Land ways, adjusting his old habits of seeing the world. He had a lot of time to think by now, especially in these relaxing days by the water. He could not help but dwell on the mistakes that brought him here. To try to stuff a ladder into a mailbox now seemed absurd. His mother had meant for him to send a letter. LLucid's presence made him painfully aware that he desperately wanted a second chance to get his life straightened out.

Oliver finally had enough of LLucid's games. He couldn't contain himself any longer. "I'm glad you came," he blurted out as he approached the swing. "Thanks so much for bringing the books. And I can't wait to eat lunch. But first, I wanted to talk to you."

LLiterally stopped swinging in order to listen to Oliver. "Lauriander explained your job to me. She said you move large groups of Ls from L Land to Word Central. My guess is you know more about this place than anyone else. Tell me honestly if you have figured out any way I can return home. Is there any way Lauriander can return with me? Could she live in Los Angeles as I'm living here? If you know, tell me."

LLiterally stretched his short legs straight out in front of him before he answered. "Only one small letter is needed to change a word. That is why every letter is important. Add the letter 'l' to word and you create a world. So perhaps Lauriander, as an L, can be added to your word to make your world. No L has tried this. Only Hs are known to move from letters to humans, and once they do they never return. But we letters are versatile. Scramble the word 'late' like an egg and you get a 'tale.' Switch 'i' with 'a' and turn 'trail' to a 'trial.'

All constructions are as fragile as that. Only the most ignorant among us doesn't recognize he is merely a lone letter, or two in my case, dependent on others for meaning.

"In many ways our value is derived only from other letters. The letters in the words we compose are like family. Since we only know as much as Big Mac allows us to know, and you are the first person from your world to visit us, none of us knows what may occur if you try to return. And none knows where an L would fit in your world if not in a word."

With that comment, LLiterally jumped down from the swing and suggested they walk to the lake to eat lunch. On the way, Oliver showed him Watchim. He told him how Watchim kept him sane, how he'd kept track of days and weeks, how he worried that the battery would run out soon, and how then he would be lost forever.

"Times time whether measured or not. You worry far too much about such matters. Lets have our lunch and a swim," LLucid said, laughing.

Oliver wanted to rectify his past, and he had spent much of his time in L Land dwelling on a future, so he said no more. He would not let his concerns stand in the way of a good time or the promise of a ham sandwich. Despite the circumstances, he intended to enjoy himself no matter what. The water looked too tempting not to jump in. So he grabbed LLucid and threw him in the lake. They splashed and played like kids let loose after a long winter. They had so much fun that Oliver almost forgot where he wanted to be.

During the rest of the visit, LLiterally LLucid, sweet and rambunctious, played with Oliver and Lauriander like any ten-year-old boy. He ran all over the place, rolled around in the water like a beach ball, and climbed around on his big, old oak tree. "What a nice break," he said, ready to leave. "I needed to have a bit of fun. But I have too much on my mind to stay any longer. Things are getting out of hand. There seems to be a sudden surge in the need for Ls, perhaps for other letters as well. I am overworked trying to figure out where to take them from. As a result of this, you may soon find you will have fewer letters available to use in your designs, Lauriander."

When LLucid disappeared, the tree vanished with him. Only the books and the extra ham sandwiches remained. But Oliver and Lauriander had to return to town anyway. They had made that agreement with Lefty. Oliver left the books inside the cabin in the hope he and Lauriander would return soon. They felt great sadness upon departing from their little bit of paradise.

When they returned to liberaltown, they found that the situation had actually become more severe than before they left. While they were playing and washing away their worries, rumors had spread like a forest fire through town. Lauriander gathered from some of her friends that Lucy had bragged about some sort of intimate moment she'd shared with Oliver. For sure, the tale had grown taller and taller. By the time they returned, Lauriander heard that Lucy had replaced her as Oliver's steady girl.

After the word spread that Oliver and Lauriander had returned, women lined up on the Littleleathers' doorstep and out through the yard to the street. Women of all kinds— beautiful, ugly, fat, famous, old, young—demanded that Oliver strut his stuff. If he could party with Lucy, they reasoned, he could give each of them a quick toot as well. After all, they were all equals as computed Ls.

The line of visitors extended around the block after a short time. "Do you know what my husband did?" Luna Lark, an exact Harriet Nelson look-alike, asked Lo-Rain from the perch she maintained as first in line on the Littleleather front porch. "Lo-Rain, do you know what my own dear Lyle Life-lite did when he couldn't get his pipe to stand up and say howdy doody? Why, he 'l'omputed himself into a lady. The cad waited until I had gone into town shopping to do it, that low-life scoundrel. Then he ran off wearing my best dress. I don't know how to find him now. He could be someone else's wife for all I know. Lo-Rain, if you ask me, this Liver's the one to blame."

Oliver refused to see any of these women, and Lauriander backed him 100 percent. The mayor needed all his sweet-talking ways to disperse the unruly line. He personally guided Luna Lark back home. But several angry women, despite Oliver's rebuff, prepared to wait forever. Their defiance left the Little-leathers shaken. Lefty inquired among the ladies that remained, only to learn that Luna's husband, Lyle, wasn't the first or the last to make a sudden gender switch. Many transformations occurred among the failed husbands of liberaltown.

Women continued to arrive at all hours at the Little-leathers' door. No relief appeared on the horizon in those tough days. Lauriander refused to let any of them inside. She told Oliver she suspected that some of those women in line had been men who had switched identities just to get a close-up look at Oliver's pipe from a different perspective.

Toward the end of August, and some time after the line of women began, Oliver and Lauriander accepted an invitation to a surprise birthday party given at the home of Lucy for Lauren, the little Mouseketeer. To avoid those stubborn women still waiting at the door, the young couple exited through the backyard and climbed over the neighbor's fence. Despite his concerns about an encounter with Lucy, Oliver went along to the party. He couldn't be sure that she had actually started the nasty rumors. "Anyone could have spread them," Lauriander told him when he hesitated. "Lots of people are angry with you, Liver," she reminded him. "So let's forget it and go have some fun. Forget and forgive. Fair is fair."

The two Lucy Ricardos, Lucy's parents—one blond and the other a redhead—had decorated their living room with brightly colored streamers that ran from wall to wall. Across the entrance to the crowded room hung a shiny purple sign reading in big, yellow letters, #span_smallcaps HAPPY 'L'IRTHDAY!span.

Lauren had never had a party before or celebrated her 'l'irthday, for that matter, because Ls didn't have birthdays. Lucy and her family only organized the party because Lauren had watched a birthday party on LTV and wished out loud for one herself. When Lauren arrived and realized the party had been planned for her, she jumped around with excitement.

A cake made from a mixture of flour and lentils and heavily 'l'alted stood in the middle of a large table. The cake had the name #span_smallcaps L A U R E N!span spelled out in light-pink glaze on top of white icing. Placed around the name were pink and yellow sugar flowers and small red flags with a white L printed on each of them. The decorations left hardly any room for candles.

The guest of honor, the youngest looking member of the group, bright-eyed and bushy-tailed in her brand-new white turtleneck shirt that Lauriander had made her, went from friend to friend, hugging and kissing each of them. On this, her first special day, she felt the full meaning of a "Happy Birthday."

Oliver seated himself on one of three couches that cluttered up the living room. He wondered only briefly why they needed to crowd three couches into a small room. Like many things he didn't understand but had learned to accept at home in Los Angeles, he'd also come to accept much of what he saw in L Land as normal.

The kids at the party jumped around with excitement. Oliver watched a dark-haired kid stuff his face with food. He looked like Beaver Cleaver, the kid in his uncles videos of *Leave It to Beaver*. The Nelson boys, David and Ricky, came as well, squeaky clean as if they d been scrubbed with Ivory soap. Their hair glistened with what looked like Brylcream. Each boy wore a blue-and-red striped tie and had a white handkerchief, folded into a perfect rectangle, sticking out from his left lapel pocket.

Oliver looked on as the group played Pin the Tail on the Llama, an L version of tag called laglag, and a most disorganized variant of Mother May I known as Let Me, Big Mac.

After the games, the group gathered around Lauren, who had her pal Lucy on one side and Lydia and Lucinda, the Hayley twins, on the other. Lauriander and Linda, the Sandra Dee look-alike, stood a bit farther back from the group. They all began to sing "Happy 'L'irthday" to a beaming but shy-looking Lauren. Oliver, still seated on the couch, observed the performance from a distance. His eyes moved from face to face as they sang at the top of their little L lungs. He had never seen a happier bunch.

Suddenly, as if a strobe flashed in a darkened room, a bright flare of light burst from the crowd. Next to Lauren, Lucy glowed bright as a star. An instant later, her body turned transparent. As the group backed off, Oliver could see the hallway right through her.

From his vantage point, Oliver saw the last expression on poor Lucy's beautiful Liz Taylor face, a terrified look of disbelief. Then a single word, #span_smallcaps LUST!span, appeared for a second over the very spot where she had sung so joyfully only an instant before.

As tragedy struck, a hush fell over the room. Oliver rushed to Lauriander's side. He wanted to speak. When he asked what happened, his voice sounded so loud in the dead silence he stopped talking.

"Poor Lucy," moaned Lydia. "I can't believe she's gone, just like that."

"Where's she gone?" Oliver asked.

The two parent Lucy's, who had been standing in a corner watching the merriment, appeared as pale as computed Ls could look. They held hands. Then the red-haired Lucy crumpled onto the floor. Like any mother confronted with the sudden loss of her offspring, she unleashed a string of "lalalas" in uncontrollable wails of pain.

"Lucy's off to Word Central," Lauriander exclaimed. She held onto Oliver as if she feared she might disappear herself.

"But I saw the word #span_smallcaps LUST!span," Oliver said. He led Lauriander toward one of the couches and sat her down. "What did that mean?"

"That's her word," Lauriander told him almost in a whisper. "LLiterally LLucid told me that sometimes during Tore-cation you see the L word the person will lead." Her voice grew louder as an L-type moan escaped her lips. "Lucy, Lucy, oh, I can't believe you're gone. Please, please let's go home," she said as she stood up, dragging Oliver toward the door. They skirted around Lauren, who stood staring at her cake with her name now spelled as #span_smallcaps AUREN!span, and all the white Ls missing from the center of the surrounding red flags.

Word spread through town in no time. 'L'orecation, the feared L Land transfer to Word Central, had never been witnessed by so many at one time or occurred to an L as young as Lucy. Most often 'l'orecation sightings were limited to noncomputed Ls. To compound the problem, all the temporary Ls used by Lauriander had disappeared right off the clothes they'd been printed on. And six other computed Ls 'l'orecated shortly thereafter, though rumors put the figure much higher.

Lauriander returned home to discover the missing temporary Ls in the words she'd put on her clothing. And the T-shirt Oliver had arrived to L Land in now read #span_smallcaps WAVE THE SHA ES!span. Oliver and Lauriander didn't learn about the other 'l'orecations until the following morning, when Lefty burst into the kitchen where Oliver sat eating a bowl of dry cornflakes from his food supply. "Big trouble brewin up," he announced. "Seems a whole mess of townfolks 'l'orecated right after poor little Lucy. Larry Languisher is so angry he's called a meeting of the council right pronto. He can't believe his little Lucy is gone.

"Gotta get back fast," Lefty sputtered. "Just wanted you to know what's goin' on since some of them dumb folks are putting the blame on you, Liver. There's lots of nasty talk among the folks out there. I'm going to try to get LLorser to agree that you should skedaddle for a while. Leastways till this here storm blows over. Even heard more talk about the legislators coming. Right now I got Lexi keepin' an eye on the post office. That's where they'll arrive if they come at all."

"But I haven't done anything," Oliver protested.

"Don't seem to matter around here," Lefty shot back. "Guess you're guilty until proved innocent."

As the mayor spoke, Lauriander looked increasingly upset. "Daddy, this is terrible. To lose Lucy is bad enough, but why would anyone think? ..."

"You know how folks are. Get something in their heads, and they get fixed on it worse than a hound dog courtin' a bitch in heat. Now, I don't say for certain anything will come about. We locals are pretty slow to take action, except LLorser, of course."

"What could they do?" Oliver asked.

"Hell, if I knew that, I'd be one of those what you call 'ems?"

"Fortune-tellers," Lauriander suggested.

Lefty ignored her.

"But I had nothing to do with Lucy's disappearance. I feel terrible about what happened to her," Oliver said.

"You know, a lot of menfolk around here are upset because you can make your pipe stand up. And the ladies all wanted to be with you, but you just wanted to be with Laurie, or Lauriander as you call her. Can't get used to that dadgum name. Maybe you should make that little pecker thing lie low for a while until all this blows over."

Lauriander's voice sounded upset. "What do you want him to do, Daddy? He can't just yank it off. LLorser tried that. Remember?"

"Gotta mosey," Lefty answered in a gruff voice. "But you two best think about heading out of town till things blow over. Don't think about Larry's lodge either. I tell you Larry's fit to be tied."

Lefty backed into the hallway. Lauriander left her chair to put her arms around Oliver.

He cradled her head on his shoulder. "What do you think we should do?" he asked.

Lauriander looked down at the table. She never before

contemplated leaving home. Until this moment, she'd never had to think about such a possibility. "I guess we should go to the lodge in LLiterally LLucid's dimension. He'll let us stay until things get better. Maybe he can tell us why this happened."

"Your father mentioned something about a post office. Do you have a post office here?" he asked.

Lauriander ignored the question. "I can pack some clothes, and we can go. We had so much fun by the lake. I know we'll be safe if we're near LLiterally," Lauriander continued.

"Is there really a post office here like your dad said?" Oliver repeated.

"A post office? Sure, the Letterland Post Office. That's the way officials travel from state to state. LLiterally says at one time before LTV, they delivered letters."

"You think they take letters now?"

"I don't know."

"You don't get letters?"

"We are letters," Lauriander reminded him.

"But letters like letters you write."

Lauriander had a hard time following the drift of Oliver's words.

"Now, if I wanted to send a note home to my mother, is there any way to write on a piece of paper?" Oliver asked.

"I don't know," Lauriander said. "Maybe the post office has some. You'd have to write without any Ls. There don't seem to be any extra Ls anymore."

"I can try to write without any Ls. I want to try to send a

letter home," Oliver said as they went off to pack. He knew his idea sounded silly. But if a measuring stick existed for ridiculousness, falling down a mailbox would be way up there. So thinking along that vein, he decided that sending a letter might be worth a try.

Bad News and Jailhouse Blues

L efty stood before the assembled council members gathered around their favorite poker table at the Lucky Lady Saloon. "We got some kind of crisis here," he said. Concern showed on their faces. Lomash's expression looked more startled than concerned. LLorser listened while he absentmindedly scratched his silver beard. Lillbzellmet had stopped his whirling motion.

"I think those legislative rats are behind the 'l'orecation," Lefty continued. "They're supposed to be here sooner or later. Seems to me we're headed for a showdown with them low-down varmints at high noon, whenever that is."

LLorser's deep voice cut into Lefty's comments. "Fortune has blessed us with the ears of a double L in the legislature. This valiant knight has furnished me an advance list of those errant knaves who will be descending upon us. They include our own representative, Lister Leeds, and a noncomputed L similar to our own distinguished Lillbzellmet. Most dangerous is that scurvy knave Lester Lisp, the notorious power broker of L Land's capital. Lisp is a ruthless, wart-faced, vicious lawyer wretch, the chief architect of the law that took away our capital L."

"Well, we got our bases covered," Lefty informed him. "Limpy's gone to relieve Lexi down by the post office to let us know when the varmints show up."

"Methinks we would be wise to keep an eye on brother Liver, lest he be snatched from us. He must not be allowed out of our sight. If it be that the legislature seeks him, so much the better. We will barter our visitor on harsh terms to guarantee our survival. In return, we will demand secure borders and an immediate retraction of the law about the capital L."

"Now hold on just a blame minute," Lefty said, standing up in a huff. Lexi made a sudden appearance beside the bar to interrupt the mayor in the middle of his retort. The gatekeeper asked for a bottle, downed a shot, and waved at the assembled group. Then, sporting a smile, he took his proper seat.

"You see any signs of the enemy?" Lance asked him.

"Nope," Lexi answered. "What enemy signs? Saw Laurie and that Liver though."

"Which way were they headed?" the ever cautious Lindsay asked.

"Why, into the post office, naturally. That's where you had me watching," Lexi answered matter of factly.

LLorser jumped out of his chair at the same time as Larry, still distraught about the loss of his daughter, Lucy. "We've got to stop him," the latter said.

"Quick, LooLoo, secure thy laser lasso. Go hither and give Limpy a hand to capture that foul knave. Make haste. There's not an instant to spare."

LooLoo took the lasso and rushed off through the swinging doors to capture Oliver.

"Goin' a little over the edge aren't you, LLorser?" Lefty asked. He knew he should have stopped LooLoo. But he had to admit, to himself at least, that Oliver had made himself more trouble than a pack of ornery mules.

"I think LLorser's right. We should keep that young 'l'elia under our watchful eye," Lomash said, his single eye staring straight ahead.

"Maybe the legislature wants him back because he's working for them," Lindsay suggested.

A few minutes later, they brought Oliver into the Lucky Lady Saloon. With his head bent forward, he looked mighty sorry that he ever entertained the idea of sending a letter home. Lauriander followed behind him, protesting loudly. Oliver had been forced to walk along Main Street with the laser lasso whirling around his shoulders. Inside the saloon, Lauriander stared at her father, but Lefty remained silent. LLorser directed the captors to place Oliver in the abandoned Linguistic Layaways shop next to the Lucky Lady. LLorser himself secured the geodesic laser structure similar to the one that caught Oliver at the crossroads when he hadn't paid his Legos bill.

"Don't worry, Liver," Lauriander had called out as LLorser, Limpy, and LooLoo led Oliver away. "I'm going to get you out of there."

Right away, Lefty decided to take Lauriander home. All the way through the swinging doors she kept pulling at him, asking him why he allowed this to happen. She couldn't believe that her own dear father would condone such a sordid act. How could he let them lock up an innocent man?

Meanwhile, LLorser took advantage of the mayor's absence to stir up his fellow citizens. "Hear me out," he bellowed.

"We must put aside our personal feelings to save our town. I say we vote to turn Liver over to the legislature."

"Shouldn't we wait for the mayor to return?" Lomash asked.

"Maybe we should talk to Liver first. Let's hear what he has to say for himself," the ever rational teacher Lindsay suggested.

LLorser stood up. He reached for his crown, which he'd neglected to wear in the rush. He cleared his throat and said, "Time is fleeting. Remember when my humble request for the council to approbate an act of measuring time was rudely rejected? Without time, we don't know when the mayor will return or when the legislature will appear or if there is time to talk with the captured Liver. We must act now, for action is eloquence."

So the council, pushed into a vote, approved a decree allowing Oliver to be turned over to the legislature in return for certain concessions to be agreed upon by all parties. When, upon his return, Lefty heard the news, he protested loudly. But deep in his L heart, he breathed a slightly gaseous sigh of relief.

Give Us This Day Our Daily Mail

Letters and the post office played heavily on Grace Sandwich's mind as well. Throughout the remainder of the spring and summer, Grace developed a daily ritual. At first, very few people noticed. Each morning, after Fred left for work, she collected her supplies: a lightweight aluminum lawn chair, Evian water, a small lunch, the morning *Los Angeles Times,* and assorted other reading material. All of this, with the exception of the lawn chair, she packed into a large bag. Each day, including Saturday and Sunday, she set up shop near the corner mailbox under a large magnolia tree, which dropped leaves continually. Nevertheless, the spot provided a perfect angle from which to observe all that went on in the vicinity.

Grace couldn't explain the internal force that brought her back to this place on a daily basis. Fred had confronted her the first time he spotted her sitting under the tree. He yelled in a loud voice that she embarrassed him because she looked like the neighborhood bag lady. While he tried to hide his face in the car, she responded from her makeshift fortress under the tree, "I know that Oliver's disappearance has something to do with that particular mailbox and your ladder. I don't know what or how or why, but I intend to find out."

Grace didn't care if Fred or anyone else thought her behavior peculiar. She intended to stay put. The next person she spoke with, after Fred, was the mail person in charge of pickups. To her disappointment, Grace had to wait almost a week before the letter carrier arrived for what should have been his daily scheduled Monday through Friday 5:00 p.m. pickup. She reasoned that if Oliver had somehow fallen into the mail receptacle, he would have been dead by the time the postal worker came around to empty out the box. As the mailman removed the letters and a couple of packages, Grace approached him to ask if he'd seen or heard any odd occurrences on his route during the past couple of months.

"No, ma'am," he responded, keeping a wary eye on Grace, who had on a large hat. He'd spotted her sitting vigil while driving past on numerous occasions.

"Did you ever find a ladder in your mailbox?" Grace asked.

"Never found a ladder," he said. "No way a ladder would ever fit in here. No way. I 'spect if someone wanted to mail a ladder, they'd lay it against the side of Old MaiLA here."

"Old MaiLA?"

"Yes, ma'am, Old MaiLA there. Like mail and LA all together. I gave all these old-time mailboxes names: Old Boxum, Old Possum, always old something or other. You kind of get to know them. This is one of the few left that still takes packages."

Grace absorbed this information with great interest and thanked him. Given the man's infrequent pickup schedule, she at least understood why she received so many late charges after she mailed her bills from the corner box. She returned to her aluminum chair to dwell on her loss. Only after the postal truck departed did she allow tears to roll down her cheeks. She picked up her book and a huge, brown magnolia leaf fell onto the open page. She didn't sweep it off.

With summer settling in, tourists flocked to Los Angeles. Two or three afternoons each week, a small tour bus would pass by, bringing American and foreign tourists through the fashionable Westside areas to roll past the homes of the movie stars. The corner mailbox, not near the home of anyone significant enough to merit a stop, stood stoutly along the route.

After a week of seeing Grace sitting alone under the magnolia tree holding her bottle of Evian water and her book, the driver's curiosity got the better of him. He pulled to a stop across the street from her. He was about to get out to talk with her when, to his great surprise, ten Japanese tourists requested permission to leave the bus to take her picture, each one posing beside her. That was how Grace's face with its melancholy smile came to sit in many homes and albums around Tokyo and Kyoto.

Soon Grace became known as the Magnolia Lady, and she became a regular stop for the tour. Always friendly, she allowed her picture to be taken by visitors from as far away as Norway and Australia. Tourists thought her a famous person, and the tour driver did nothing to discourage the idea. When they asked her why she sat there, day in and day out, she replied, "This is a lovely place to sit."

One of the tour drivers had a friend who worked as a fledgling reporter for a local TV station. One day, in desperate search of a filler story, this reporter showed up to interview Grace. He'd learned that his two-hour, five-day-a-week evening news program accepted almost any story as "news." In front of the camera, Grace spoke openly and gracefully about the loss of her son and how she hoped to find a clue here by the mailbox where he had last been seen.

Following the first reporters lead, three other reporters from local stations appeared. The following week, a frontpage feature complete with photos of Grace and Oliver was published in the local news section of the *Los Angeles Times,*

All through the summer, Grace wore her hat, drank her water, and waited. A modicum of fame descended and brought its rewards. People offered her cookies and lemonade. Drivers stopped their cars to visit. Neighbors would drop by to chat. One woman invited Grace to use her guest bathroom each time she needed to relieve herself. Many people told her how they sympathized with her quest. They left her good-luck charms including rabbits' feet, horseshoes, and even a postcard from Lourdes.

Then, one hot August day, an unexpected break came out of the blue. A big tour bus stopped to let tourists photograph and visit with the Magnolia Lady. Off the bus descended a tall man with a horseshoe ring of auburn hair framing a freckled bald spot. Freckles covered his reddish face and bare arms. He carried with him a large wrapped package that contained dirty laundry that he intended to mail home to his own mother for washing.

As he approached the mailbox, Grace's eyes followed him. She could see the package he held would be much too large for the opening. She expected that the man would find out soon enough and abandon the idea of forcing his package into the mailbox. Instead, he bent over to look at the pickup times posted on the front of the box. Then he opened the package door. Grace followed his actions out of the corner of her eye and, mouth agape, saw how the package disappeared easily through the door of MaiLA.

Seven tourists recorded on digital cameras the instant of Grace's wide-eyed discovery.

Showdown and Turnaround

Limpy could be heard banging along the wooden sidewalk a short time after Oliver's confinement in the Linguistic Layaway shop. The doors swung open and Limpy entered to announce the arrival of the legislature. "Marshal, Marshal, they're headed this way," he called out. "LooLoo's with them. One of them is as mean-looking an L as I ever did see anywhere in L Land."

"No doubt you refer to the villainous Lester Lisp," LLorser warned. "Steady now, liberaltown men, women, and non-computed Ls. Stand firm. We shall vanquish the foe." He stood up, and Lomash stood up with him, momentarily facing the bar by mistake.

As LooLoo hurried through the swinging doors to resume his place behind the bar, Limpy approached the bar from the other side to down a shot of whiskey. A moment later one noncomputed L, five computed Ls, and the town's own representative, Lister Leeds, appeared. Each had computed himself as an identical tall and thin version of the young Jimmy Stewart. Each wore the same blue pinstriped suit.

Together, as one, they strutted into the Lucky Lady Saloon. Upon entering, the legislators spread out a few feet apart in a straight horizontal line as if to block off the entrance. They all sported white Panama hats with dark hatbands. At the end of the line stood the noncomputed L, strangely out of place as it whirled back and forth on its hockey stick. Like the others, the L had also been fitted in a blue pinstriped suit that came up as high as its slit mouth and down as far as its joint.

"I have been looking forward to returning home for a long time," Lister Leeds, the elected representative of liberal town, said, stepping forward with a friendly smile. His straightforward mannerisms resembled those of the vibrant title character portrayed by Jimmy Stewart in the popular film *Mr. Smith Goes to Washington.*

"If I should have need of a fork, I would borrow thy tongue," LLorser informed Lister Leeds. "You, churlish knave, have betrayed your own town. Do you deny you have sold out the name of the very town that sent thee to represent us?"

Lister fiddled with his tie. "I did everything in my power to stop the law they passed. May I remind the esteemed council members that when I became the first representative of liberaltown, I was elected on only two votes, my wife's and my own? Lethargy carried the day."

"We just want to be left alone," Lexi said. "Don't want no pokety pokes from the legislature running our town or telling us our beeswax." He clamped a hand across the top of his ten-gallon hat, as if someone might try to snatch it away from him.

Lester Lisp, the leader of the group, with big black warts covering both cheeks despite his Jimmy Stewart appearance, now prepared to speak. Since he despised most Ls, he refused to use the letter L in his speech, giving his words an intentional lisp. "Wet's get the show on the road. We wegiswators don't have time for smaww tawk."

As he spoke, Lester Lisp took a step forward. The entire group of legislators closed ranks, all lining up beside their leader. Six Jimmy Stewarts standing side by side looked quite imposing to the locals.

"Please, have a drink on the house," the mayor offered, disarmingly. "LooLoo, set up some whiskey for the boys, will you?"

"Forget the whiskey, WooWoo," Lester growled. "My father

was the wegiswative bartender. We had the wegiswature over a barrew. I had enough of that cheap rotgut whiskey to wast my whowe wife. However, we wouwd certainwy enjoy a gwass of fine champagne."

"Ain't got champagne," LooLoo shot right back. "Got beer, gin, and pure rotgut-knock-you-on-your-ass he-man-drinkin' whiskey here. This ain't no pantywaist legislature bar like your daddy ran."

If the warts on Lester's cheeks could have stood on end, they would have. Instead they began to vibrate from anger. "WooWoo, a bar without a bwottwe of champagne shouwd be cwosed. Don't you remember that program where the orchestra pwaywed bubbwe music on WEWTV? That was cwass. Every bar in the Wand shouwd have champagne on ice just waiting for wegiswative visits."

"Nobody waits for wegiswative visits," LLorser mocked.

Lefty bit his tongue because he didn't like where this conversation was headed.

"You boys need to shape up," Lister, their own representative, said in a whiny voice that caused the council members to exchange looks.

LLorser responded with a mocking laugh. "And thou, Lister, and thy blackguard friend, Lester Lisp, need to move to Wawyertown."

Lindsay put on a stern, schoolteacher expression as she spoke. "You should all be ashamed of yourselves, going at each other like a group of children. We've come together to solve a problem, and that should be the focus of our discussion."

"What probwhem might that be?" Lester Lisp asked.

Lindsay looked toward the others for support. "Well, I don't know exactly. I hoped somebody did."

"We have been notified about the sudden disappearance of citizens from wiberawtown, and we have come to hewp," Lester Lisp said.

"Did you say whip?" Lomash asked.

"HEWP, HEWP," yelled the frustrated Lisp.

"Why is it, methinks, thou hast come to bury liberaltown rather than to praise it?" LLorser asked.

"We know you're after that LTV man named Liver," Lomash blurted out. "Well, you can have him. He's in jail next door. We voted on it. But in return we want …"At that crucial moment he forgot what he intended to say.

Lester Lisp adjusted his Panama hat, and each of his fellow legislators did the same. "Who is that one-eyed cat?" Lester Lisp asked. "He gives me the heebie-jeebies."

"We call him Womash," the mayor said. Then he corrected himself. "I mean Lomash. Then you didn't come here looking for Liver?"

One of the other pinstriped legislators stepped forward. "I have heard from my band, an LTV man is loose in the land. My name is Ryan Cryin' from the town of Lyin'. Another Lyin' told me so, a 'l'elia really in the know."

The council groaned. They had dealt with Lyin' people before.

"I cannot waste more time on a pwace that doesn't have champagne," said Lester Lisp. "Here are our demands: First, we want you to put wiberawtown under the controw of the wegiswature on a temporary basis so we can sowve this mystery of sudden 'w'orecation. Second, cwose down the Wucky Wady Sawoon forever. Third, turn over to us whomever you want to turn over. The wegiswature is awways happy to take whatever extras our woyaw taxpayers want to give us."

The council members stood up, turning in the direction of the legislators in a face-off.

"And what if we refoose, er, refuse?" the mayor asked.

Lester Lisp dug into his pocket and extracted a long, narrow dark object similar to a pinstriped flashlight. He pointed the device at LooLoo's shot glasses. An instant later he pushed the trigger. All eighty-three precious glasses, minus the two that Lexi and Limpy held in their hands, vanished in a single shot. If Ls ever fainted, Looloo would have dropped to the floor in a dead faint.

"We don't wike to use force because it's uncouth. But the wegiswature must have some method of backing up our power. That's what governments do."

Several council members sat down. LLorser and the mayor continued to stand. Both of them turned their attention from the demonstration to the visitors. Behind the bar, LooLoo sat down in shock.

Aghast, everyone had lost the power of speech. Right at that moment, LLiterally LLucid materialized out of nowhere, still in his boyish form, his head barely reaching to the top of the bar. Dressed all in white, he held in his small hand a thin white pencil-shaped device similar to the one in the hand of Lester Lisp. "Why do you come here to threaten violence toward my peaceful townspeople?" he addressed the leader.

"Chiwdren are not awwowed in bars, sonny," Lisp sneered.

"There are waws against that. Go home to your mama."

"My name is LLiterally LLucid," the boy informed him. "Perhaps you've heard of me in the legislative corridors."

"Wwiterawwy Wwucid, go home to your mama wike a good boy."

LLiterally turned in the direction of the bar. He pointed his white object straight at where the glasses had stood. One zap restored all eighty-one precious glasses. Limpy helped raise LooLoo onto his feet to observe the miracle for himself.

"There are many forms of power in Letterland," LLiterally LLucid stated in a strong voice.

The council looked back and forth during the exchange. Lester found it difficult to believe a small boy dared give him so much lip.

"I awways try to be nice to young 'w'omputed ones wike you. But you are pushing your wuck, sonny boy. I don't know why the counciw wets a young boy carry such a dangerous object or wets him speak for them."

LLiterally Lucid stood up full size. "I may be small, but I can state our case clearly. Your requests have ulterior motives and are unacceptable to us. I suggest you take your boys back to the post office and ship out before someone gets hurt."

"Sonny, you must have some wrong ideas about who is in charge here. We come from the wegiswature, and no undersized constituent says what we can or can't do. You are not even of voting age. We decide what is for the town's own good, and that's why we do what we do," Lester reminded him. "You did a nice job restoring those gwasses. Wet's see if you have the power to bring back one of your counciw members from Word Centraw."

Before anyone could respond, Lester pointed the thin, black, pinstriped object directly at LLorser. Instantaneously, the large double L radiated a doubly powerful burst of light, grew transparent, and vanished with only the word *pill* lingering in the air.

Everyone in the room gasped. Even the cool LLiterally LLucid couldn't believe his own eyes. Never had any of them seen or imagined such ruthlessness among Ls. LooLoo, who had picked up one of his glasses to inspect it, dropped the precious object on the floor, where it shattered into a thousand pieces. Lillbzellmet kept opening and closing its support stick in a fit of pique. Lomash blinked his eye as if LLorser might reappear at any moment. Lefty scratched his head, wondering if he might be next.

"Hey, wittwe boy. Wet's see you bring that fat one back."

LLiterally LLucid stood as tall as he could. He spread his legs apart, arched his back, and raised his elbows. The banana tie on his chest swayed back and forth. "You know," he said, "and I know, that once your word comes up, nobody can bring you back. But let me clearly explain to you and your clones that I have enough authority to give my lost LL friend some powerful company."

With those words, LLiterally LLucid lifted his long white object. Just then Lester Lisp pointed his own object in LLiterally's direction. But Lester's timing proved a shade slower. With a quick movement of his small finger, LLucid sent the powerful legislator off to Word Central in a heartbeat. Lester Lisp flashed brightly, became transparent, and suddenly became only a wart-faced memory. The word #span_smallcaps LOSER!span hung in the air, then quickly vanished.

"Yeah," cried Lexi with a wave of his ten-gallon hat. In his excitement, he used his free hand to wave at all the remaining legislators.

"Thanks for the hand, Mr. LLucid," the mayor said. Not only did he know his own life had been spared, but he also realized that his remaining days would be far easier from now on. "What are you gonna do with the rest of the varmints?" he asked LLiterally LLucid. "I've heard it spoke somewhere that 'l'orecated Ls don't tell tales."

The other legislators, minus their leader, appeared frozen in place.

"I thought you should all know your 'l'orecation problems have nothing to do with Liver or Lauriander or any of you," LLucid said calmly to the council members. "The problems have to do with an unexpected excessive demand for letters. School has begun around the LTV world. I have learned that other letters are experiencing this same sudden volume demand. Vowels have been hit particularly hard." He looked at the legislators, who all, except for the noncomputed Lawtonzell, showed glum Jimmy Stewart expressions across their faces. Lawtonzell showed no expression at all.

"As for this bunch, I think they may reconsider their illegal actions and show a willingness to leave peacefully if we allow them to do so," LLucid said, lacking any desire to annihilate the others. His nature tended toward violence only when he deemed violence necessary.

"I feel weak, for myself I speak," said Ryan Cryin', delegate from Lyin'. "I feel as frail as a snail. I'll happily disappear if it's legislators you fear. If that is all you require, your wish becomes my desire." Then, with that talent Ls from Lyin' have, Ryan Cryin' vanished into the air.

Liberaltown's representative, Lister Leeds, bowed in

LLiterally LLucid's direction. He produced a wide smile. "I will quote an old Leeds family saying that big things come in small packages. Thank you for rescuing us from the tyranny of Lester Lisp. He has forced us to do many things against our wills, and we are all grateful for your decision to get rid of him. I cannot speak for the others, but it is an honor for me to return to Legistown to work on behalf of my wonderful liberal town constituents. My first action will be to introduce a law rescinding the earlier law about the capital L in the towns name. Without Lisp around, I'm sure the law will be reversed."

"A capital idea," Lomash cried out.

"I think we're out of here," said another legislator, the first words he'd uttered since his arrival.

With a sudden rush, the legislators crammed through the door all at once. Bringing up the rear came the whirling Lawtonzell.

Lexi jumped up in the air, clicked the heels of his cowboy boots, and shouted, "Whoopee!" His ten-gallon hat flew right off his head.

"Can't thank you enough," the mayor said to LLiterally LLucid.

"I would request that you release the young 'l'ella you are holding next door. He is innocently trying to find his way home. Both Lauriander and I would be happy if the council agreed to do that," LLucid implored.

"I vote we rescind our previous vote," Lindsay called out. Immediately, the council raised hands to support a voice vote rescinding the previous vote. Even Lillbzellmet, with no hand to raise in support of the request, called out an affirmative "La."

LLiterally waved goodbye. A sudden pop, and he faded like a sunset.

A Time for Goodbyes

Life settled down in the town and residents of Liberal-town even changed their tune toward Oliver now that the legislature righted their wrongs, permitting the capital L to face right as Big Mac intended. All animosity soon vanished. The citizens even accepted, or at least tolerated, the presence of Oliver's extraordinary appendage. When Oliver and Lauriander jogged through the streets in their matching Lauriander-designed jogging suits, or walked about town visiting shops, folks treated them much the same as any other couple.

Though he remained focused on returning home one day, as September came, Oliver found himself, finally, falling into a daily routine with some ease. However, to accomplish a normal life and a sense of privacy, the young couple decided they needed a home of their own. To look for a house, they paid a visit to the offices of Liberaltowns 'L'ouse and 'L'ome Finder. There, they hired a 'L'ome agent.

Assigned to assist Oliver and Lauriander, Lob Loper, a young, jovial Bob Hope look-alike with a long ski slope of a nose, greeted them in a friendly manner. Agent Lob, as they called him, told them what approximate Lego price they could expect to pay once he found them the house that lived up to their specifications. They, of course, would have no trouble getting the Legos necessary to purchase their dream house from the local bank. No need to worry. He would guide them through the process.

Agent Lob took them to see several vacant houses around town since there proved to be a glut on the market. Though the 'l'orecation scare had finally settled down, a feeling of uncertainty remained. Since Ls were free to move anywhere in L Land, many Ls had chosen to return to their Lecturetown or Lawyertown roots, or find another living area altogether. Most of the abandoned houses turned out to be traditional homes similar to the one Lauriander lived in. As a girl with modern ideas, she had her L heart set on an ultra-modern chic 1960s house.

Agent Lob explained that no post-and-beam houses from that era were currently on the market. He told them to return from time to time to check the listings. "One is sure to come up down the road," he assured them, patting Lauriander's hand and smiling in a pleasant way.

Some time later—a few hours, according to Watchim, which to Oliver's good fortune still worked—the young couple returned. Agent Lob's office looked abandoned, as did the desk of the receptionist. Oliver and Lauriander agreed that their absence seemed odd. But since they had already walked all the way into town, they decided to wait a while longer.

As they sat, Lauriander concentrated on her new house. She chattered on about what furnishings they planned to buy. She couldn't wait to decorate each room. She talked about getting one of those wall sconces shaped like two large leaves with star holes in the shades. She had seen a perfect one in the window of Larry's 'Hardware Store. She asked Oliver, "Wouldn't pretty wall sconces look nifty if placed on the wall over the couch? Should they be in black or white?"

Oliver didn't answer, while Lauriander's mind raced on and on, going over every detail of their future home. After an endless hour counted almost minute by minute on Oliver's Watchim, neither Agent Lob nor the receptionist appeared.

"We'll come back another time," Oliver finally suggested.

Much to their surprise, on their return home, they noticed that the mood in the town had changed. As they walked from street to street, they spotted a number of computed Ls milling about randomly. A few stood silently in front of their houses. The scene reminded Oliver of his own street in Brentwood after the big earthquake some years earlier. There had been an eerie silence then as well. Now, he detected low levels of sounds that indicated an undercurrent of L laments.

"Something's going on," he told Lauriander.

"I don't like it," she answered.

A few blocks from their house, they stopped to ask one of the mourners what had happened. The man could barely talk from the shock he had suffered. During the time they had waited in the real estate office, a large number of Liberal town citizens had 'l'orecated suddenly and without warning. Apparently almost everyone in town had lost a loved one. Sounds and cries filled the streets all the way from the 'L'ouse and 'L'ome Finder office to the Littleleather house.

Oliver realized his worst fears had come true. His heart began to bang against his chest. He felt a sense of panic he'd never felt before—at home or here. Nausea overcame him, causing him to pause in the street.

Lauriander rushed home ahead of Oliver. By the time Oliver reached the Littleleather house, he found her sitting on the couch next to her father in stunned silence. Lefty held his arm around his daughter. On the coffee table stood an empty coffee cup.

"What's the matter?" Oliver asked the moment he saw them. He sat down next to Lauriander.

Two stricken faces greeted him. Finally, Lefty found the

words. "My sweet Lo-Rain has gone to greener pastures," he said in a heartbroken voice. Oliver looked stunned. Tears welled up in his eyes. He couldn't have felt any greater pain if he learned his own mother had died.

"Just a bit ago, she looked happy as a lark, cookin' up a storm in the kitchen for our dinner tonight. I went in there just by chance, mind you, went to ask her a question, when I saw the 'l'orecation before my very eyes. Your poor mother," the mayor moaned, as he covered his face with both hands. "Why, I watched your ma pull a loaf of 'l'alt bread from the oven. A flash of bright light, and the pan tumbled onto the floor. Your ma, that poor, dear woman who wouldn't harm a fly, if we had any of them little critters, departed for Word Central. Laurie, if only I could have gone off in your mama's place."

Lauriander said nothing. She stroked her father's hand and stared down at the floor.

"Your dear departed ma would be happy to know she's the lead letter in a word that can brighten up anyone's day, '#span_smallcaps LIGHT!span,'" Lefty whispered. "Saw the word flash myself. I thought you should know."

Lauriander and Oliver agreed that the best idea would be to get away from the house for a while. The mayor wanted to head for the Lucky Lady Saloon to drown his troubles like a man. Before they left the house, he placed his worn cowboy hat on his head. On the walk into town, he said to their surprise, "Never thought I'd see the day I wished for LLorser LLitebrite. Never thought I'd miss the old geezer. At least I could have talked to him about what's goin' on here. The rest of them are just a bunch of 'l'omputed nitwits."

All the way into town they passed groups of people standing

dazed on the street or scurrying about. One person after the other approached the mayor to share some personal tale of grief. Lefty would listen and then tell them about his own loss to reassure them none had been spared.

Finally, after many interruptions, they reached the wooden sidewalk in front of the Lucky Lady. The bench usually occupied by Larry, Lowen, and Lew now held only Lowen.

"Lew and Larry?" the mayor asked. Alone and sad, Lowen shook his head.

"Well, LooLoo's behind the bar," the mayor sighed in relief after he'd poked his head through the swinging doors of the saloon. Limpy, who often hung out with the bartender, was nowhere to be seen.

"We'll see you later, Daddy." Lauriander hugged him, planting a kiss on his cheek. "Everything will be all right. We'll visit LLiterally LLucid. Maybe he can explain what's happening."

"Maybe you should stay there a spell," Lefty told his daughter. "I don't want to be thinkin' about losin' you, too."

"Don't worry, I'll be just fine," she told him.

Oliver felt his heart would break in two. He'd come to love Lefty like a father. Now he thought Lefty looked like the loneliest cowpoke he had ever seen. He felt bad about leaving him there. But the mayor insisted they go ahead with their visit.

Literally a Brief Visit

Lucid sat with a small monitor in one hand on the front porch of his cottage. Soft music played from somewhere, the first music Oliver had heard since his arrival in Letterland. Weary, LLucid watched them approach his house up the garden path. He didn't stand. He looked old and tired for a kid.

"I wish I could say your visit came as a surprise," LLiterally said when they reached the porch. Standing up at last, LLucid embraced them and welcomed them into the house. No acrobatics this time. No walking on air. He followed them through the doorway like any other computed LL. Upon entering the living room, Oliver looked at the three clocks on the back wall. None of them worked anymore. "Are you all right?" LLucid asked them. Oliver, unable to speak for the moment, nodded his head. "I'm afraid I'm rather unprepared to make you a meal," LLiterally LLucid said in a vague voice that seemed to be coming from elsewhere.

"We didn't come here to eat," Oliver finally answered. "Terrible things have happened in town. I'm scared to death. Lauriander's lost her mother. I'm worried she or her dad could disappear too. We need to know what to do."

"Lauriander," LLiterally said, sitting down on the couch, "I'm so sorry about your mother. What's going on is totally beyond my control."

She turned to him. Then, sitting down beside him, she buried her face in his small shoulder. "She just vanished when baking 'l'alt bread," she whispered.

"I'm going to take a walk," Oliver said. He couldn't stand the pain any longer. He walked through the garden until he reached the big oak tree holding the swing. Sitting down on the ground, he leaned back against the trunk.

"I'm afraid you'll have to get out of town quickly." Clear as a bell, the voice of LLiterally LLucid appeared like the wind.

"Where are you?" Oliver asked, looking around. He stood up. Was the boy hiding behind a tree?

"Time is short. I've split my double L so that one half of me can be with you and the other with Lauriander at the same time. Somehow, in an unexpected way, our little world has shifted out of control. Order has turned to chaos. Demand for letters is overwhelming, causing a great struggle for us to keep up. These sudden surges are both unexpected and new. You have so many ways to write words now: computers, text messaging, e-mails—and I have been told books are printed faster and easier than ever before. And in your September, countless children return to school. I don't know which of these could have prompted this sudden, insatiable need from Word Central. I have lost contact with my counterparts in other letterlands. Stop looking around trying to find me. If you prefer, I'll swing as we speak."

Sure enough, an instant later, Oliver watched the empty swing move slowly back and forth. He could hear the groan of the rope against the branch.

"I want you to promise me something," the voice now came from the direction of the swing a few feet away. "Promise me that you'll take care of Lauriander and that the two of you will try to reach your home."

"Of course," Oliver said. "Why are you saying that? You know that I love her and will always take care of her." He listened to the sound of his own words, the first time he had shared his personal vow with someone else.

"You might get home. You might not get home. Once you leave L Land, I have no more influence. I wish I had the power to send you all the way back where you came from, but I don't. At least I can help you get out of here though. And with a bit of Letterland luck, you'll be delivered to Los Angeles.

"But first, you must try to understand what you are up against," LLucid's voice warned him. "As I told you once before, the letter of the land dictates the characteristics of the people. If you cannot 'l'ompute yourself to Los Angeles, and I hope you can, then you will most likely go to A Land. Watch out for As if you find yourself there. They can be avaricious, autoerotic, astute, aesthetic, acerbic, assertive, and aggressive, a bad combination at best. Seek out the art dealers there. They remember me and will help take care of you.

"If you return home, you must remain on the alert. Watch out for the feared Hs, who can hide among your kind. 'L'omputed Hs are the only letters that can switch to human forms, though not back again. Hs can be heartless or humane, hateful or harassed. Like here, they are often found in government positions. Like so many, they do harm while pretending to do good."

Oliver tried to follow the conversation. "Do you think Lauriander and I can leave together?" he asked.

"You must try. Listen, your time is short. You may not be able to 'l'ompute yourself at all. I have given Lauriander codes to attempt to send you both to your home through the Letterland Post Office. That is the only possibility. There is a risk Lauriander will leave, and you will stay. There is a risk that Liberaltown and Lauriander will be deleted before you can reach the post office. There is even a risk much of L Land will disappear. We have attempted to put double and triple shifts at Lettering Heights to try to process all the dead letters, but the noncomputed Ls are disappearing faster than we can replace them. That is how desperate the situation is. I only know that, at any instant, my dimension will be closed off to protect me from this deletion risk, and we will never see each other again."

"Shouldn't I come into the house?" Oliver asked. "Shouldn't I be with you and Lauriander?"

The swing stopped. "Endings are not always easy or neat," the sad voice said. "Your job is to find a way to get Lauriander out of here," LLucid went on after a short pause. "You two have much to share. As long as she remains in L Land, Lauriander might vanish. Outside L Land, she's far more difficult to locate. I've warned her on how to prepare for the journey. As for you, you must take care of yourself. There is something you must do that can help you leave. That is…"

In mid-sentence, the voice vanished along with the swing, the oak tree, the garden, the lush forest, and all signs of LLit-erally LLucid. Oliver found himself standing in the woods amid laurel trees near the oleander. Close by, Lauriander sat alone on the ground in the very spot where LLiterally LLucid's house stood a moment before.

Comings

*L*ight of my life. Fred read the words incredulously. What else but those hormones again? No doubt about it. What nonsense blabbering about Oliver falling into a mailbox.

Fred sat in the kitchen. He had awoken during the night, wandered into the kitchen for a glass of water to wash down a couple of aspirins for his headache, and found Grace's letter. Now he read the letter through for the third time. He couldn't believe the words in front of his eyes. Oliver's departure had driven her completely bonkers. She had become stark raving mad. He always suspected that she lived on the edge. Now he held proof in his hand that she had gone over the top.

#div_bq #bq-right *September 25*

#bq-indmargbot *Dear Fred:*

#bq-noind *In order to make sure that I didn't do anything rash, I have thought this decision through long and hard. Your indifference to Oliver's disappearance has been evident for a long time. As a matter of fact, you have been indifferent toward Oliver and me for years.*

#bq-ind *The truth is, as strange as it may sound to you, I have concluded that Oliver somehow slipped and fell inside the corner mailbox. I know this for a fact. That mailbox is not like any other mailbox around Brentwood. If you don't believe me, I challenge you to climb inside yourself.*

#bq-ind *With various crimes in the area, the police have more than enough to cope with. And if I went to them with this information, they would think me crazy sooner than pursue a lead that required a detective to climb into a mailbox. No other choice remains for me but to get to the bottom of this. Oliver has always been the light of my life.*!div

When, an hour or two earlier, Grace had written out the word "light," she paused as she felt a wave of hope wash over her. She sensed she had somehow crossed a language barrier that brought her closer to her son. She didn't know why. But the word "light" seemed to glow on the paper, as if a sacred meaning rested in those five beautiful letters.

#div_bq #bq-ind *Anyway, you know where to find me. Once I am inside, I will do whatever is necessary to find Oliver. Either we will return together, or you will be able to live your life out in peace exporting, importing, watching Dodger games, and drinking Southern Comfort.*

#bq-noind *Your wife Grace*!div

Fred swallowed his aspirins, and despite the headache, thought for a moment after his third time through the note. Should he go out in the dark of night to look for her? Should he go back to bed? He decided she would soon find she couldn't descend the corner mailbox. At that point she would undoubtedly regain her sanity and return home. He decided to go back to bed.

Grace finished writing the note sometime around 2:15 in the morning Watchim time. A few minutes later, she stood before the corner mailbox. The ocean damp had rolled in from the coast, chilling the air and making the night silent and dark. She knew the instant she walked out the front door and slammed it shut behind her that she would not return again.

"I know you're different from other mailboxes," she told MaiLA in a voice barely above a whisper. "I saw what you did with that package. I know you took Oliver and his ladder. I'm coming in to find them."

She waited a couple of minutes, almost as if she expected a response. The only sound came from the high-pitched yowling of a cat. With a final shift of her hand, she pulled open the package door as wide as she could. She bent forward, putting her head and shoulders into the slot.

When a lonely car passed five minutes later, no activity could be seen around MaiLA.

And Goings

Lauriander and Oliver spoke their final farewells to Lefty at exactly 2:18 a.m. on the very same September night Grace Sandwich checked into the mailbox. A more difficult farewell could not be imagined. The three of them hugged and kissed. Oliver left behind his #span_smallcaps WAVE THE SHA ES!span T-shirt. Lefty had asked for it as a memento. After all, just as Oliver had begun to think of him as a father, Lefty had come to regard Oliver as a son. And more importantly to an L, he had come to think of Oliver as a true 'l'elia.

When Oliver and Lauriander took one last look back, they saw Lefty still standing on the front porch. Next to him stood a newly computed Edith Bunker. While she looked the same as Lo-Rain, she knew that she acted only as a replacement. Lo-Rain had taken her rightful place in the word "light." As a matter of fact, Lefty's newly computed companion was none other than Luna, the former Harriet Nelson.

Luna decided, soon after she heard about Lefty's tragic loss, to compute herself into Edith Bunker. Ever since her Ozzie had run off and left her alone, she had contemplated a change of identity. "I'll give it a try," she told a friend. "Perhaps Lefty will accept me. That's a better life than sitting around the house alone waiting for 'l'orecation or for that lowlife vermin husband of mine to return."

Oliver had difficulties when he witnessed firsthand the new Luna arrangement. After all, Lo-Rain had vanished only a short while earlier. Even by Los Angeles standards, this transition had been lightning fast. When he thought about the details, he realized he retained many of his mother's old-fashioned American values, and that they probably appeared outdated in L Land.

Now, as they started down the street, Oliver discussed these concerns with Lauriander. "Don't you think this is all too soon? Lo-Rain has just 'l'orecated. Lefty should have waited a while longer—in respect to her memory. That would be the decent thing to do."

"Daddy should do what makes him happy," Lauriander answered. Frankly, she didn't like the idea that Luna had become Edith and moved in, but she knew that in her L heart, the original Lo-Rain would always be her mother. She would remain number one in Lefty's L heart as well. No doubt about that. And Luna's sudden presence, she reasoned, made their departure easier.

Right before they turned the corner, Lefty raised Oliver's T-shirt and waved his hand for a final time. Once the house passed from sight, the young couple paused to share a somber moment, for they knew as sure as shootin' they would never see Lefty again.

As Lauriander and Oliver made their way to the post office hand in hand, Oliver's head began to throb. His heart began to thump. Nerve ends tingled down to his toes, his feet moved forward heavy as lead. As they passed through town, Main Street looked deserted, chillingly identical in appearance to that first day the street showed on the monitor at the crossroads. Oliver checked Watchim: 2:44 a.m., September 25, in Los Angeles.

Lauriander sensed his concerns. "We'll be okay, Liver. LLiterally gave me the codes we need." She squeezed his hand in an attempt to reassure him.

"I feel so shaky inside," Oliver explained.

"Don't worry. I know what to do."

Lauriander and Oliver paused for a moment in front of the Letterland Post Office. The place looked deserted. They looked at each other, shaken. What did the future hold for them? Would they be together? Would they be apart forever? With their eyes locked in a long embrace, they knew in their L and human hearts that no matter the outcome, their love would last for all eternity.

Upon entering the building, they recognized the room that resembled any small post office in an old Western town. To their surprise, they encountered postal officials wearing little hats with visors. The lone man behind the counter sported a dark, bushy moustache. To the left of him sat a keyboard with an official sign stating #span_smallcaps FOR 'L'OFFICIAL USE ONLY!span. Lauriander approached the keyboard to punch in the first code.

"Destination?" the clerk asked.

"Los Angeles," Oliver blurted out. He checked Watchim again. His faithful companion had finally stopped working. The time sat suspended at 2:47 a.m. The date no longer showed.

Without moving, the clerk activated a monitor on the ceiling above their heads. A notice came up on the screen: You #span_smallcaps HAVE BEEN CLEARED FOR INTERPOSTAL TRAVEL. INTERACTIVE TRAVEL IS PENDING. APPROVAL IS EXPECTED AT SOME TIME. PLEASE PROCEED TO CHAMBER LLLAAA FOR TRANSMISSION!span.

As the monitor shut off, a door leading into a long, dark hallway opened up.

Hand in hand, they started down the passageway. A loud monotone voice froze them in place: "A disk is being prepared for transfer. The post office assumes no responsibility for errant delivery. If you wish to return to L Land, you may do so at this time, or you may advance to the transformation center dead ahead. The post office will make every effort to transmit your disk to your primary destination. This is a recording.”

“Do you want to go back?” Lauriander asked.

Oliver couldn’t see an inch in front of his nose in the darkness. “No, but whatever happens, I just hope somehow we’ll stay together,” he whispered.

Lauriander squeezed his hand. A light shone in the distance. A moment later a beam of pulsating light encircled them.

“I’m scared to death,” Oliver whispered. He could feel his body trembling.

“Whatever happens, I love you,” Lauriander whispered back.

The voice from the passageway drowned out Oliver’s response. “Your destination disk for Los Angeles has been activated,” came the flat announcement.

In a sudden move, Oliver grabbed hold of Lauriander. He pulled her close to him. Her L heart, which didn’t beat,

pressed up against his heart that thumped hard enough to push through the flesh. The beam of light intensified. A second later, in a dizzying whirl, he no longer knew if Lauriander remained beside him in that instant of their final embrace.

The words #span_smallcaps SAFE JOURNEY!span flashed in the darkness. Oliver’s body moved along with the pulsating motion of the beam. Only a black void hung, like a threatening cloud, above him.

Then the beam vanished.

De-liverence

Lauriander! With his mouth pressed against the concrete, he whispered, "Lauriander. Where are we?" Oliver felt the cement sidewalk press cold against his cheek. After blinking several times, he opened his eyes. A throbbing pain ricocheted back and forth from one side of his head to the other. He lay on his stomach on a bed of concrete.

An eerie morning light descended across the scene. No sound could be heard. Then came the noise from a passing car. Tension gripped his body. He jerked his head to one side, blinked several times more, and tried to focus on the scene around him that seemed familiar but not like Letterland.

Across the street a house, then another house, and when he twisted his neck the other direction, he saw before him the very same fat corner mailbox that had opened itself to swallow his ladder and himself months earlier. From this place he'd begun his adventures. Now he'd returned from the land of dead letters. He pulled his body up into a sitting position, then sat cross-legged on the sidewalk to stare at the mailbox.

"Lauriander," he repeated aloud, this time pivoting his head, first left, then right. He surveyed each inch of the surrounding terrain in the hope of sighting his love. *How had he arrived here?* he wondered. Letterland seemed as distant as a foreign land. Once familiar, Brentwood now seemed equally distant, as if he'd returned to a world far removed from his consciousness.

No Lauriander! No L or human in sight. With the exception of the single car that had passed, nothing stirred anywhere in his vicinity. In an attempt to release the cobwebs clouding his mind, he shook his head vigorously. How odd his body felt, light, as if he were an angel descended from the stars only to sit cross-legged on a sidewalk a short block away from his home.

A sound startled him. His heart leaped. Lauriander, Lauriander. Was there ever a name more beautiful?

A repeated thud appeared to come from within the mailbox nearby. Oliver cleared his throat and tried to raise his voice above a whisper.

"Lauriander? Are you there?"

A muffled response sounded like a cry for help. A high-pitched whine preceded another thump. Oliver's heart burst with joy: Lauriander had survived the perilous trip from L Land, but landed inside the mailbox rather than on the sidewalk. Oh, he knew the depths of this mailbox, Oliver did. For a moment he viewed that archaic government issue with both disdain and admiration.

A moan coming from within set Oliver into motion. With a great effort, he managed to pull himself up from the sidewalk. His stance proved as wobbly as that of a newborn calf. Rubber legs kept the mailbox at a distance. He sank to his knees, and like a baby, he crawled forward along the sidewalk until he reached the mailbox.

Oliver felt damp sweat spread across his body. That oh-so-human sensation brought him back to earth. No longer in L Land, he became just another human returning from a long trip. Home again—and yet not home at all.

"Lauriander, I'll get you," he called out, unsure of how to proceed. Though he knew this mailbox literally inside out, he realized the path within could be treacherous and deceptive. But the thought that his beloved could be so close filled him with true grit and determination. He grabbed hold of the cold steel corners for support and hoisted himself to his feet once more. Leaning against the front of the receptacle, he felt a million tiny pains shoot through his body. Face-to-face with the wide entry door, he pulled the handle back to peek inside.

"Help," came the weak cry from within. "Help me please, I'm stuck."

The voice struck him with the impact of a bucket of ice water. His mother inside the mailbox? When a feeble hand appeared to wave through the open doorway, he saw an all-too-human lined hand that did not resemble Lauriander's. The hand that appeared had once rocked his cradle.

A different person might have paused a moment to question why his mother would be stuck inside the mailbox. But not the reborn Oliver, who now took hold of his mother's arm with a gentle motion and made a determined effort to extricate her. As he worked, he felt himself consumed by grief, for he sensed his Lauriander had somehow not reached their destination. As his mother's head and arms appeared through the entryway, he gripped her solidly under the arms. A gentle edging forward produced her waist, and finally both legs inched their way safely out through the flexible door. As his beloved mother—and his former life—returned to him, all the joy he should have experienced lay in a quiet pool inside him, buried deep beneath a mountain of great sadness and sudden grief.

Grace, freed at last, swarmed all over him. As he helped her down onto the sidewalk, she yelled, "YAHYAHYAH," seeing the identity of her rescuer clearly in the early morning light. In between outbursts of joy, she moaned about how she'd been stuck in the box for hours. Her need for attention allowed Oliver no time to think.

After perhaps a hundred stifling hugs and a million

unanswered questions, his weakened body folded itself into a lump on the curb. In a flash, his mother dropped down beside him, driven by curiosity as to how he happened to appear at this very moment to rescue her. "I'd decided you'd fallen down through the mailbox," she said. "I went inside because I intended to look for you. But you couldn't have been in there because you didn't return that way. I know. I've been stuck in there for hours. Nothing could have gotten past me."

Oliver could only shrug his shoulders. He had no idea how he'd managed to return, or even where he'd been for that matter. Despair tempered any happiness he would otherwise have felt upon being reunited with his mother again. For her part, Grace did not see his pain, wrapped up in the joy of his return and in her own unexpected rescue. "What a story," she thought, as visions of appearances on *Oprah* played in her mind.

She put an arm around him. "Oliver, my dearest boy, this is truly a miracle."

Side by side, they sat on the curb in front of the mailbox, each recovering from a different ordeal. Together they looked like two sides of a coin, one pumped with joy, the other sagging with sadness.

She took his face between her two hands. "Can you believe I got stuck in there looking for you? I'm sure someone would have heard me or that the mail person would have come along to rescue me eventually. But this is so much better. A perfect ending. I'm dying to know. Where did you go? Where have you been?" In a gesture of motherly affection, she took both of Oliver's hands in her own to hold them in her lap.

Despite Grace's intention never to return home, they went back as soon as Oliver could walk without a wobble. Early morning light crept through the window. Fred had not yet been awakened with the news of their return. Grace sat alone in the kitchen with a steaming cup of coffee, dreaming of Saturday afternoons together with Oliver, a far different future than she'd imagined only hours earlier. And she noted, for future reference, that Fred had read her note sometime during the night, and then returned to bed.

Dazed from his ordeal and grieving from his loss, Oliver sat on his bed for the longest time before he could stir himself. A bath seemed in order, perhaps the only way to properly drown his sorrows. He set the bathwater running while the heaviness of his despair continued to weigh on him like a boulder. As he undressed mechanically, his eyes and nose stung from the agony of his tears.

Just as he turned toward the tub to step into the hot water, he caught a glimpse of his naked body in the bathroom mirror. He paused to stare. At first glance, he saw no changes from the body he had before he fell into L Land. Despite the limited supply of food, he had not even grown thinner from the ordeal.

Then what he noticed made his heart stop. His eyes widened as he stared into the mirror. A small heart faintly visible now appeared on the left side of his bare chest. Clearly outlined over his own heart, this token of true love sat etched in red, just below the surface of his skin. A neatly centered single letter showed within the small ♥: a capital L.

He blinked. He blinked again. The heart remained.

He could not believe his eyes. Lost and found all at once, Oliver peered at his reflected body while his eyes read the clear message of love present on his chest. He knew in his heart that the sign, sweet and pure, would remain part of him forever under his skin. Lauriander had found a way to write her presence into his life.

He felt a warm glow rising in his chest, and then a new flood of tears began to cascade down both cheeks.

At that moment, the embedded heart began to pulsate as if infused with a life of its own. The color red intensified, then faded, then intensified again. "Lauriander," Oliver whispered at the mirror, bending forward to give the reflection of the L a quick kiss.

"Lauriander. We'll be together forever." And with that he sank down into the warm water to soak and dream in a state of pure bliss and lunatic love.

#end LLITERALLY NOT THE END